Intention Implication Wind

Intention Implication Wind

a novel
by Ken Sparling

Pedlar Press | Toronto

ACKNOWLEDGEMENTS
The publisher wishes to thank the Canada Council
for the Arts and the Ontario Arts Council for their
generous support of our publishing program.

LIBRARY AND ARCHIVES CANADA
CATALOGUING IN PUBLICATION

Sparling, Ken, 1959-
    Intention, implication, wind / Ken Sparling.

ISBN 978-1-897141-41-0

    I. Title.

PS8587.P223I68 2011   C813'.54
C2011-901089-5

COVER ART
Drew Khan

BOOK DESIGN
Zab Design & Typography, Toronto

TYPEFACE
Matt Antique

Printed in Canada

THE CANADA COUNCIL | LE CONSEIL DES ARTS
FOR THE ARTS | DU CANADA
SINCE 1957 | DEPUIS 1957

ONTARIO ARTS COUNCIL
CONSEIL DES ARTS DE L'ONTARIO

What will you do with your life right now? Not in the long run, but right now, after you brush your teeth. You must know: just as the kiss is coming, other things are coming too. But what do you do till the kiss arrives?

I was in a cave. That part, at least, was true; the part about Mary felt utterly brilliant, but it was only utterly. I felt like God. I tried to write a duet for me and the woman who I was going to love when I found her.

God's angels wrote songs across the clouds with their pee.

Part One

Chappy left early in the spring and there was a feeling he would be back. Mirror felt he would be back. But the summer passed. The owl-eyed boy was young. Mirror waited through winter, but when the second coming of spring came, when the second spring of Chappy being away arrived, Mirror decided she would have to go off and try to bring Chappy home.

She found Chappy in a cabin in a town where music fell from the sky on a certain night each year. Chappy had made a life for himself in this town, and his past was like a dictionary, charting the distant memory of various words used in various settlements since late in the eighteenth century.

But Chappy remembered Mirror. And he remembered the owl-eyed boy.

He saw them outside his cabin one afternoon in the earliest months of winter. He closed the curtains. But he could not continue the charade. He opened the door.

Eventually, Mirror convinced Chappy to come home. He wanted to go home from the start, from as soon as he'd walked away from Mirror and the owl-eyed boy. By the time

Mirror got to him, though, the desire to return home was an impulse deep inside that he didn't recognize anymore; but Mirror helped him recognize it, and he went home with her.

Or maybe it was that Mirror used her presence and that of the owl-eyed boy to shape an amorphous clump of feeling that Chappy had but couldn't name. Perhaps the feeling Chappy felt really didn't have a name. Perhaps Mirror manipulated Chappy by recognizing the namelessness of the feeling Chappy was having, and the terrible hurt the namelessness caused, and she simply stepped up and gave Chappy a name for the feeling. There's no way to know for sure. Maybe Chappy went home because he chose to, or maybe he was entirely manipulated. Probably it was a combination of both.

When Mirror fell off the house, she came to a decision. What if someone else fell off the house, or worse? she asked herself. And whose house was it that Mirror fell into when she fell off her own house? For isn't the earth itself someone's house? And so, when we fall, are we not falling into another house, a house that is a step or two away from the house we're used to living in?

I love the silence of snow falling outside the big front window of the library. Big flakes drifting. The sound implicit in bigness; the silent betrayal of that implication through plate glass.

I love the silence of machinery. The humming of the candy and coke machines in the front lobby of the library. Or the silence of the furnace kicking in at home. The whispery silence of air through a vent in the floor.

I love the silence of sun through the kitchen window, and you lie under the light angling in over the counter to touch the wall above the breakfast nook.

I love the silence of Mirror entering my head, the silent sibilance of words made quiet, invasive flashes of scarlet thought through the winding passage of my inner ear.

God's angels ran across the clouds, leaving footprints, like dents in smoke. Falling into Mirror's face, I could feel the falling music making Mirror understand.

Those are my clouds up there, today, Mirror.

How secret is the secret I am saying? The secret I am saying right now? Sentences that never should have been suddenly are.

Chappy's amazing clouds flew over Mirror like race cars in a race where the TV is on mute.

God's binoculars have infinite zoom.

When I locked my bike to the post, I thought: It can be the most significant day of your life, and yet you don't want to get out of bed.

I finished locking my bike to the post.

When I looked at the clock in my West Coast home, I saw for the first time that it was the number five that mattered most. It was five minutes later than it had been five minutes before.

When I look out my window, I feel the heat of everything rushing up to the glass, but never getting past the glass to touch me on the face, or on the arms, or on the chest. I put on a t-shirt and go out into the street once again to face the day.

I call Jonathan Goldstein.

Go to sleep, dude, Goldstein tells me.

My neck is getting tired, so I put my head back on the pillow and think: Soon I will go to sleep.

She wrought the lawyer in canyoned snow.

If life was so good, why did you make up your mind to go to hell when you died? Why did you spend time thinking about dying at all?

Dad had this cool way of cutting up peaches.

It's because I can't see with my glasses off, he told me. But I didn't believe him. It was something else. I watched him. I tried to emulate him. I could not come close.

Be constantly resurrected and in need of being killed again, Dad told me.

And now I monitor whatever god my father is worshipping. I monitor God and my father. I hate Dad. And I fear, most out of all the gods, the god Thor. I fear his war hammer.

I was in love with this woman I had never met, but knew that when I met her I would love her.

If it was so good, why couldn't I remember exactly what it was I actually wrote down? It always felt safest when a thing was written down, but what does writing something down actually accomplish? I'd read the passage. I liked it. I tried to rephrase it as I sat on the toilet, but I couldn't get it any better than how I'd written it down the time before.

I opened my eyes to find I was nowhere near the intersection of Davenport and Yonge. I was on page 132 of Greg Gerke's book. Marvelling at the distance I had travelled, I shut out the light, grabbed a pillow to hug goodnight, and closed my eyes, wondering where I was going to wind up tonight.

Greg Gerke phoned.

I fell out of bed trying to get the phone.

Greg and I, we hadn't met, but we had each other's books. Let's go to sleep, we each thought, and I took off my glasses, and Greg did whatever it is he does just before he goes to sleep. This would sever the connection, of course. But that was okay. It wasn't like another connection would suddenly rise up. It wasn't like Napoleon rising from the sea, with seaweed and salt water dripping from that cool sideways of his.

I wonder if Napoleon wore that hat to bed. Is that something you could research? I would research that, totally.

Once upon a time, I was asleep. A voice came soft, like the sound of trumpets.

A voice like a can opener opening a can of trumpets. Trumpets with their mutes on.

Yes, this is how I will go out into the world today, you tell yourself. But you run a risk. When you go out, is it always like that? Is it always a terrible risk?

After they got off the bus, they were walking down the stairs, and when they got to the long corridor leading to the subway, Chappy had a thing to say: You have to be able to laugh, he told Mirror. You have to be able to do that, don't you think, Mirror?

Chappy and Mirror were together on the bus. They'd seen the lad with the hat numerous times before. And not always on the bus! You've got to have a good sense of humour, whispered Chappy.

The time machine story reappeared above Chappy's cabin as

a red star in the sky, which Chappy went out to look at some nights.

Chappy was anonymous as a hill. Anonymous and still. He hardly dared breathe. His anonymity couldn't hide him. He hardly heard a thing and he didn't understand. He rang out like a note. He wrote to Mirror, but hoped that she would never read the note.

It was so cold that winter they came back together after Mirror's long journey. Chappy wore a thick layer of clothing, yet he felt utterly exposed. He stood sideways next to Mirror, twisting his fingers of his one hand with the fingers of his other hand. His hands felt big, awkward. Swollen. He felt like he still had mittens on.

Chappy felt his tongue push against the top of his mouth. He felt his tongue grow fuzzy. He felt his mouth open. He felt his lips encircle words. He felt his tongue caress sounds, the sounds of a language he had been given. Still, he felt obscenely mute.

When Chappy slept, he slept like a baby. When he woke, he woke as a man terrified and devoid of hope. Clouds were yellow where sun splashed through. But the sun never quite pushed all the way through. Chappy began to wonder. Had he moved into a different universe, a parallel universe, a universe where the atmosphere was so different it wasn't like being with Mirror at all?

Chappy wanted to tell on someone. He wanted to tell on everyone.

But there was no one to tell on and nothing to tell. There was only him and whatever it was he told himself today.

Until he told what it was he was going to tell today, Chappy knew there would never be anything to tell. He knew that telling was just his way of creating what had to be told. If he didn't tell it, it didn't exist. Chappy didn't exist, except in the telling. But, in the telling, he came to exist only as what he told. He, therefore, didn't exist at all in the telling. All that could exist in the telling was what telling had told. And if people confused Chappy with what was told in his telling, it negated the nothing he'd never been.

Chappy closed his eyes and tried to remember.

The woman Chappy imagined looked interesting enough.

The story of Chappy seemed to go on forever, although actually it was only one song among the many Chappy knew. Days would pass. Then, suddenly, the story of Chappy would begin again.

They drove down to the beach and opened the car doors. Mirror took off her shoes. The sand was cold. Mirror sat sideways on the seat of the car, looking down at her feet. Chappy hadn't moved since he stopped the car. He was facing forward, his hands on the steering wheel. You didn't say good morning this morning, Mirror, he said.

This is the worst day of my life, Chappy. Mirror's head sank down till her forehead touched her knees. She was so thin. She could barely feel her body where it pressed against her thighs.

If you can say good morning on the worst day of your life, Mirror, that says something about you.

I know that, Chappy, Mirror said. Her voice was muffled from her lips being pressed against her knees.

Chappy was feeling fastidious, and it was making him sick. He untied his shoes, took them off, tucked the laces neatly inside the shoes. Then he pulled off his socks. They were brown socks, brand new. He folded each sock once and laid it on the corresponding shoe. Mirror had her head turned sideways, so that her ear was on her knee. Her eyes were slanted tight to the corners of her eye sockets, trying to see what Chappy was doing. What are you doing, Chappy? she asked.

Folding my socks.

Mirror sat up, put her hands on her knees, stood. She brushed the tops of her pant legs to get the wrinkles out. She looked down the beach toward the lake. There were two birds high in the sky above the lake. Lazy, low waves capped about a foot from shore and rolled onto the beach. Mirror walked down to the shoreline. Chappy stayed in the car and watched Mirror through the windshield. I should get out of the fucking car, Chappy said to himself. But he didn't move.

Mirror had her feet in the water now. She was drifting south along the shore. The lake came to meet Mirror with its little bit of foam, then left Mirror. Mirror counteracted her feeling of abandonment by moving down the beach. She was moving forward, leaving Chappy behind. Goodbye little bird, Chappy whispered. He put one foot out the car door and set it in the sand. Cold, he whispered.

Mirror kissed Chappy quickly, then ran back into her dream. She ran down hills and into forests. She ran down halls limned in early morning light that came through the windows like terror.

After she'd gone into the bathroom and peed, Mirror got back in bed with Chappy and tucked herself in tight to the covers. She turned her back on Chappy as a kind of safeguard against him reading her dreams. It seemed to Mirror, as she fell back into her dreams, that the apartment took its location from the sound of her footfalls.

In the morning she relented and told Chappy part of her dream.

They could hear me coming, Mirror said, and they placed little selves at the end of wherever it was they thought I was going. They didn't seem to know I had no idea where I was going. I was just running, trying not to take the same turns as the night before.

But aren't they just bits and pieces of me, Chappy, all these people in my dreams?

Chappy didn't speak. He couldn't speak. He opened his mouth, but nothing came out. He felt like he was in Mirror's dream waiting for Mirror to fill his mouth with words.

They always thought I was going directly to where I was actually going, but how could there even be a place I was actually going if I didn't know where I was going? Do you think there can be such a place in the world, Chappy?

The world is a very different place when you go about smelling things more deeply than other people. You start to hear sounds other people don't hear. Sounds locked deep inside walls, stirring to get out. Sounds in the chests of the people you pass in parks. Sounds deep under the ground, where darkness covers men skinned in humid walls, clambering into endless circles, looping endlessly back on themselves, till they turn their ways of being inside-out.

When you smell the world more deeply, you see things you weren't meant to see. You keep your nose low to the ground, except on rare occasions when the winds drift new-made overhead at a certain height. Then, you lift your snout and breathe.

I often feel as though the world is coming to an end, Chappy, said Mirror. They were in the mall. Mirror had a knitting book in her hand. She bought two beige sticks with hooks on the ends at a store Chappy had never been in before.

What are those things? Chappy asked. They were going out of the store, into the vicious light of the mall.

Crochet hooks, Mirror told him.

Do you know how to use crochet hooks, Mirror?

No.

Unexpectedly to me was the fact that it mattered how you went about doing your work. Things can sneak up behind you, no matter how you approach what is approaching you, but you can miss seeing what is sneaking up behind you if you don't turn around sometimes and cease your approach.

There was a second day when Chappy didn't want to get out of bed. And there was a second day when Mirror rode. There were two riders on the bike, Mirror, and the owl-eyed boy. There were two reunions pending.

Chappy got out of the chair he was sitting in. He went over to the door. He took hold of the doorknob. He gave it a twist. He pulled. The door came open. He stuck his head out in the hall.

A lady wearing a grey skirt and a pair of white nurse's shoes came running out of the ladies room. Fire! she screamed. She ran down the hall. Chappy went back to his desk.

Chappy left his cubicle on Wednesday. He opened the door

all the way. He went into the hall. The door hissed softly closed behind him. It snicked as it came to. The carpet in the hall smelled like kerosene. It was very soft to walk on. Chappy touched the elevator button with the down arrow on it. He waited. There were three elevators. Chappy watched the numbers light up above the elevators. Elevator one was coming down. It would get there soon. It was stopping at some floors on the way down. It would stop at a floor, then skip down a few floors. As it skipped floors, the numbered lights above the elevator door flashed quickly on and off. Then the elevator would stop again at another floor. Eventually, the elevator door slid open. Chappy stepped inside. Touched G. The door slid closed. The elevator dropped.

Whenever Mirror stood upon her uncertainty, she always felt certain. But when she looked down, she always fell. And she always looked down.

Mirror could smell spring coming through the trees. Spring smelled like a whisper.

Chappy sat alone in his small cabin. Only the surface of the table was lit. The remainder of the cabin lay in shadow. Outside, music fell like rain. It fell like leaves dropping from autumn trees, like petals from a dying flower.

The people of the village called it the night of falling music. It was like some monstrous guys up in the sky had got hold of musical instruments they didn't know how to use and were firing on Earth, trying to destroy it with music.

Mirror could hear crackling. Like the sound you get from a fire. The sun was just above the trees to the west of where they sat and the flames were getting drowned in the bright light of the sun. It was awkward sitting with these people. Mirror was glad they were with her. She'd been getting lonely on the road the last few days. The owl-eyed boy sat behind Mirror on the bike everyday, but most days he stayed entirely silent.

The man and the woman got up. They went into their

tent. Mirror could hear sounds of the man and woman going through bags and moving across their air mattress. The tent walls bulged. The tent was a big creature that had eaten the man and the woman. The man and the woman were inside the tent's big belly, pushing around. Not trying to get out, either, Mirror thought. It was a gentle bumping around they were doing. Like swimming, or treading water in the creature's stomach.

When the man came back out of the tent, he was wearing sunglasses. The woman came out behind the man, also wearing sunglasses. They had packs of cigarettes. They brought the packs of cigarettes over and set them on the table. After they'd set down the cigarettes, they themselves sat down.

The sunglasses were mirror lenses. Mirror could see herself. She couldn't tell if the man and the woman were looking at her. She could only approximate that they might be looking at her. When they pointed the mirrored sunglasses at a certain angle, they might be looking at her, Mirror thought.

The man and the woman smoked their cigarettes and pointed their mirrored sunglasses across the campsite. They might have had their eyes closed, for all Mirror knew. They pulled in smoke from their cigarettes like it was something they needed. They blew smoke and sighed. Mirror felt nervous for the owl-eyed boy. She felt nervous at the sight of these two people slipping cigarettes between their lips, sucking cigarettes like tiny white-papered penises.

The owl-eyed boy didn't seem to notice the cigarettes.

The smoke from the cigarettes rose to join the smoke from the campfires that were burning all around the campground.

It seemed like a fairly new campground. The trees were saplings. Weed trees. You could see everybody else in their campsites.

Off to the west, where the sun was setting, there was a stand of more mature trees. There were arrows on the signs Mirror had passed coming into the campground pointing toward the stand of older trees. The signs said there was a nature trail and a lake.

Have you been to the lake? Mirror asked.

Oh yes, said the man. He slipped the cigarette between his lips, held it. It seemed as though he might be afraid to inhale. The cigarette, which had been about the longest Mirror had ever seen when the man first lit it, was dwindling. There was not much left of it. Soon it would be gone.

The man inhaled. It seemed he had nothing more to say about the lake.

How is the lake? Mirror asked. She faced the woman. She hoped the woman might volunteer more information. They had been quite talkative before they went into the tent. But the cigarettes seemed to have quieted them.

The woman said nothing. She held her cigarette aloft, her hand limp, bent at the wrist. The cigarette was a few inches from her mouth. The woman seemed reluctant to move it any closer.

The lake is beautiful, said the man. The woman nodded. They faced each other.

Mirror could not tell if they were looking at each other, or at themselves in each other's mirror sunglasses.

The man dropped his cigarette, pushed it into the dirt with his toe.

The woman did the same.

They bent to retrieve the butts. They stood, went over to their own campsite, dropped the butts in the fire.

They walked back over and sat down again with Mirror.

Would you like to share our dinner this evening? the man asked.

Yes, said the woman. You should.

Mirror looked from one to the other.

The man took his sunglasses off and put them on the table.

The woman followed suit.

They both looked at Mirror.

Mirror saw now how gentle their eyes were.

That would be nice, said Mirror.

We have to buy groceries, said the man. Would you care to drive to the mall with us? The boy would be welcome, as well, of course.

There's a mall? Mirror asked.

Oh yes, said the man, and the mall and the lake took on an equivalency that made Mirror afraid to ask the man about the mall, lest he pronounce it beautiful, as he had the lake.

They kept their windows open in the car as they drove along the highway. The wind bit Mirror and the owl-eyed boy, hit them in the face, like chubby fists on a kid who is hitting his parents but doesn't really want to hurt them. There was both a gentleness and a violence, Mirror realized, to wind that came into a car through open windows on a highway.

Everyone wore their seatbelts.

At the mall, they drove up and down the aisles, looking for parking spots.

Men and woman and children who had already found

parking spots and parked their cars walked toward the mall. There were men and woman of all shapes and sizes. They were fat, or skinny, or neither. They wore polyester or wool or cotton. They wore jackets and blouses. Some smoked.

The man accelerated. He slowed. Started up again. He was watching for a good parking space.

The woman pointed and gestured, but said nothing.

There was absolute silence in the car.

The man rolled up the windows.

They were sealed in.

The man parked as close to the mall as he could get. Before he shut off the motor, he leaned forward and listened, as though the car might have a message for him, something he needed to know before he went into the mall.

The man and the woman carried jackets and wore their sunglasses on the tops of their heads.

It was already growing dark. It was that moment at dusk where the people around you disappear into the vaporous light that presages night. But the people scuttling across the mall parking lot were lit by overhead lights. As they got closer to the mall, they were lit by bright neon signs over stores.

The man and the woman looked up at the signs.

We're looking for a grocery store, the man said.

Yes, said the woman.

The two looked away from the signs and faced each other to nod, as if they'd reached some significant decision they hadn't been sure they would ever be able to make.

They stopped just short of the mall doors. The man pulled out a pack of cigarettes. Offered one to the woman. The woman took a cigarette. They put the cigarettes to their lips. The man pulled a small package of corn chips from his pocket. He had the cigarette in his lips. It bobbed as he focused on getting the corn chips package open. He offered the package to Mirror. She took one. He offered it to the owl-eyed boy, but the owl-eyed boy said no. He said it very quietly.

Mirror looked at the owl-eyed boy.

The owl-eyed boy looked nervous.

The man gave the package of corn chips to the woman, who held it while the man took a drag on his cigarette, and then removed the cigarette from his lips. The man held the smoke in his lungs for what seemed like a long time. When he blew the smoke back out, he tilted his head back and pursed his lips upward to point a stream of smoke at the sky.

Mirror was running, dark hair bobbing in the breeze, feet pounding. She felt light, a slight wisp in the wind, mingling with the other wisps in the wind, no more than a scent, the scent of pine, the powerful odour of damp. The trees rose high behind Mirror, like window frames, great cathedral ceilings of green spread out above, thin shafts of sunlight piercing shadows, like knives wounding her fatally.

Surely this is fatal, she thought. This running, this terrible, wonderful running.

Mirror would be late. Already the sun was down below the canopy of leaves. Her father would be mad.

Without slowing, Mirror tilted her head back, let the leaves spin above her. She made herself dizzy. She knew this part of the path well. Years later, she would understand other paths, see where they were leading, but she would never understand a path the way she understood this one, the way it supported her, moved her along, whisked and whirled her.

Mirror fell, lay silent on the ground, breathing, chest heaving, world spinning. The dew fell like sparkling wind onto grass, covering Mirror like a midnight blanket.

Mirror charged in through the front gate, not bothering to close it. She stood in the front yard braying until her father came to the window to see what was happening.

I'm a horse, Mirror whispered. She reared onto hind legs.

What time is it? Mirror's father called, his voice distant and small, the outline of a book cut into his cheek from where he'd been sleeping with his head down on his desk. Shouldn't you be in bed, Mirror? What are you doing outside? Your sister is in bed. You have to go to bed when your sister goes to bed.

In my mind, Chappy and Mirror speak.

It was Mirror. I was not imagining this.

Mirror was in my head.

Mirror was my head; Chappy my hands.

Mirror was on her way to try to get out.

Chappy was waving.

Chappy knew he should try to meet Mirror. He knew what direction to travel. He walked on my knees, tapping his feet.

We separate at opposite ends of a lake, two waves; the same wave, separated by time. The closer my hands get to my head, the less strength I have to reach up and touch my face.

It was during the day, and I was in the cats. Braun and I were in a door. Maggie was tinkling through the cracks. Braun opened the door like something human. Like a whole human world. I must not have closed it right, I thought. I was climbing the hill. I was spring. I smelled of morning. I was porcupine.

Who's Braun? Mirror asked, but at the same time she was

thinking: If this boy, Chappy, asks me to marry him, I will say yes. It was the first time she had thought this about Chappy. The first time she had thought this about anyone.

Chappy continued. He seemed not be aware of Mirror, and Mirror was glad. As glad as a time when she stood on her front porch in the shadows. Near the cone of porch light, beside the statue of a dwarf with a brush at its base for wiping the mud off your shoes in springtime.

Chappy's next-door neighbour had pieces of equipment and wires. He pointed cone-shaped instruments at the sky, and out toward the perimeter of his property.

A family sat by the river, in the dark, and felt the music fall around them. Kids slept on blankets, while parents communicated by touching each other's hands.

A professor from the university took his followers out to a point that shot like an arrow into the sea. They tried to capture the music in custom-made recording canisters fashioned from seashells and gold plated speaker wire.

The relentless hunt for the rational came on like logs running blind through shipping channels, running madly past forests, through towns, running straight into people's hearts.

The man in the bicycle shop asked Mirror if he could help. Can I help you? he said.

Mirror said nothing. She stood in the dusty light coming in the front window and looked around the shop.

The shop had wooden floors.

The stretches of empty beach told Chappy that the people were gone. Occasionally, an old person drifted by in the sand, like a tumbleweed rolling away on its way to nowhere. It made Chappy feel strange to see these solitary old people lost on so much beach.

Mirror woke. She told Chappy something. Something in a voice so sleepy, it made Chappy sit up and listen. Chappy had been drifting into sleep. He didn't know what Mirror said. He thought she was still asleep, that she was saying something in her sleep. He touched her arm. Go to sleep, he told her.

Investigate what it means to begin, Chappy whispered.

I'm tired, Chappy. Can you just tell me what it is you want, exactly, and not go through all the theoretical posturing.

Mirror's voice seemed to be coming from somewhere in the mass of hair that lay scattered across her pillow. Mirror's pillow had a message for Chappy. Mirror's pillow had taken possession of Mirror's hair to deliver a message to Chappy.

After sobbing for a half hour or so, the owl-eyed boy went into the bathroom. He looked in the mirror for confirmation of his pain. He saw it in the red blotchiness of his skin and in the red blood lines in his eyes.

He washed his face, then dried it vigorously with one of the white scratchy towels. He went into the living room, turned on the TV. The owl-eyed boy didn't tell Mirror that he'd seen Chappy that day. He didn't tell Mirror anything.

Mirror was in the living room crying. The owl-eyed boy was in the kitchen pulling things out of drawers. He got the scissors. Chappy took them away. The owl-eyed boy lay on the kitchen floor. He looked up at Chappy. He started to cry.

Chappy was grating cheese.

After a time, Mirror came into the kitchen. She looked at the owl-eyed boy. She looked at Chappy. I have to go to work, she said. Her eyes were red and her face was puffy. She went upstairs and the shower came on.

Chappy felt the steam in his blood. He thought for a while about the trip home from work that night. He'd got on the wrong bus. Two men in suits were standing in the aisle of the bus, talking about fuckers. One man told the other man about one fucker he knew, and he talked about that fucker for as long as he could, till the other man interrupted to say, Oh yeah, well I knew this one fucker... and they talked about that other fucker for a while.

Chappy sprinkled grated cheese onto baked beans and ground beef he'd mixed together with ketchup and mustard. He put Pillsbury crescent rolls in the oven. He went in the living room and sat on the couch.

The owl-eyed boy stayed on the floor in the kitchen. He'd stopped crying.

Mirror came down the stairs. Said goodbye. Went out the door.

The door closed. The house felt lit. It felt lonely.

Chappy went through the hall. He put on the lights.

Now all the lights on the lower level were on, except the one in the bathroom.

Chappy went in the bathroom. He turned on the light.

He felt even more lonely.

He went in the kitchen. He sat at the kitchen table.

The owl-eyed boy was lying on his back, eyes wide, staring at the ceiling. He wasn't moving, except for his chest rising and falling quietly from his breathing.

It was seven-thirty. Chappy turned off the lights in the kitchen. The blinds were open. Chappy saw the girl across the street come out her front door in moccasins. It was almost Christmas and the Christmas lights were on in the tree outside the house.

Chappy went in the living room and plugged in the Christmas tree. He turned off the bathroom light. He turned off the floor lamp in the living room. He looked at the Christmas tree. It needed tinsel. But the owl-eyed boy ate tinsel, so they didn't put it on anymore.

The owl-eyed boy saw a strange looking boy. The boy had a hat on his head. The boy had hats in both his hands. There were more hats on the ground, all around the boy. The hats were red. Each hat had a white feather in it.

There are books that promise hope just by the fact of their existence.

The owl-eyed boy lifted his head off the pillow.

Chappy tipped the book.

The owl-eyed boy tried to tell if he felt hope just by looking at this book, but he couldn't tell. He wasn't sure what hope felt like. He wasn't sure he'd ever felt hope. Or not felt it.

This kind of hope is a slim hope, bound in a cover. It is hope as slim as a poem. Chappy looked at the dark square of window above the owl-eyed boy's bed. He looked back at the book in his hands.

The owl-eyed boy kept his head raised off the pillow, only now he wasn't looking at the book cover, he was looking at Chappy.

The poem, Chappy said, is a desperate falling off from the page. It is a renaming of the hunger that won't let go.

Chappy. Mirror was standing in the door. Are you trying to put the boy to sleep, or make sure he never goes to sleep again?

Chappy looked up. He held the book between his hands like a prayer. Perhaps this isn't the best book to read tonight. Chappy looked toward the owl-eyed boy. He put his hands on his knees, pushed himself up from the edge of the bed.

Will you read me a poem by Souvankham Thammavongsa? The owl-eyed boy was the one in the family who could pronounce Souvankham's name. When Souvankham came to visit, the owl-eyed boy greeted her at the door. He led her into the house. Mirror and Chappy greeted Souvankham with a silent hug. It was okay, because Souvankham carried a kind of silence with her wherever she went. Even her name produced a kind of silence, followed by a song that itself was a sort of silence.

Chappy went to the bookshelf and ran his finger along the volumes, stopping at the thin blue spine that belonged to *Found*. He pulled the book from the shelf. Is there a particular poem you'd like to hear?

The Sun.

Chappy read:

The Sun

      built

        shafts

          and sent them

down to harm you;

but you,

    you lifted

        from dirt;

    took each

        one down;

    and built,

          to survive

Chappy held the book open a moment, looking up at the darkened window. He thought he could see the shape of the tree out in the yard behind the house, but it was dark and Chappy might just have been remembering the shape of the tree, projecting it, the way Souvankham projected the sun.

The owl-eyed boy had his head on his pillow. He looked at peace.

Chappy closed the book. He slipped it back into the little space on the shelf where it had sat before he pulled it off.

Goodnight, said the owl-eyed boy.

Goodnight, said Chappy.

Goodnight, said Mirror.

I love you, said the owl-eyed boy.

I love you, said Chappy.

I love you, said Mirror.

See you in the morning, said the owl-eyed boy.

See you in the morning, said Mirror.

See you tomorrow night, said Chappy.

See you tomorrow night, said the owl-eyed boy.

Chappy and Mirror went out of the room. Closed the door most of the way. They went into the kitchen. They sat in the breakfast booth under the sixty-watt lightbulb.

Mirror looked at the clock over the sink. It said ten o'clock. You need to get him to bed earlier, she said.

When Mirror came home at night, she brought cold air from outside with her. Mirror came home several hours after the owl-eyed boy saw Chappy. She entered the house with an energy that made the owl-eyed boy feel better. Mirror didn't take her shoes off, just crossed the living room and kissed the owl-eyed boy on the face. The owl-eyed boy felt the cold Mirror carried with her from walking up the street from the bus. He smelled bus on her. And the cloth of her coat. And the shampoo she used. The shampoo smelled green.

Whispering in the silent, I try to feel my way. Bicycle Shop God spoke softly.

Mirror leaned forward to hear. Pardon?

People will often tell you whatever it is they feel they need to tell you, said Bicycle Shop God, with no regard for anything you have just told them.

Waiting for Chappy to kiss her goodnight – waiting for him to kiss her, so that he could hurry up and go down the concrete steps and around the corner of the house and get on his bike and go home so that Mirror could go in the house and hide under the covers of her bed – Mirror wanted nothing more than to not be noticed.

Being with Chappy tonight was like being with a book. You could open it, see it, read what it said – but the book couldn't see you. It couldn't notice you at all, because it was a book, and, like all books, it had no sentience.

I was a porcupine pursuing a girl, Chappy told Mirror. A girl who looked a lot like Cathy. We were lonely together, like bits of cheese melted into different dishes. God persuaded me not to listen. I fell to the floor and slept. Someone opened a door upstairs. It started to snow. I thought, Who put the chair in the middle of the room like that?

Mirror felt herself swoon. She wanted to touch Chappy. If she opened her mouth, she wanted to pant.

The dogs went out the front door tragically, Chappy said.

His face was crumply, like he no longer understood the game he was trying to play. Cheese was melting into people's eyes. God caught onto what we were doing. God smashed us. It was what he decided to do. Old people fell open in snow. There were lilies in their hair.

Mirror looked at Chappy's face. Chappy was looking straight at Mirror out of eyes as round as owls. Mirror felt caught. She lifted her hand to touch Chappy, but then she stopped. She had no idea where to touch him. Her hand hovered like a hummingbird. It vibrated like a hummingbird. Fast. As though it would hover for a brief moment at great speed, then die from the very speed of itself.

Squirrels arrived in the morning. Ears down. Eyes blank. Silver lakes sparkling in the valley below. Mirror sat in the crook of a tree. The owl-eyed boy played in the dirt below. It was early morning. The boy talking quietly to himself. Or to a friend that Mirror couldn't see. Or to the squirrels. The boy's voice was hushed. He whispered. Squirrels watched. They sat at the edge of the clearing. They chattered. Something was going on. The boy lifted something Mirror couldn't see and proffered it to the sky.

Mirror saw a tall, dark-haired man with heavy whiskers. The man was holding a pair of binoculars. He kept the glass to his eyes for a time, then dropped the binoculars to his side. His lips moved. He was a far ways off from Mirror. He wasn't speaking loudly. He might not have been speaking at all, just forming words in his mind, lips miming thoughts. But Mirror could hear what he said: You're so sweet. You're so fine. Just like a car, you're so pleasing to behold. The man was part of the trees. His hair caught in wind and curved like glass. His hair waved like grass in fields behind him.

Red tractors rode the horizon like it was a road.

See Mirror now. She is having an effect on this man. He is phasing out like a man on the transporter pad in a science fiction movie. He is becoming one with the air, then returning, joining trees, waving arms like branches reaching for clouds.

Seeing you again, Mirror heard, is doing things to my heart and the palms of my hands.

God had his own pair of binoculars. He held them to his eyes. He was watching the tall, whiskered man, whose name was Everett. God hadn't seen Everett for fifteen years. God was bigger than a planet, but smaller than he'd ever been before. He'd been bigger than a supernova at one time. A not so very long ago time, God thought whimsically. God was infinite at the start of time, but he had been giving pieces of himself away ever since.

I won't last forever, God thought. He lowered the binoculars from his eyes. He tapped them against his thigh. What is it that makes me so interested in Everett? God thought. Everett is a good man. But there have been plenty of good men over the years. They slip away. More good men slip away than even I can know. More good men will come. There will always be good men. But I won't be here forever. If I latch onto Everett now, what will I miss?

Morning slipped by. God remained where he was. Now and then, he lifted the binoculars to his eyes. Located Everett.

Everett, in the meantime, had slid off the rock. He began to walk. He walked along the ridge, toward Mirror and the owl-eyed boy. He moved slowly.

He looks tired, God thought.

God zoomed his binoculars. He zoomed in close on Everett's face. God's binoculars have infinite zoom.

*

Everett's face doesn't look tired, God thought. There is light in his face this morning. He is moving slowly now. It has nothing to do with fatigue.

The last time God saw Everett, Everett had a great deal going on. He used his movement to quickly, but always agilely, seem agitated. Now he seemed content.

Chappy saw the blood fish. He sat on the street. He felt his feet. His feet hurt. A door opened. Wind. Cheese melted. God felt sad. That's weird, Chappy said.

Chappy ate. Bread. Toast. Drink this coffee, a man told Chappy. Chappy remembered Mirror, briefly, like a flash of fish in a darkened lake. His fist hammered. This will be a letter to Mirror, Chappy thought. But one she won't ever read. I'll say anything I want in it, so it won't really be a letter to Mirror, because I can never really say what I want to Mirror.

What I want to say to Mirror can't be said, Chappy thought. But if I wanted to say it – if I really wanted to say everything I want to say to Mirror – I couldn't even say it if I tried, even if it could be said.

We circumscribe ourselves. We stop one another from saying certain things. We stop ourselves. We hear ourselves within the framework of what we want to say. The project, you see, Chappy told himself, is to see. Beyond the moment is the plan. To fix up, to alter the moment, that is the plan. To adjust the moment before the moment becomes. To make the moment what it will eventually become. That is the project we plan for all our lives. We never know the moment for what it is in the way God knows the moment. The way God is the moment. God is everything the moment had that we never saw because of our plans for the moment.

Mirror was about to mount her new bicycle. Before she got on it, though, there were details to be hammered out. It was a beautiful machine, the new bicycle. There was no doubt about that. The colour was good. Solid. It was blue. But a special sort of blue. A blue that meant, for Mirror, something beyond blue. Beyond sky. Beyond ocean.

The font they used to paste the name of the bike on the crossbar was an airy sort of font, one Mirror could appreciate. Mirror showed this font to the owl-eyed boy. That's a good font, don't you think, she said. The owl-eyed boy nodded. Mirror couldn't tell if he really liked the font, or if he just wanted to get this over with... get this bike, get on this bike, ride this bike, ride to find Chappy, find Chappy, and bring the sonofabitch back home where he belonged.

The gleaming silver wheel hubs. The cables disappearing into the tubing, reappearing just in time to connect to a derailleur or a brake assembly.

*

Chappy and the owl-eyed boy walked from Chappy's sister's place to the beach. The beach was empty. It was February.

The owl-eyed boy got huge rocks. He got them from the beach. He dragged the huge rocks across the park to the harbour. Then he and Chappy threw the rocks into the harbour and talked about the sister's boy, the cousin, who the owl-eyed boy had seen in the park a few years earlier, playing with kids from a camp. They took the big rocks and hauled them across the park past the harbour condos and tossed them into the canal that runs up to the place where the boats are docked. The ice was thin in the canal and the rocks smashed through with a pop. Splumes of water shot out the holes made by the rocks. The owl-eyed boy threw giant sticks in, too. The giant sticks broke through the ice, then popped up a few feet from where they broke through, trapped beneath the ice. Chappy and the owl-eyed boy could see the sticks, drowning stickmen under the ice, trying to break free, their silent mouths open.

Chappy and the owl-eyed boy walked out onto the ice, to the place where the ice and snow welled up like a huge wave frozen close to shore. The huge wave ran the length of the lake, as far in either direction as Chappy and the owl-eyed boy could see. It made a kind of mountain. Chappy and the owl-eyed boy climbed the mountain. They stopped at the top of the mountain. They looked out over the lake. Beyond was ice for a long way out. They couldn't see where the ice stopped, where ice turned to open water. They could only see the open water from up the hill in town, but not from this mountain of ice they stood on at the edge of the lake.

The boy is too large for a bicycle seat. Bicycle Shop God stroked his chin. There were some hairs on his chin. You either have to buy the child his own bicycle, or you could buy one of these things. Bicycle Shop God raised his finger and opened his eyes wide. Mirror looked into his eyes. She felt like she was peering into hollow metal, a light alloy structure with lots of air streaming through.

Bicycle Shop God turned. He moved across the wooden floor of his ship. He was a mariner, propped up on deck in a storm. He stared at the back of the shop like he'd never seen it before, pointed to a smallish contraption that looked like a bicycle with an apparatus on the front for connecting it up to a bigger bike.

Will you hook it up for us? Mirror asked.

Bicycle Shop God looked surprised to see a woman on board his ship. He made an elegant turn, shifting his feet gracefully in a way that did not make the deck of the ship creak. It will cost you extra, he said. For the labour.

Hallways are frightening places. Hallways narrow down possibility, funnelling one room into another. For a brief moment, between rooms, the walls seem too close.

Then you step through a doorway. A room opens. Light spills through a window. Furniture sits patiently in corners. The frightening hallways are forgotten.

I'd much rather wander the fields of a poet's words than follow the train tracks left by a novelist, Chappy said. The curtains were shut, but for a foot-wide gap in the middle. Light from the gap made Mirror's eyes shine like empty tunnels with floodlights shining out from inside.

What are you reading? asked Mirror. They were in the living room. They were on separate couches, each curled up with a book and a cup of coffee.

I'm reading Kurt Cobain's journals, Chappy told Mirror. And then I've got this other book with pictures of sheep and mountain goats.

Chappy didn't welcome the night of falling music. He didn't try to explain it. He was pretty sure he feared it. He was definitely angry with it. He felt powerful in his way. But the night of falling music felt more powerful.

People told Chappy about the night of falling music. They told him it was a thing of beauty, a thing that defied description. You will never really understand it, people told him. And then they went away. These were people he'd met on the street, in front of the barber shop, at the post office, the places a person feels safest when he comes to the middle of town on a day when the sun is shining, and the people stand on paths that cross the park in the square at the centre of town.

For it is said that the falling music has no melody, no rhythm, no pattern.

Yet the falling music is perfect in its form, which is no form at all.

Most people won't understand what I am saying, but the music exists as music because it can't be said. Anything you say about the falling music is better said by the fall and clamour of the notes. Anything you think about the falling music is better heard by the fall of sound in the inner ear. Anything you feel about the falling music is better beat out in the beat of your heart.

Winter was almost here. The people of the town told Chappy he wouldn't understand the falling music until he actually heard it, but Chappy thought the falling music would sound like an attack. It would sound like a truck had hit him.

Here's a goat. Chappy held up the book. His eyes closed for a moment, a slow motion blink. He needed to comb his hair. Pages and pages of goats. Did you know the modern horse started off as a mini-horse, about the size of a jackrabbit? I forgot the name of the thing – epo-something. Did you know that the hippo is actually a giant pig?

I had Sally Carth meet me at the ice bridge, said Chappy.

What ice bridge? Mirror asked. They were staying out by the lake, near Chappy's sister's house. There was no ice bridge near Chappy's sister's house. No ice bridge Mirror knew of, anyway. Why did you call Sally Carth? Mirror asked. We haven't seen Sally Carth in years.

I didn't call her, Chappy said. I conspired with the universe to bring her to the ice bridge this afternoon at precisely two o'clock. The same time I arrived. Chappy was in his pyjamas. He needed a shave.

I like it when light comes into the sky, Mirror, Chappy said. He was looking out the blurry motel window at the motel parking lot. There weren't a lot of cars in the motel parking lot. It was early March. No one was travelling.

Things – that house across the way, I mean – look solid against the sunless dawn. Look, Mirror. They're like things hungry for light. Things stopped dead in their anticipation.

These were the words of a poet, Mirror knew. She wondered what Chappy saw out there. She wondered if Chappy was in some other universe, if his soul was somewhere north, near an ice bridge, near Sally Carth.

It was a noisy place that Mark went to live during his nineteenth year. On summer afternoons, in the parking lot below his window, there were boxing matches. Rings of people surrounded boxers, who wore new red boxing gloves. Cheering rings of people undulated as boxers danced. Mark stayed alone in his room, devising soundtracks for the drama unfolding all around him.

The owl-eyed boy sat on the little pseudo-bicycle behind his mother. His head pivoted slowly. He was taking in the scene. He was learning that the scene spread out in all directions, on both sides, like butter on a grilled cheese sandwich, with he and Mirror the guts, slapped onto the long roads of bread that Mirror travelled beneath the endless sky.

Mirror made no effort to hurry. She made no effort at all. All effort was effort of will, Mirror saw.

When she came to an uphill section of road, Mirror dismounted. She lifted the owl-eyed boy off the bike. They walked. Mirror held the T where the bike's handlebars connected to the frame.

Mirror held her son's left hand in her own right hand. They travelled each day till the sun set, at which point they found a place to roost.

Chappy's job was a secret job. Chappy's job was to screen people before they went to see the human resources people. The people Chappy screened had come to see about getting jobs.

I played the snare drum from grade five to eleven, a man told Chappy. Then I got a part-time job at Dunkin Donuts. The man handed Chappy a piece of paper. This is an overview of my life just after I gave up playing the snare drum.

Chappy found himself in the living room with Mirror again. The curtains closed. The lamps in the corners lit. The Christmas tree was up, decorated by the owl-eyed boy on the weekend. Chappy couldn't focus on the book that sat in his lap. He was thinking about the words inside him that he couldn't put into words. He was thinking about the rain that would come later in the week, and the wind that would steal leaves from trees, leaving them naked and bereft.

Mirror wrote: Yesterday, I thought to make a wildlife journal. It almost seems too late, though. We've been on the road for days. I should have been writing down what I saw all along, since we started this trip. I want to say what all the wildlife we've seen already was.

The owl-eyed boy was asleep in the tent. Mirror was out by the fire. She felt less afraid.

We saw two snow-white dogs in a ditch at the side of the road this afternoon. I hope they're somebody's dogs, the owl-eyed boy said. He worries for the dogs. He thinks they might be alone, with no one to take care of them.

I saw a bird with a wide wingspan that made its body look small. It seemed to grab the air with its wings, then pull hard enough to leave its body behind. Then it caught up to itself and pulled again.

The owl-eyed boy saw a hippo. I didn't see that. But we passed some farm zoos. There could have been a hippo. We passed some llamas yesterday that both I and the owl-eyed boy saw. We saw a horse hitched to a sign post on the shoulder of the road. There were Mennonites standing on the shoulder of the rode, across the highway from their horses, with a table, and bottles of maple syrup lined up on the table. I wanted to stop and get some maple syrup. But the owl-eyed boy said no. And then I just wanted to keep going. I didn't want to stop anymore, ever again. We saw horses by a barn, just standing still in front of the cold, windless sky. I saw two Canada geese standing on the ice in the canal that leads to the dock area. We were at the beach. I was going to show the geese to the owl-eyed boy, but he was too far away. He was hauling big logs. He wanted to throw these big logs onto the ice. By the time the owl-eyed boy got to where I was, with the big logs he was hauling, the geese had flown away, honking with a sound that echoed like we were in a cave.

Last year, I went Christmas shopping very early in the year. I don't usually do this. Suddenly, for the first time, I had to find places to hide things so that no one would find them. I kept telling people to stay away from the places I was hiding things. Danger! I said. There is danger if you open that closet door. But no one listened to me. No one took me seriously. They laughed when I said it. Danger! I said. And they laughed. It was funny.

No one cared about Chappy at that moment and it was perfect. He sat in a dark room alone – unknown, unmourned, uncelebrated. He disappeared, and in the moment of his disappearance, he died.

He listened to what the others said about him and none of it was true, but he said nothing to correct them. It was like he had become a character in one of their stories, and it pleased him. It was a heavy pleasure, one that made him breathe faster, almost like sex, but something else. He thought, This is not me, it is a character in a story, and so he said nothing, for how do you correct a story when there was never really any story to begin with.

Chappy stood. He tried to figure out ways of reacting. He touched the tops of his thighs. He was still there.

Picture it, Chappy said to himself. But what was he trying to picture? He was trying to picture something he could not quite picture. It seemed a lofty enough pursuit. It didn't seem unrealistic, no matter what Mirror tried to tell him. He was trying to picture something he could almost picture. If he could picture it completely already, what kind of pursuit would it be?

Anyway, said Chappy, looking down at his feet. If you could just help me out here. Just help me out a little.

The man on the corner stroked his long, white beard, and looked thoughtful.

Wait a moment longer, but when nobody says anything, and everything seems in danger of no longer being dangerous, remember.

The old man turned and wandered away in the direction he'd been going before anybody ever thought to stop him.

June 2008. Mark is preparing to go to Humber jazz school. I've finished reading the biography of Lenny Breau and I'm starting a book about Jackie Du Pré, written by her sister and brother. A windy thunderstorm is tearing at the trees in the ravine. I can see the tops of the biggest trees where they rise above the townhouses across the playground from our backyard. They bow like giving benediction, swaying in the savage wind.

A Texan dying in the sand beside his hovercraft, so far from water it makes no sense. Mirror rides on, hoping her heart won't stop her. She has only the boy to sway her. But the boy remains behind, a reminder.

Keep moving, Mirror murmurs. Stay ahead of what your heart demands.

I live in the writer's vault. Don't think of this as a set of instructions, though. You're so carefully prepared. You could easily make a mistake.

The maps you buy at the gas stations look so clean the first time you open them.

Bicycle Shop God was lost. The clearings were getting fewer. He could barely see his way clear to the woman and her boy standing on the worn wooden floor of his ship.

Never read into the random breaks a system of authority.

He had to make everything clear quickly. He had to win back her confidence.

It's not as though someone puts the paths and clearings in the forest to make things easier for you, is it.

He tried to smile. The woman's hand went to her child's head. She spread her hand across her child's skull like a bicycle helmet.

Read the map as though you were entering a forest with no instructions for getting out alive.

*

Keep your notes.

Help sense the vaguely savage.

From somewhere deep in the back of her mind Mirror let out a final little cry. All of this is not some sort of joke, she hoped.

When Chappy had got himself arranged in what he felt to be a reasonable facsimile of the way the owl-eyed boy was arranged, he looked sideways at the boy. The owl-eyed boy looked at him and smiled. The smile didn't last.

The boy looked down at his lap, then away. He looked toward the window. The back of his head was facing Chappy. Chappy heard music. It was outside the cabin. It was almost tuneless. It was an eerie rising and falling. Toneless. No discernible rhythm. No apparent purpose.

The music seemed happy sometimes. It sounded like something Chappy had heard before, a long time before, like a song he'd grown to love and was hearing again for the first time in years. But this time, with the owl-eyed boy here beside him, the sound seemed not to be so happy. It seemed merely to exist, and then fade away, and then reappear, to exist again briefly, only to fade away again once and for all.

There was something compelling about the falling music. Chappy found himself perched on the edge of his bed, waiting to hear it again. It left him feeling emptier each time he heard it. The lack of substance, this hollow thin wail, it made Chappy feel that, even alone in this cabin in a town far away from Mirror and the owl-eyed boy, it might be worth seeking his own elusive substance.

The sound emptied Chappy entirely.

Part Two

October 2008. I'm in bed. It is 2:30 p.m. Sunday. I've been sick. Mary says to stay in bed. So I do. Voovie is snoring. He's on his side, a puff of fur rising and falling near the foot of the bed. His front paws twitch, then fall still. His head is tipped, not quite upside-down. I can see one of his fangs.

Outside, it might be raining. I can see the roofs of the units across the street. The tiles look wet. But I hear no rain. It might have stopped. Or, it might be a light rain still falling.

Voovie's little breaths are just audible over the seemingly constant hiss of cars on the street. The window is slightly open. It is warm for October 26.

The sight of Voovie so comfortable reminds me how sick he was not long ago. It makes me feel safe and happy to know he is well now.

But I love him too much.

Voovie's paws twitch again. His breathing takes on a harsh, ragged quality, but still remains soft and comforting to hear. Voovie wakes up suddenly, probably from a dream, lifts his head for a moment, then settles back down, chin nestled in the rumpled covers. After a while, he stretches. His head tips as his body shudders in the vortex of his stretch. He pulls what would be his wrist – if he had hands – up to his cheek, and rests it there, soft fur on soft fur.

That's when I go back out in search of Chappy and Mirror and the boy with the owl eyes. They come to flickering almost-life in the deep spiralling cone of Voovie's new breathing, which sounds now like a pneumatic pump cycling far off in the distance.

That's where I became the day, Chappy told Mirror. The day I wasn't me. You were still you. Also, I could smell the man.

What did the man smell like? Mirror was lying on her side, her head resting in the crook of Chappy's arm, her body loosely curled, knee touching Chappy's thigh, arm draped across Chappy's chest, fingers in the hair between Chappy's nipples.

I could smell his whisky skin, said Chappy. I could smell his deep pockets. He smelled like not-me. This man was a smooth rock near the shore of a lake no one ever visited.

There is this guy. This other guy. This so totally not Chappy guy. This guy is so completely someone else. This guy is standing on a beach. Beside him is a woman. The woman, who is feeling something, is not Mirror. But it might have been Mirror. And the man might have been Chappy.

Or it might have been that the woman was Mirror, and the man was not Chappy.

Or that the man was Chappy, and the woman not Mirror.

Any of these permutations are possible in the sprawling future not yet seen.

Mirror tried to think of things to do down at the river. She wanted to throw sticks in. Or stones. She wanted to catch bugs. Like a little kid, she wanted to catch fish. Like a burly man in a lumber jacket and baseball cap, she wanted to stick her bare feet in the river. Like an eleven-year-old girl, the year before she becomes a woman, knowing she is becoming a woman, Mirror wanted to be a stick. She wanted to be a puck. She wanted to slide on ice in winter. She wanted to see herself. She wanted to be that person who sees herself by a river.

Look in the river, in the eye of the river. Try to be a person who loves the river for no reason. Try to be a person who loves the river for the silver sliver of river at noon. Try to be the person who loves the brown river at dusk. Try to be the person who can simply watch the river. Watch the sparkle of river rippling in sun on a windy day. Watch the pock pock pock of river hit by rain. Watch the torrent of river on sunny days with snow melting. Be the buzz of bugs over river heat. Be that person. Be envied for it. Envy motionless forever staring somewhere far ahead. Be a Zen master practicing the art of being river. Be anything inside this world. Be a way of being outside of the world.

Chappy heard bells. He heard Mirror's voice. He saw horizons. Saw Mirror's eyes. He saw wind. He lay on Mirror's horizon. Heard wings flap inside her words. Words slipped past Mirror's lips. Love filled her mouth. Her words spilled, trotting like fillies toward Chappy's naked ears, eating Chappy's head.

Chappy went into the bathroom. He turned on the water. Rolled out some toilet paper. Blew his nose. He flushed the toilet. Paced. Looked up at the ceiling, then down at his toes. He wrung his hands. He sat on the toilet lid and wept. When he finished weeping, he left the bathroom. Mirror called him into the kitchen. He had lemonade. They sat at the kitchen table reading grocery flyers.

Mirror called him the dictionary man.

Who is he? Chappy asked.

Mirror felt so much a part of this life with Chappy. When she talked about the dictionary man, or similar subjects, it made her feel more a part of Chappy than she was a part of herself.

The way the flaps of her housecoat lifted slightly when she leaned over the sink to look at the tomato vines outside the kitchen window. The way the sun tapped her in the morning when she stood at the counter waiting for the coffee maker to finish making the coffee.

I feel like a part of a life, Mirror said, irrevocably, the way an actor is a part of a movie.

Chappy was looking at flyers. He looked up at Mirror now. He looked at her skin. Then he looked at her back. Then he looked at the place where the skin on her back showed between her hair and the collar of her housecoat. Why do we live here, Mirror? He looked back at the flyer laid out on the table in front of him. He moved his head closer to the flyer. He looked up at Mirror. Everything is so cheap in Cambridge, he said.

When the owl-eyed boy was born, I felt a kind of love or something. It felt like something growing inside me, like a tumour.

If the weather was good, Chappy and Mirror went out on the balcony. They looked across the parking lot at the railroad tracks. If the weather was lousy, they went and got groceries. They took the owl-eyed boy when they went to get groceries. They got him a free cookie from the bakery section of the grocery story, then they sat him in the buggy, his legs hanging out the holes they put in grocery buggies for legs of kids to hang out. Mirror moved around the grocery store like a machine, picking out lettuce, a loaf of bread, other things, all the time going through her coupons.

You wrote this?
　Yes.
　Why?
　I had some time.
　You could have done anything, said Chappy. You could have done nothing.

The owl-eyed boy said nothing. The words he'd written stood on the page, unretractable.

They would be filed. Forgotten. Found one day, perhaps. But by who?

Chappy shook his head. What should I do with it?

File it, the boy said. But it might have been more of a question than a command. It might have been a denial.

Will you remember it? Chappy asked.

The boy hesitated. What did this man want? Yes, he said, finally.

Chappy also hesitated. He looked at the words. Pulled out a lighter. Lit the page. Held it till the flame approached his fingers, then dropped it on the floor. He stepped on it.

The boy went out of the room, closed the door, leaned back against the door, tipped his head back till it touched the door. He tried to remember the words he'd written on the paper. Already, some of them were gone. He tried to picture them. He saw the spaces in between, where flame had licked away all meaning. He felt the beauty rush in.

The owl-eyed boy looked at Chappy. You're on a mission, he said. Aren't you?

Yes, said Chappy.

The boy nodded. Looked at Chappy's hands. His legs. His face. Where are your weapons? he asked.

Chappy shrugged. He looked confused. He shook his head.

You need a weapon, the owl-eyed boy said. He turned and crawled across his bed to where a poster was stuck to the wall above the pillows. This is where I keep my weapons, he said, lifting a corner of the poster. There was a hole in the wall behind the poster. The owl-eyed boy reached into the hole. His arm disappeared up to the shoulder.

The pool supervisor was a balding fellow, lean, wiry, friendly. He asked if Chappy and the owl-eyed boy needed help. What level is he in? the fellow asked.

Six, said Chappy. He said it on the spur of the moment. He had no idea what level the owl-eyed boy was actually in.

Three, said the boy.

What's your name? the pool supervisor asked.

Owl, said the owl-eyed boy.

The pool supervisor ran his finger down a list. That's an unusual name, he said without looking up. Here you are. You'll be with Rag. That's him over there. The pool supervisor pointed to a boy in the pool surrounded by mothers and their infants. That's Rag, said the pool supervisor. The pool supervisor had POOL SUPERVISOR sewed into the side of his bathing suit.

This is a deeper meaning, Chappy said. This is a meaning that is hard to get at. This meaning is buried. You know this meaning, Mirror. It is there. It is always there, if you want to go looking for it. It is always there. Somewhere. Under the ground. Begin digging. Be prepared to do some work.

You have to finish your mission, the owl-eyed boy told Chappy. But Chappy didn't see this. He wanted to stay here with his head in the owl-eyed boy's lap, with the boy's hand in his hair.

You can't give up now, Chappy, the boy said. You've worked too hard.

Chappy had only started his mission that morning, but he knew the boy was right. He'd been on this mission forever.

You feel safe here with me now, said the boy, caressing Chappy's shoulder, massaging his neck. But you have to leave me sometime. You can't stay here forever.

Chappy kept his head in the boy's lap. He closed his eyes. He might have been asleep. He might have been dreaming.

Video games are played mostly for entertainment, Mirror said. Some players do not realize it, but video games help you adapt to many skills. She held the paddle in her hands, pushing buttons.

Chappy sat beside her.

Video games help you build hand-eye coordination, Mirror said. When you see something on the screen, your hands react and push a certain control that will affect what happens on the screen.

I don't care about this, Mirror, said Chappy, sitting back onto the couch.

Mirror pushed her paddle toward the TV. She jumped to her feet. The more you play, the faster your fingers react to what you see on the screen. Mirror's character looked like a little fox on two feet with a metal box on his back. The metal box had a hose attached to it. The hose shot fire. Mirror's character sprayed Chappy's character with fire. Chappy's character turned black and fell over.

Video games can also help you with reflexes and quick thinking, Mirror continued. She turned briefly to look at Chappy. If things in the game are jumping out at you...

Mirror pushed the joystick and hit a button on the controller and her character jumped forward… then this will help you react quickly.

Chappy's character lay on its back, still black from the earlier burst of fire.

The silence lasted only a moment. Chappy was not more than a few feet from the men. He did not want to be seen by the men. He did not wish to be disturbed. He hung a do not disturb sign on the nose of the Chappy within. This made him laugh. He must not laugh, though – the men would hear!

Chappy felt within himself his mission. He did not know exactly what his mission was. But he could feel it, like a pressure in his stomach.

He did not know exactly what Chappy was. In substance, he was, perhaps, nothing.

The men certainly didn't seem to see him. They talked quietly among themselves, as though alone, each with his thoughts. As they talked, the men moved along the path. Occasionally, one of them laughed softly. They passed so very close to Chappy.

Chappy saw himself. He saw himself ensconced in a little town, known to exist, but never bothered.

One of the men seemed to look directly at Chappy. For a moment, the man seemed to see Chappy. His brow darkened. He looked from the field of gold cast by the street light, into the dark. But then he turned quickly away, speaking to the other men.

The men moved within their laughter. Each went to a car parked along a street. Car doors slammed. Engines started.

One man stayed on the curb.

Cars pulled away.

The man on the curb waved.

When the cars were but sounds in the distance, the man on the curb stopped waving. He turned, walked past Chappy, went into his house. The porch light went off. It was truly night now. Chappy stood alone in the darkness.

For two months, Chappy had lived in the empty lot at the end of the street. Nights, he came out onto the street and stood under the owl-eyed boy's window. He saw the light behind the curtains. He imagined the owl-eyed boy sitting on the bed – just as he'd left him so many nights before – staring into space.

The street was wet tonight. The sky clear. Chappy could see the few stars that were visible in the city. The moon was high. It must have been full just a few days before.

Chappy turned, began walking. He walked toward the ocean. It was fifteen hundred miles to the ocean.

Chappy had no idea where he was going. He had no idea how he would get to where he was going. When he got there, he had no idea how he would know he had gotten to where he was going. It was a long walk. Chappy had time to think. He knew the ocean was deep. The owl-eyed boy had once said to him something about the ocean. Chappy tried to remember what the boy had said. He tried to remember as he walked past dark houses. He looked back. Saw that the owl-eyed boy's light was still on. It was the only light in any of the houses along the empty street. When Chappy looked back again, he had gone beyond the place where he could see the owl-eyed boy's light.

Mirror felt wide and calm, like a lake. She spread herself flat and featureless, a mirror to the sky. She could feel Chappy on her shores, dipping into her... hesitant. He's afraid, Mirror thought. Afraid of me. Chappy's fear and hesitation made Mirror feel calmer still, and the stillness of her heart and the slowness of her breathing radiated, touching Chappy as no embrace ever could, and he crumpled into Mirror like a drowning man sinking, at last hopeless, into a bottomless lake. But Mirror remained buoyant and Chappy did not drown. He held on tight to Mirror and together they made a lake of their combined tears.

What the scientists now call radio waves were, in the time before time, wind of mind. All mind flowed in this wind. When, at the dawn of time, a bit of the wind fell away, it died in a swirl of writhing evil. For, to be apart is what we today think of as evil. These bits of unexpected evil, which died practically in the moment of their conception, brought good into existence. What had been just wind was now good, in the way poet, or anti-scientist – or simply tenaciousness – suddenly is real poet.

Chappy put another log on the fire, then went over to the window and looked out into the night. Mostly, all he saw was himself reflected back in the window, but there were some shadows of things he could make out if he pushed his forehead to the window and held his hand above his head to block out the light reflected from inside the cabin.

I don't want to live here anymore, Chappy said.
    Can you tell me a story?
    I don't know a story.
    Yes, you do know a story.

But it might not be a very good story.

It doesn't matter. I just want a story. Any story.

All right, I'll tell you a story. Is there a particular story you want to hear? Chappy had learned a long time ago that in times of mind a particular story in a particular mind could mean something quite different from the same particular story in a different particular mind.

One story that Chappy had told before had a particular favourite character from one of Chappy's other stories that he told before. If you told a story and it wasn't the one people wanted, would the people wait to hear another story, or would they just walk away? If they just walked away, would other people come to stand in the space where the people who walked away had been, so that you could tell another story to another group of people and try to make it a story this new group of people wanted to hear?

Theodore would wait till Chappy finished the story and then ask for another. He would make Chappy tell stories till Chappy told the one Theodore wanted to hear.

Tell one about Princess Mirror, said Theodore.

Okay.

It made Chappy sad to tell stories about Mirror, but he liked telling them. Telling stories about Mirror made Chappy remember how much he missed her.

Princess Mirror lived in a far distant land, Chappy began, across a great ocean. But the vast expanse of ocean was nothing compared to the universe of distance that stood between the lands the princess and her prince inhabited each in their own mind.

Theodore sat back on the couch. He closed his eyes.

Distance, it turns out, was the beginning and the end. The first and the last. The only. All else was just distance from this only moment that began and ended the story.

Everything Chappy was saying these days was becoming an afterthought to what he'd said just a moment before. Everything just arrived. Theodore just arrived. Night just arrived. Chappy felt lost. He had to remind himself that this was a story.

Theodore had his eyes closed. Chappy was able to fixate on his face, to examine his face closely. To focus on the way Theodore's nose sat on his face.

Since this is a story, mostly out of fear we will begin at the beginning and make our way back. For, in order to make this a story at all, we begin by throwing ourselves to the far end. We then attempt the difficult return to our beginnings.

Theodore sighed, sank deeper into the couch.

Chappy wondered what was coming next. And then, suddenly, what was coming next came, and Chappy was waiting to see what was coming next.

Each word we lay upon together grasps again for beginning. To say we are to begin at the beginning is only a commitment to reach with each of our collective utterances for that beginning we so long to repossess.

The owl-eyed boy told people his hair was gold. My eyes are pink, he told people.

You have beautiful blue eyes, Mirror told the owl-eyed boy, holding his head between her hands so she could gaze into his eyes.

The boy shook free. No, he said. My eyes are pink.

The teacher in a story creates an equivalency. Creating an equivalency is the only thing teachers know how to do.

If you know anything about equivalencies, you know that, at bottom, the story of an equivalency is a story of love. Two things, such as Mirror and Chappy – or Mirror and the owl-eyed boy, or the owl-eyed boy and Chappy – move toward each other, seeking equivalency, examining equivalency, moving together toward something beyond them that represents equivalency in its absolute oneness and its utter, unquestionable resistance to duality.

From the position of duality, equivalency seems like the only resolution for oneness. But from the position of oneness, duality never existed at all.

One side of the equation does not authorize the other. In a terrible sense, equivalency causes one side to cancel the other out.

Chappy and Mirror certainly gauged value by the standards of love. Which is a mistake. It is a mistake that the teacher must not make.

Chappy could not get the owl-eyed boy's bicycle into the garage because of the way Mirror had parked the car. He took the bike around to the back of the house and threw it over the fence. It bounced onto the lawn.

Chappy went back around to the front of the house. He went into the house.

What's he saying up there? Mirror asked when Chappy came back.

I don't know, said Chappy. I don't think he's saying anything meaningful, Mirror. I think he's just practicing talking. I can't make out a single word he's saying.

Whatever he's saying, Chappy, I think it must mean something.

Yes, Mirror, but it's a secret meaning.

It means something to him.

But he's so far away from us in the world he inhabits at this point in his life that what he says means nothing to us.

I don't want to know the secret, but everything I say gives it away. I want to keep the secret from myself, so I try to talk myself away from it. But everything I say is just the same secret being said again in a different way.

Mirror was silent. For many days, she said nothing. She tried to think what her secret secret might be. But if her secret secret was something she was keeping secret even from herself, how could she ever know what her secret secret was.

Mirror showed Chappy things in the flyers she kept beside her whenever she went to bed. She talked about other people's laundry. The neighbours have some nice red towels, she said. I've seen them hanging on their balcony.

Chappy was waiting for Mirror. He parked, and waited, and the street filled up with people. He was meant to wait, he knew, but part of him wanted to leave. Part of him didn't believe Mirror would come.

He was waiting one corner before where you would turn to go to the museum. The road to the museum looked like a truck depot. There were trucks parked at odd angles all along the street. Chappy had been on this street before, but he couldn't remember when. He wanted to tell Mirror about this street, about how much this street looked like a truck depot.

When Mirror finally arrived, she looked breathless and beautiful, but before Chappy could say anything to her, Mirror said, This street looks like a truck depot, Chappy. I've been this street before, she said. I remember this place.

Chappy was also going across fields. He had to get over three big floppy pipes. He might have been looking for the owl-eyed boy. Mirror never showed up. Chappy thought he might be on the wrong street.

Chappy went looking for Mirror again on another day.

When he went to sleep that night, Chappy found himself lying on a bed with Colleen. Colleen snuggled onto him, handled him. Chappy and Colleen had just been reunited after thirty-four years, and Chappy thought they could get married and have kids. They were both in their late thirties. It wasn't necessarily too late to have kids. As Chappy climbed over pipes, he remembered Colleen's husband. He remembered that Colleen already had kids. Two kids, Chappy remembered.

I was riding a little kid's thing. It looked like a cross between a big wheel and a trike. A tractor trailer truck nearly backed over me. Way up high in the cab of the truck a Russian woman with wild hair looked down at me and laughed.

Chappy was furious. This is like a movie, he thought, with the Russian woman and her two cohorts – one skinny, the other a big, burly, bearded Russian guy – were doing something illegal in a house. They were installing art pieces. One of the art pieces was a bed they were hanging from a tree. The skinny guy fell and was killed. It was Chappy's curse on them for laughing. The fat guy and the woman were still in the house. The fat guy was freaked out about the curse. He jumped through a huge window and fell toward a fence with animal horns and other pointy things attached to it that were going to impale him. As he fell toward the fence, Chappy thought, Change the scene, change the scene. But no one heard him. He woke up and realized that he'd slept in his clothes again.

He'd gallop at first, running faster and faster, feeling light without the cart, not knowing what it was that was making him feel so free. But then he'd slow down. He'd stop, eventually. He'd look back at us.

The horse won't be looking at us now, Chappy told Mirror. He'll see the air all around him, like an all-embracing friend. He'll dip his head quite slowly. His mane will quiver with flies.

She died, of course, said Mirror. She's gone. But where is she now? Mirror cut Chappy another piece of cake.

Chappy knew he had made a fatal mistake. He had opened a back door on a place he should never have even ventured into. He was in a neighbourhood he had no business being in. This was a door he should not ever have opened. Fear trickled down the valley in his back where his spine ran the length of his upper body.

Chappy wouldn't sleep at all now, he knew. He knew this as perfectly as he felt the tingle in his fingertips, making it hard for him to feel anything but his fingertips. He tried to feel what should come next for him, but he couldn't feel anything. The numbness in his fingertips felt like the end of all accomplishment. The word accomplishment sat in Chappy like some god bound to limit his vision. Eyes down, blanket up to her neck, Mirror looked at the clock that was blinking red at the far end of the room. Morning hadn't come yet, but Mirror was afraid that it soon would.

Mirror dances. Her heart beats harder. Chappy's heart beats harder, too. Harmony, my love, Mirror says. We miss each others' notes. We sing our separate songs. We hear each other sing. Placate those who are not prepared to sing. Sing quietly in your head. Kill those who sing without hitting any note. We are inside our naked noises, deep inside the hollow echo of our selfhood.

Chappy was smitten with the new toaster. And to think we've done without this for so long, he told Mirror. How did we even live without this thing?

There's an engine, they say, Chappy, that keeps us alive when we haven't got these gadgets in our lives.

The toaster had a small computer chip that allowed a person to interface with it. Chappy pointed to the tiny keyboard that was included in the cost of the toaster. Type in the colour of the toast you want, Chappy told Mirror. Watch what happens. This will fundamentally change everything, Mirror. This toaster should make things more simple.

God is most simple, Mirror whispered, because God never tries.

Harmony made itself plain in the lines in the sky. Mirror felt love in the grass beneath her feet. We miss each other, Chappy. I miss you. Do you miss me?

Chappy was on the front porch, watching Mirror. I'm right here, Mirror, he said.

We each sing our separate songs.

Chappy was humming, but he stopped now to try to hear what Mirror was saying. But he saw her dance, and the humming he had been making had its source in the dancing Mirror made.

There are many who are not prepared to sing. They are in the offices in the east end of town. The offices rise into the sky like crystal spires rising higher than small mountains. They are too skinny to last forever.

Watch the sky, Mirror, Chappy said. He could feel the desperate hopelessness of the limitless hope he felt. With Mirror dancing in the front yard, it flung out of him like he'd opened a window in his soul, but at high altitude, so instead of fresh air rushing in to sate his hunger, his guts got sucked out and dropped a thousand feet, from high above the clouds, spattering on the earth like a lamb dropped from the peak of a mountain, high above the clouds, to splatter on the rock near the alpine tents.

Chappy and Mirror's day was at an end. In the end, they had decided to go down the hill to the river. To let the cart roll. To give the horse its freedom.

Now they were going home. They were trying to get back up the hill. Finally, Chappy gave up and sat down on the sidewalk.

Fuck it, he said. I'm going back down the hill. I'll sleep by the pond.

What about the mosquitoes? Mirror asked. She was looking down the hill toward the pond. When she looked back over her shoulder, the hill was gone.

Technology, Chappy said.

The sky was dust-coloured.

You know that man who writes the column in the newspaper, Chappy asked Mirror. We have his book.

Finally, the two of them slept the sleep of babies with nothing in their heads. When they woke, they woke with the hunger of babies, with nothing to do but eat.

You remember that guy who could hold his breath underwater longer than anyone? Chappy asked Mirror. They had the light on in the living room. It was almost winter. It got dark so early.

You mean Simon? Mirror asked.

No, said Chappy. Fuck, Mirror, are you even listening to me? The guy who could hold his breath longer than anybody. Simon could hold his breath about as long as a cat.

Mirror was listening, as it turns out. As it turns out, she'd been listening all day. She'd been listening since the day she met Chappy. She'd been waiting, listening, hoping to hear Chappy say something she'd never heard him say before. Something no one had ever said.

How long can a cat hold its breath? Mirror asked.

Do you remember, Mirror?

Vaguely, said Mirror. But she didn't. She didn't remember at all.

The guy stopped holding his breath when he was twenty-two. He said he didn't want to do it anymore. He gave up holding his breath. When he died, there was no one who remembered exactly how long he could hold his breath. At the funeral, the two factions took up positions on opposite sides of the grave. One faction claimed that in the time since the guy stopped holding his breath no one had ever held his breath longer. The other faction claimed a nineteen-year-old guy in Germany had broken the dead guy's record and was still increasing the time he could hold his breath by a series of chest expansion exercises.

The mute being. The hollow ringing. Sound of people singing quietly. And their voices echoing off the walls.

The subway is a funny place. People's hair goes funny in the subway. Look. Mirror pointed. And nobody seems to be able to fix their hair once it goes like that. No matter what they try. Mirror looked at Chappy's hair. She touched it.

He imagines the old man is dying. Say something to that guy in the hat. He imagines that the old man feels irresistible.

People hurry and bump into each other. And when they bump into someone, they don't turn around to see who it was. They just keep going. Wouldn't you want to see who it was?

Did you walk all the way to the subway? the old man asks.
    Yes, says the boy.
    It's so cold, says the old man.

You might want to go to dinner, Chappy, Mirror says. Or you might just take a little walk. You could wash the car. Or just eat something you find in a garbage somewhere.

People know your secret. As soon as you open your mouth to speak, people hear your secret. That's why it is so scary to open your mouth.

There was something horribly exhausting about raising the owl-eyed boy. About the time he turned two, Chappy found it became more and more difficult to negotiate the line between what the boy wanted and what he could safely have. Chappy set the owl-eyed boy's bottle down on the coffee table. The owl-eyed boy pushed it.

Up until the kid was two, he stared at everything with his owl eyes. As he got older, it no longer seemed to be enough for him to see the world. He wanted to touch it as well. The owl-eyed boy looked at Chappy. His eyes big and round and watching.

I thought, Chappy told Theodore, that, by leaving, I might find another approach, a way to capture that elusive something I was feeling inside me and put it on display for others to see. But no one can hear what I'm talking about. Can you hear what I'm talking about, Theodore?

Theodore was playing with two twigs that had fallen to the floor as he brought in the firewood.

They don't know when they've heard me, Chappy said. I am able to say things that sound to me like the things I'm trying to say, but, whatever it is I am trying to say, it seems I am unable to say it in the things I actually say.

Chappy was cold, so he went into a video store. It was the only store open at that time of night. The store was busy.

Entire families, many of them in flimsy clothing not suited to the weather, were in the store.

The adults seemed most lost. They were lost in the shadow of a world of woe that held only the slimmest of hopes. Hope sat about their eyes, a thin, evanescent light surrounding the shadows deeper inside their eyes.

The only ones in the store who seemed comfortable were the kids. The kids were running around like maniacs. They were picking up videos. They were yelling: Can we get this!

On a street far from the video store, after the video store had closed and Chappy had had to leave, Chappy saw a woman sitting on her front porch. The woman was peeling the outer layer off an onion. She put the onion in a pot that was sitting on a small portable element on the end of an extension cord that ran through the front door of the house. Steam rose from the pot, touching the ceiling that hung over the porch. The steam condensed on the overhang and dripped onto the wooden porch like little tears. A child, sitting cross-legged on the floor beside the woman, put his finger in the little puddle that the condensing steam had caused.

Chappy travelled to Carmedy, a small town on the north shore of Lake Prouseau. He walked the gravel shore road, walled on one side by a thin veil of scrub and scraggly trees. On the other side were the homes of the wealthy.

Chappy's eyes closed and he walked as though asleep. The sun was a dull throbbing red thing pulsing over the dark blue water, chopped as it was with whitecaps. The road wound gently along the shoreline of the lake, meandering in unpredictable ways, yet Chappy was able to navigate it perfectly with eyes closed.

It is the violence of the margins we are trying to live up to. To make the words capture the power of the space in the margins.

Maybe it's the violence of the margins you're trying to live up to, Chappy, said Mirror, but that isn't what I'm trying to live up to.

The blank page is the best you'll ever get, Mirror.

Again, I say, that may be the best you'll ever get, Chappy, but it isn't the best I'll ever get. Mirror gave Chappy a look. I've already got better.

Really?

Really.

The word is titled and desperate, Chappy says.

Mirror listens. She hears something, something trapped behind Chappy's words. Fear. She has no idea what he's talking about. She wants to tell him to smarten up. Speak sense, she wants to say. But something keeps her from saying anything.

The word strings and loops itself to other words, Chappy says. Already the sentence freaks me out.

Chappy? Mirror says.

Chappy doesn't answer.

Chappy? Are you all right?

Filling the falling sky with solder, grey and fusible. Do I seem encrusted to you, Mirror? Chappy looked directly at Mirror.

But when Mirror looked back at Chappy, she thought Chappy was looking through her, and she felt like a ghost.

Do I seem unleavened? Unlovable? I seem to see the scenes through the seams. Like I'm looking through the zipper of my pants.

I don't understand.

Neither do I, Mirror.

I got these pretty good sunglasses while we were away on holidays for a week at the cottage, Chappy told Theodore. Foster Grants.

Theodore looked over at Chappy. Those are good sunglasses, he said.

Twelve bucks.

That's a good price, said Theodore.

I got them in Hanover. We went to Hanover because of the rain, and because we found ourselves staring at each other vehemently between meals. My sister told me about Hanover. She said it had a Zellers. So right away, when it started to rain, Mirror said, Let's go to Hanover.

Nice, said Theodore.

Is the owl-eyed boy dead? asked Theodore.

No, said Chappy.

It's not a good rejection if it doesn't kill him, Theodore said. You haven't done your job if he's not dead when you're done.

I'm not trying to reject the owl-eyed boy, said Chappy. Or Mirror.

You have to know who killed you, Chappy.

I'm not dead.

To reappear in the right guise, said Theodore, at the right place, you have to do your job, and, in the end, you have to know who killed you.

But Chappy didn't understand. He didn't care that he didn't understand. The sun was shining. Chappy could see the cabin on the other side of the meadow. There was snow on the roof. There will also be snow on the roof of my cabin, thought Chappy. He was so certain of the existence of snow on the roof of his cabin, even though he hadn't seen it there, that it made him feel certain of other things, and he ceased to pay attention to Theodore. In his mind, Chappy was walking across the meadow, past the cabin with snow on the roof. Past other cabins – and every one of those cabins had snow on the roof, that was the incredible thing – until he had walked right out of town. And then Chappy would be finished with this foolish town and their obsession with the falling music. Ah, thought Chappy, happily. He felt satisfied as he sat at the table across from Theodore and the two men drank their coffee.

Chappy sat at the table in the kitchen with a cup of coffee set in front of him. A wisp of steam rose from the coffee. Sun slanted in the window above the sink. Mirror was at the counter, leaning her hip on it, humming. She blew a wisp of hair away from her eyes. She set her hands on the counter. The dishes were washed. There was nothing left to do but wait. Mirror felt satisfied. There was an absence of pain. It was the absence of the pain of needing to know what is coming next.

Chappy was doodling on a piece of paper.

What are you writing? Mirror asked.

Chappy looked up at Mirror, surprised. He'd forgotten she was there. Do you need coffee? Chappy asked. He picked up his own mug of coffee and took a sip. He slurped it. Mirror heard the noise he made as he drew the coffee into his mouth.

No, said Mirror. I don't need coffee. What are you writing, Chappy?

Chappy set his mug down. He looked at the piece of paper he'd been doodling on. Nothing, really, Mirror. I'm just practicing my handwriting. I want to be a writer.

No writer seeks to improve his handwriting, Chappy. Yet this is exactly what Chappy set out to do. Writing has nothing to do with handwriting.

Who was Chappy talking to? Not Mirror, certainly. Mirror knew this, but did nothing to try to stop the thing she felt growing in the pit of her stomach when she watched Chappy talk.

Chappy now heard the music every day. It entered his consciousness slowly. When he woke in the morning, it was like knowing a radio was playing in another room, not because you could hear the music, but because you could feel the vibrations in the walls.

As the day wore on, the walls came down. The music was like cymbals made naked. Behind them, the music pulsed, the rasping sizzle of cymbals set into the mix too dominantly. The sound of guitar, the sound of drums, the sound of piano were all like sounds translated into the language of cymbal.

Chappy understood that Mirror was on her way. He began to feel as if he were on the cusp of invasion. He felt that the townspeople were more his allies than Mirror. The wind picked up overnight. Now flakes of snow tore past the window, fleeting white moments fleeing sky, separated by sky, and by leaves that only now were being ripped from trees, the final survivors of the fall.

Chappy thought that Theodore might be his friend, but he knew, deep inside, that he had no friends. And again, no matter how he tried to protect himself in unreality, he saw that the arrival of Mirror could not be judged – her arrival with the owl-eyed boy would be neither invasion, nor reunion, but something outside the simple boundaries defined in these ideas.

Chappy wanted only to do what he'd set out to do today. He put on his plaid jacket. He stepped out the front door. Closed it. Locked it. He stood on the porch and watched the pulse of the woods in the place the path emerged and entered his year. He waited on his porch a long time. The sun burst from the clouds, then disappeared again, and bits of ragged snow raged quietly, never quite able to mass into a true snowfall.

Chappy grew cold. He unlocked the door, went back inside. The warmth swooned over him, smothered him. He experienced a feeling of false security. He needed more sleep, but he never seemed to get enough sleep.

It seemed Theodore would indeed be late. All Chappy wanted now was to get to the pile of wood they had chopped two days earlier and load it into the wheelbarrows and bring it back home. Then he would sit by the fire and read. If Theodore wanted to stay, fine. He would have to remain silent. Theodore never read. He sometimes did crossword puzzles. As soon as he finished a crossword puzzle, though, he would throw it into the fire and watch it burn. He would hold his hands near the flame, as though the work of completing the puzzle had been merely a prelude, a way of bolstering the fire to warm his hands.

I met Stephen at the front door. He was getting his socks on. I already had my socks on. I had my coat on, too. My coat had been hanging downstairs all along. The whole time I had been looking for it, it had been hanging downstairs on the hook by the door. I pulled my shoes on. I opened the door. Looked out. It was snowing. This was the third day of snow. Stephen said not to open the door yet, so I closed it. He finished tying his shoes. Pulled on his coat. We went out. I turned back to the door. Put the key in the lock. I turned the lock in the front door. Heard it click. Pulled on the door. It was locked. I went down the steps to the garage. Pulled the car out. Stephen went to get in the car. I gestured to him to close the garage. He turned back. Closed it. He got in the car. I don't know where my head is these days, he said.

Mirror and her boyfriend had broken up. No one had ever met Mirror's boyfriend. He might have been an invisible friend, except that Mirror didn't seem the type to have an invisible friend. She was sixteen years old, too old to sustain the kind of magic it takes to maintain relations with someone no one else can see.

In the mornings, during the winter, after all the lights in the house were on and Chappy had the coffee ready, Mirror came down the stairs looking serious and sleepy.

Sometimes in the morning, when Mirror was sitting in the kitchen, not saying anything till she could drink some coffee and get herself woke up a little, the cats did something that made her laugh.

Call me Angel, Mirror told Chappy. So, for a while, Chappy called Mirror Angel. But then one day Chappy forgot to call Mirror Angel. He called her Mirror. Mirror forgot she wanted to be called Angel and she was Mirror again. For a long time after that, Mirror was Mirror. Then, one day, when all the lights in the house were on and Chappy had the coffee ready, Angel came down the stairs and said to Chappy: Please, Chappy, call me Mirror. That's my real name. I don't know why you insist on calling me Angel. Chappy looked into Mirror's eyes and wandered there a while.

A broken heart doesn't last. It would be too hard if it did.

It was cold enough inside the fridge to keep things cold. Near the back of the fridge it seemed to keep things colder. Things put in the rack on the inside of the door hardly stayed cold at all.

It was like a volcano getting ready to erupt. When Chappy thought back, it seemed as though there was a low rumbling noise that accompanied the moment. Hands were rising, and a boy named Ed swung from the clotheslines behind everybody's house. Everyone in the class would turn and look at Ed. It happened two or three times a year.

But that year, the teacher stopped speaking. All the kids in the class traced paths in the snow with their eyes. It was like the start of winter, or the start of something revolutionary.

But the kids would only go so far in anything revolutionary. Then they would start to laugh nervously, until they were laughing all out in an effort to crush the fear they were feeling too intimately.

It was enough to break through a mountain. It was as though a mountain were about to speak. All of them saw this, but none of them wanted to admit they believed a mountain could speak. Not even the teacher.

Start up in a slow deliberate voice. Talk about some girl you've seen walking to school. Talk about the shape of that girl. All the time, listen to the way you never have admitted love. Listen to the way a kid loves another kid and wishes he could do the things that other kid seems able to do without even trying.

Many years later, Chappy told Mirror about Ed, admitting his love for the other boy, his desire to be like Ed, to reveal himself so guilelessly. To not care that a class full of kids was laughing at you.

The night makes admissions to Mirror. They are at the cottage. The fire is dying, the lights are out. Sometimes, when Mirror turns her head a certain way, Chappy can see her eyes glow from the light of the moon through the window. Chappy lays his head in Mirror's lap.

Mirror says very little. She strokes Chappy's hair. She lays her hand along his cheek gently, as though comforting a child. And so Chappy is a child again.

Back in the classroom, afraid, listening to the teacher, wishing he were someone else, Chappy believed it was like there was no wall between the subconscious and the things that people told him.

He'd talk about his home life. He'd talk about his feelings for milk. About the way he sometimes noticed his mother's breasts when she was wearing certain clothes.

When it was so late into the night that morning was already a threat, and Chappy began to feel the damp dread that sat at the base of his spine, making him clench his buttocks, he turned his head in Mirror's lap and looked at her face. Mirror looked down at Chappy. She seemed like a stranger. She seemed to have no expression at all. Her face seemed featureless, not so much ghostlike as utterly unformed.

Mirror laughed. Let's go to bed, she said.

Chappy and Mirror had their library cards. They were at the library. They looked at each other.

Inside the library, they met a woman. The woman started talking. She looked at Chappy while she talked.

Mirror was devastated with the course of the day so far. She was filled with the amazement of seeing the day inside out. At the second stroke of the town clock, Mirror thought: No one ever talks to Mirror or Chappy. Out of all of them who went to the library Saturdays, it made Mirror howl inside. She made her way to the shelves with the DVDs on them.

When the woman who talked to Chappy was gone, Mirror stood in front of Chappy with a book in one hand and a DVD in the other. You wanna go home now? she asked. She had her head tilted sideways and all her weight on one foot.

You're back.

Yes, said Chappy. He looked away from Mirror, then back at her again. He felt like a reward for something, but he didn't know what, and he had nothing to give Mirror.

Mirror had a look like she'd seen a little dog shit on her lawn while she looked out her kitchen window.

While I was gone, things happened, Mirror. You know, the way things do.

Yes, I know how that happens, Chappy.

People died while I was away.

People do that.

Other people grew old and helpless. Some of them were my relatives.

Mirror shifted her weight from one foot to the other foot. Chappy thought she looked like someone who had recently lost some weight. She didn't look any thinner. She looked less rooted, like there was less of anything holding her to the earth.

The ironing board screamed downstairs, like someone was killing it. Chappy's mother was ironing.

After Chappy's mother finished ironing and closed down the ironing board, Mirror got out of bed and closed the bedroom door. She came back and fell onto the bed with a whumphing noise of disgust. It was a very warm noise she was able to make when she fell onto the bed like that. A noise of total abandonment. It was a noise that seemed not to come out of any opening in her body, but straight out of her chest, like the woomf of something heavy landing in a mountain of feathers.

All my memories are motionless, Chappy told Mirror. They sit like a lump at the back of my biology. They might well be dead, Mirror. I might well be dead. My memories might as well be that dog out on the street that I've never seen before, or that cloud scudding across the sky, that I'm not looking at, shifting and dissipating even as we speak. Could a frog we were dissecting in high school really be the central core of my memory system? Or one of the desks we sat at in biology?

Once in a while, on a very rare occasion – and who knows what causes it? the weather? the phase of the moon? – someone will get this look on his face, like he is going to cry and, you know, if you happen to be looking over his way when this look comes on his face, you know that that person just thought of something very sad.

Chappy watched his own hand rise up toward the ceiling, like it was some exotic bird he was watching, only it looked more like a big ham. He'd raise his hand like that, very slowly, watching it the whole time, and somewhere in the middle of his hand's ascent, close to its apex, when his elbow was almost straight, and his hand was not quite at the top of its trajectory, but almost, and Chappy had judged it too late to retrieve his hand from its wayward journey – or maybe he saw it as something independent, doing its own thing, beyond his control – at this point he would panic. He'd pull his hand back down out of the air. He'd look down at his lap. But it was too late.

You could see it in his eyes that he'd realized he was in big trouble. Nothing he might have to say could possibly be of any interest to anyone.

Mirror felt soggy. Like sod in the rain. Sod that hasn't taken root, so there's nowhere for the water to go. Let this feeling fill me as I listen to Chappy's stories, she silently prayed. She thought her prayer went away into the sky, the way fish swim away into the deep part of the lake after diving for the surface to catch a bug. She felt the danger of getting to the surface to capture this thrill. Chappy stopped telling his story. Mirror got up slowly, like an old woman, and went to the kitchen. She leaned on the counter and contemplated making something with food.

Chappy's stories seemed to go on forever. Although, really, it was just one song among the many Chappy knew. Days would go by, then suddenly the story of Chappy would return.

Say you've followed your dreams as far as you can follow them, Chappy said. By this point, Mirror had given up listening and was just staring at Chappy's belt buckle, waiting to see what he would say next.

Chappy was not looking at Mirror at all. He was staring out the window, grasping for something so far beyond him, he had no idea where to start looking.

Mirror took the sewing machine into the sewing machine shop. She couldn't get the sewing machine to work at all anymore. She wanted a new one.

I want a new one, she told the guy in the shop. She was trying to be nice to the guy, even though she didn't feel like being nice to him.

She left the sewing machine at the shop and went home.

The guy from the sewing machine shop called the next day. There's nothing wrong with this machine, he told Mirror. I tried it. As far as I can tell, there's nothing wrong with this machine.

Mirror tried to think of what to say – how could she have overlooked the fact that it worked perfectly? Why can't I get it to work? Mirror asked the guy.

I can't answer that question, ma'am, the guy from the sewing machine shop said.

Mirror pictured the guy. She imagined him wearing the same not-quite-white t-shirt he had on yesterday. It was a thinning t-shirt through which you could see the guy's chest hair. He wasn't an old guy, but he had a lot of hair. His hair on his head was bushy and unkempt. He'd needed a shave yesterday, too, when Mirror was in the shop. Mirror wondered if he might have shaved and changed his shirt, in which case she was picturing him all wrong.

Alls I know, ma'am, the guy continued, is that I didn't do anything to the machine, I just turned it on, and it seems to be working fine.

Mirror put the phone down gently into the cradle. Fuck, she whispered.

Mirror held her left hand up, palm flat against the air in front of her. The subway whispered, hissed its motion under their seats. Mirror used her right hand to poke the air around her left hand. There were rests here, here, here and here, she told Chappy. She poked the air each time she said the word here. Her left palm was the solid substance among the rests. There were rests everywhere, she said.

The emptiness inside Chappy was pushing him aside, desperately seeking substance. He watched Mirror, trying to capture the substance of the things her hands were making.

A poem is a conversation you have with yourself in public, where the poet answers questions no one else has heard, Mirror said. I saw that time was running out, which is how I knew to slow down, let the tracery of lies unfolding slip by lazily, like water in a summer river. And, indeed, time did run out, like water running from the shore after the final big wave, signaling God's intention to go for coffee.

Chappy tried to see each moment as his goodbye to the world. He cooked by a tree in the middle of each month, till December, when he finally came inside. You can try to defeat God by trying to look like you planned it all along. But God never planned anything. And the only way to defeat that bastard is to do exactly what he does, only do it better.

Mirror was doing something, but Chappy had no idea what she was doing. She was in the living room. Chappy was at the table in the kitchen with some food on a plate. They couldn't see each other. Chappy pictured Mirror. In his mind, he saw her. She had her face turned toward her work, but he didn't know what she was working on.

I was in between everywhere. Everything I get these days looks like a book.

I was a lot of things, but I wasn't looking like anything in any conventional sense, Mirror. I wasn't looking at anyone's tits. Chappy looked down at his plate. I was having this love hanging out of me, hanging out toward some low point I could see out there but I didn't want to touch it.

Derek was getting ready to go to Thunder Bay on the weekend. He didn't want to die on his way to Thunder Bay. He said he didn't mind dying, but not on his way to Thunder Bay. He said he wanted to die in the city. Maybe in the very coffee shop we were sitting in. Or in Queen Video.

You saw Derek?
He's the one who gave me Michael's book.
Why's he going to Thunder Bay?
I don't know.

He had strong legs and pink shorts and he was pouring oil into an opening in the engine where he was leaning over the front of his car with the lid up. The clouds just ended at the blue sky the way land ends at water, except for some shreds of cloud that had somehow ripped away from the main body. On the other side of the blue there were other different kinds of cloud and a plane flying under a cloud and Chappy could smell his past loading itself into the present like it was the chamber of a gun. When he looked up again, everything had changed. Chappy entered that territory where everything has changed.

When a baby dies, everything has changed. Chappy didn't look at Mirror, he looked at his feet. Chappy's feet were stretched out on the road in front of him, with the sun on the tips of his boots. Kimball is about the death of something in language, Mirror. Something hopeful.

Mirror listened.

Something as hopeful as the stretch of life out in front of a baby. Kimball is about a new hope. Chappy turned his head. He looked at the side of Mirror's face.

Kimball is about defeat. He's about the defeat of linear hope. He is about the defeat of the up and down, left and right hope that moves toward the back of a book.

Chappy knew about concrete and he knew about coffee – or worse – but it was impossible to know what Kimball was saying. The ants massed at the curb. Chappy tried not to step on them.

Mirror sat next to Chappy on the curb, felt the cold concrete on her bottom. There was a woman further along the sidewalk, walking. The sun got through the clouds, but then got covered up again by new clouds.

They were trying to pretend that the sound wasn't actually there. But it was there, and they could hear it. Then it got too loud to ignore. Mirror said, What's that sound? It's freaking me out.

I don't know, Chappy said. It sounds big.

You think it's a squirrel?

It sounds like a dog.

They'd had squirrels in the roof before. In the roof, squirrels sounded like someone throwing something onto the roof, like acorns, or something hollow, something light that could bounce. This sound was not in the roof, though. This sound was in the floor.

It's under the fridge, Mirror said.

Chappy went outside. He opened the garage. The garage was directly underneath the fridge. There was nothing in the garage. No squirrel. No anything. Chappy went back in the house.

What the hell is it? Mirror looked scared.

There's nothing in the garage, said Chappy.

They didn't hear it again for weeks. They'd forgotten about it by the time they heard it again. Chappy felt sick when he heard it again. He felt hopeless.

Mirror found pellets. She showed them to Chappy. She had them on a dust pan. She held the dust pan out toward

Chappy and looked at him.

They're small.

A mouse?

Yes. Probably.

How does a mouse make so much sound?

Chappy went to Canadian Tire. He took the owl-eyed boy. There was a large display of different traps, as well as some rows of poison. Chappy took a trap off a hook.

The owl-eyed boy said, No, Daddy. He picked up a trap that would capture the mouse alive. It was a thing that tipped when a mouse went in and a door fell shut. You put peanut butter in. Or cheese. Peanut butter, it said on the package, was best.

Mirror put crunchy in. Do you think it will work? she said. Dad says those things don't work. He says you have to kill it.

The owl-eyed boy wouldn't let me get the one that kills it, Chappy said. He still had his hood from his sweatshirt on and his face was shadowed. The owl-eyed boy was in the living room watching TV. Mirror and Chappy were in the kitchen, under the big combination triple light and ceiling fan.

Dad says we shouldn't let the owl-eyed boy tell us what to do.

We'll just try this, Chappy said. Dishes were drying in a drainer on the counter beside the sink. Chappy put the trap in the cupboard with the pots, near where they'd found a lot of droppings. If this doesn't work, we'll get the other one.

Later, after they went to bed, when Chappy was just drifting off, he could hear the trap tipping back and forth. It wasn't loud. You had to really listen. Chappy and Mirror were in their bedroom, above the kitchen. They were reading their books. The owl-eyed boy was asleep.

Do you hear it?

Mirror didn't hear it.

Chappy went downstairs. He picked up the trap. He could feel the mouse inside, the weight shifting as it moved around. The warmth of it. It scared Chappy and thrilled him.

The owl-eyed boy was with his cousin, Miranda. I can't wait till I can drive, he said. He kicked the ball. Miranda dove onto the floor.

You have to get lessons before you can drive.

I know.

Miranda was on her belly on the floor. You have to have a car, she said. And keys.

I don't have to have a car.

You have to have keys, though.

I know.

How old will I be when I finish high school, Daddy?

Seventeen.

I'll have a job. I'll be making seven dollars an hour. How much do you make, Daddy?

I'm not sure.

A thousand a month?

Maybe more.

More than a thousand a month?

Maybe.

That's a lot.

I guess it is.

Hey Owl, pass!

Chappy looked up. The owl-eyed boy's friend took a shot. Missed. The friend climbed out of the pool and sat on the ledge, his legs in the water. The owl-eyed boy climbed out of the pool and sat beside his friend. The instructor yelled for them to get back in the pool. They slipped back in the pool. Chappy looked back at his book. Someone scored. Shouted. Chappy looked up. It was impossible to tell who had scored.

Cam got a new baby brother and now the owl-eyed boy wants one, too, said Chappy.

No way, Mirror said, but she was talking more to herself than to Chappy. She'd thought of it before, of maybe having another child, mostly for the owl-eyed boy, so he wouldn't seem so alone.

Chappy was on the other side of the living room, cloistered in his corner of the couch. He was holding a book open in his lap, a book of poems. These poems are beautiful, Chappy said.

If anyone's poems are beautiful, Chappy, it's because they do something to consequences. They act like consequences don't exist.

Chappy looked up from his book. Something in Mirror's voice made him listen.

They ride in the face of consequences, Mirror said, sticking out her chin.

I don't know what that means, Chappy said. He thought Mirror seemed very brave right now.

They make consequences seem like a good thing, Mirror said.

Some consequences are a good thing. Aren't they? Chappy truly wasn't sure. It seemed like a sure thing. But it sounded like Mirror meant something else when she used the word consequences, though, something terrible. Something irrevocable.

They put the fish tank on top of the little bookshelf Mirror had placed against the wall in their bedroom. If they sat up in bed, they could see the fish tank over top of their feet.

Their feet looked like soldiers standing on guard for the fish.

That's where the dead fish was when I woke up this morning, Mirror told Chappy. It was floating overtop of my feet. The other fish didn't seem to notice the dead one. Don't you think that's weird, Chappy? The live fish all swam around the dead fish like it was just another one of their living friends swimming around with them.

Mirror saw the dead fish before Chappy did. Chappy was still asleep when Mirror woke up and saw the dead fish floating at the top of the tank, above her feet. Mirror thought she should take the dead fish to the toilet and flush it down, but she stayed in bed till Chappy woke up.

Chappy's dad called to say he had cancer. He told Chappy he loved him.

I love you, too, Dad, Chappy said.

Chappy's dad started to cry.

Chappy had never heard or seen his dad cry.

Chappy took the owl-eyed boy to Niagara Falls once when the owl-eyed boy was two. Chappy put the owl-eyed boy's wagon in the back of the car and drove for two hours. He tried to do the driving when the owl-eyed boy was supposed to be having his nap. But the owl-eyed boy only slept for five minutes. He woke up when they were in Vaughan, about two miles from home. Chappy fed the owl-eyed boy crackers and other food to try to keep him from crying all the way to Niagara Falls.

In Niagara Falls, they stayed at a hotel with a pool. They went in the pool. They could see trains going by just outside the window at the end of the pool.

For dinner, Chappy got the owl-eyed boy Wendy's. He got the boy a Frosty. At midnight, the owl-eyed boy woke up sick to his stomach. Chappy tried to think what to do. He turned on the TV. He held the owl-eyed boy over the toilet. He tried to imagine where he could find a doctor in Niagara Falls at midnight. He figured he'd have to go to the hospital.

The next day, the owl-eyed boy slept till ten in the morning. When he finally woke up, Chappy put him in the wagon and dragged it down Clifton Hill. He pulled the owl-eyed boy across the Rainbow Bridge. He pulled the wagon halfway across to the U.S., but the wind was blowing and it was cold. The Canadian customs guy seemed to think Chappy was kidnapping the owl-eyed boy. When the customs guy let Chappy and the owl-eyed boy go, finally, they went back to the hotel and went swimming again.

For three years, right after Chappy and Mirror got married, Chappy never stopped. He would always think about what he had to do next. He got mad a lot. He'd come home at night and sit in the bathtub, planning how long it would take to put a deadbolt on the back door. Mirror was afraid people were breaking in. She thought people were breaking in during the day, while she and Chappy were at work, moving things around in the house.

Then one day Chappy stopped for coffee. After that, he couldn't get started again. He went to sleep at night knowing that he would soon lose his job, and he'd wake up in the middle of the night and stay awake worrying. When he finally did lose his job, though, it felt good, and for months he slept like a baby.

The problem is, Chappy told Mirror, once you get started looking, you can't stop. You keep looking and looking and before you know it, all you're doing anymore is looking. And even when you stop looking, you're still looking. There's no longer any such thing as after the looking, or thinking about the looking. When you think about looking, you're already looking, and when you close your eyes, you're still looking. And when you pee, you're not peeing, you're looking.

If you could read every line at once, said Chappy, you might get what the poet is trying to say to you. Mirror sipped coffee. They were sitting up in bed together, the pillows behind them. Chappy had a book in his lap. Mirror had coffee. The curtains were open. The light through the window was soft. It daubed the side of Mirror's face, gave her features a blurry glow that made Chappy feel less substantial. Membranous. He felt like he was, once again, falling into Mirror's face.

The owl-eyed boy came into the living room. He was dragging eighteen years behind him like the wake from a big ship. Are we going to shovel Papa's driveway? he asked. His eyes weren't as owl-eyed as they once had been. They were veiled, Chappy thought.

Yes, Chappy said. You want to go now?

Yes.

You want something to eat, first?

No. Let's just go.

Are you coming? Chappy asked, looking at Mirror.

No, said Mirror. She looked out the window. She held her mug between her hands. She looked lovely, Chappy thought. He wanted to stay with her in the bed and feel her warmth, even if he didn't touch her at all. She didn't look like she wanted to be touched. She looked sad, but in a very lovely manner. Her face drenched in emptiness.

Chappy put his legs over the edge of the bed. The owl-eyed boy was gone, off getting dressed. They could hear him moving, pulling out drawers, closing the bathroom door, running water. They could hear his pee hit the toilet. Then he flushed. The tap ran. Chappy stood. He turned. He wanted to say one more thing to Mirror. Just one more thing before he went downstairs and got ready to go.

Mirror was looking out the window. It was like she was somewhere else altogether, but her body remained in the bed, like a bridge to whatever place she was currently inhabiting. Chappy knew that if he spoke the bridge would collapse. But there was no way to get across the bridge without speaking.

He tried to think of words that would maintain the fragile substance of the bridge, and at the same time open a space for him to step onto it.

There were no words that could do that, except maybe
cloud.

Why do you think Chappy reads all that poetry? Do you think that he's looking for the right words, the few correct words, the secret key to the meaning that will open a space in the soul of the other?

There are no right words.

But that doesn't mean it can't be done, Chappy.

Don't give up.

One time, you'll get the right words, but you won't be there to see the soul you open.

Another time, you'll start to move toward the other, but you'll say the wrong thing at the last minute and be locked out again.

Being locked out, Chappy felt, was like being assigned to some frozen wasteland. He saw himself as an Eskimo. He didn't even look like Chappy anymore. He looked like some guy in a movie about Eskimos. What makes this distance possible? Chappy wondered in the kitchen. He went to the basement where he kept his snow shovelling equipment.

Mirror breathed so tenderly, as though every breath were a supreme gesture of communication, bringing to Chappy a new and radiant version of Mirror. Chappy felt he could weep. He should have shut up and gone to sleep, he knew, but he found he just could not. Mirror suddenly sucked in a breath. You're dreaming, little ghost, Chappy said inside his head.

Chappy had no idea what it meant, to say things to someone who was sleeping. He thought of trying to step into Mirror's dreams. There were people who believed you could do that. Enter another person's dreams.

You need to stop now, Chappy, said Mirror. Stop and listen. I'm going away. I don't know when I'll be back. Stay here and read poems till you get it figured out. Okay?

Mirror slept with her mouth open. She was in a story.

When sleeping adults are woken suddenly, they emerge from a place of frightening intensity, their eyes either overly bright, or utterly veiled.

The owl-eyed boy lay in his bed, leafing through picture books. This is for babies, he thought suddenly, thrusting the book closed.

Mirror dreamed the way a melody finds its way through rhythm and harmony. The owl-eyed boy was in her dream, appearing regularly, like a series of quarter notes. Like a toccata.

If you want to kill God, Chappy told Mirror, check your watch.

Mirror waited, but apparently Chappy was through. I see, she said. She wanted to hear if her voice still worked. She lowered her legs over the edge of the bed. She was in a nightshirt and her legs were bare from mid-thigh. She pulled on her bathrobe, went into the bathroom. Chappy heard water running.

One night, the owl-eyed boy told Chappy to take his pillows downstairs when he went to the foldout. Take them all, he told Chappy.

Every night, I come into your bed, the owl-eyed boy told Chappy.

I know, said Chappy.

Every night, you go down to the foldout bed. Usually, you leave one of your pillows behind, because I like to have a pillow for my head. But today you should take all the pillows down to the foldout. I'm bringing my own pillow to Mommy's bed.

Okay, said Chappy.

For some reason everyone was pretty restless one night. The owl-eyed boy was rolling around in his crib making it creak. Sometimes he cried. Mirror and Chappy stayed in the kitchen, under the light. They didn't go up to get the owl-eyed boy. They were both too tired.

Eventually, Chappy started looking for patterns. He tried to see if all the grass was dying, or was it just that one small patch over there by the tree? He asked himself: Was it this hot last year? What he was really wondering, though, was, were these just the first symptoms of his death?

The young girls sing a song called, Is This the Death of My Loved One. The youngest girl is singing her own song, though. The words to this song go: I can sing any song that

I want to. La la la la la la la la la la la. I can sing any song that
I want to.

The girl gets in the swing. She sings and swings in the
swing.

The oldest girl is looking out for a place to escape. Her
mother is twenty feet off, telling her to come in the house.
Yelling. Telling her: Come in the house!

The youngest girl goes on singing: La la la la la la la la la
la la la la la la la la la.

Mirror came down from the cottage wearing her blue terrycloth shorts and her bra. There was no one at the beach this time of the week. It was the middle of the week. It was almost October. Kids were back at school.

There was one guy staying up at number 413. But he slept all day. Then, around five in the afternoon every day, he stumbled down to the beach.

He lay on the beach for a while every afternoon squinting up at the sky. His dog came with him. While the guy lay on the beach not moving, the dog ran up and down the beach peeing on every log he came to.

If you could describe the owl-eyed boy in a single sentence, Chappy said, what would you say?

Why would I want to do that, Chappy? Tell me. Why would I ever want to describe anyone in a single sentence? Mirror didn't so much stand there looking at Chappy, as she hung. She seemed to hang on the air, waiting to fall from the stupid things she heard coming out of Chappy's mouth.

Unless you'd just met the person, Mirror said. If you'd just met a person, you'd only have a sentence to say. Just what their name is, maybe. If I'd just met you, for example, and I had to describe you in a single sentence, I'd say: This guy's name is Chappy and he has shit-brown hair and blue eyes.

That's nice.

I'd want a whole book for the owl-eyed boy, said Mirror. And he's not even a year old yet. When he gets older, I'll want an entire set of encyclopedias to describe him.

Okay.

I'll want a whole library full of books to describe the owl-eyed boy.

Okay.

At night, tractor-trailers pulled into the parking lot of the post office, which was behind the house where Mirror and Chappy and the owl-eyed boy lived. The owl-eyed boy was very small, and for a few months one summer, when the windows stayed open all night, the owl-eyed boy would wake up to the hiss of air brakes as tractor-trailers slid into their docks behind the post office. He would lie awake, his eyes wide, unfocussed, and, for a moment after he woke, he was someplace else; he was nowhere; he was in between.

There might be another hiss then, or the clap of the truck door slamming, and the pat, pat, pat of the driver's feet on the parking lot pavement. And sometimes a voice. The dark was a forest. Primeval. Dripping vines, thick in steamy mist that rose slowly from muddy soil. The owl-eyed boy's feet sank and he pushed himself along, but he sank deeper with every step. He struggled and grunted and, finally, called out. He called out only when he could no longer move. He was sinking, slowly, and voices dropped out of trees like monkeys, brown and indistinct, thousands of monkeys tumbling onto the forest floor, touching down each with a thump, then rolling away, chattering and hissing at one another, tumbling, and frightening.

Mirror would rush in. She would sit on the edge of the owl-eyed boy's bed, stroke his forehead. She would remain long after the owl-eyed boy had fallen off, stroking his forehead, calming herself.

Chappy called his dad to see how he was doing. Already something had changed. His speech was very measured, very careful, as though his dad had given up on everything, not just the possibility of living forever, but the possibility of living now, in this very moment.

Chappy figured he should try to see his dad at least one more time while he still seemed like the dad he'd always known, before he got so sick that Chappy didn't recognize him anymore.

The owl-eyed boy knew only his music and his mother. The two were inseparable. Inseparable, not because they'd been welded together through association, but because they had never been taken apart.

The owl-eyed boy had watched the elements of his world disassociate themselves from one another. He heard birdsong through his open window one early morning and knew it wasn't a part of the air he swam in. The milk he got from his mother's breast wasn't coming from his mother anymore, he understood, but from some alien source. Whether the music remained a part of his mother by the owl-eyed boy's choice was not clear, but they were truly inseparable.

I'm going back to Earth, Chappy told himself.

I read about a woman who married on November 14, 2359, Chappy told Mirror. And I thought to myself, when I read about that woman, I was three months old to the day when that woman got married.

Chappy, that's more than 300 years in the future. What are you talking about? You weren't even born then.

The man this woman married, said Chappy, was a musician, a guitar player, and it seemed to me, even if someone wrote down on paper the date I got married, or the date I was born – or whatever – it would mean so little. Everywhere on this planet, and on every other planet, there are people reaching milestones; and every milestone one person on one planet reaches lessens the significance of my milestone.

Chappy, stop. Mirror had the baby to her breast. She was in the chair at the back of the room, where the light was least. Her face shredded by shadow.

Chappy knew that this memory he was having was a stand-in for something deeper inside him than any memory ever could be. A stand-in for something so deep inside him he could never quite touch it; but something he knew he would long for until the day he died.

He couldn't see the face of the person in this memory; he didn't know who the person was. Chappy tried to think of himself and the owl-eyed boy together, but it felt like reaching across time to touch a memory. It hurt, this distance Chappy felt. In his mind, he forced himself to touch the owl-eyed boy on the shoulder. Maybe this would be enough, Chappy thought. Maybe this single touch would make the difference. But, as soon as he had this thought, Chappy knew that a single timid touch, such as the one he had imagined, would never be enough.

It had stopped snowing sometime in the night. The owl-eyed boy awoke fully alert. He raised his head off the pillow.

Mirror and Chappy lived well north of the city in a small white house that sat in the middle of a large field that was long gone to weed and now rapidly returning to wilderness. There were subdivisions, close-packed housing, all around the field. But almost no one lived there anymore. Everyone was gone. It was too far north of the city, this place where Chappy and Mirror lived now.

Chappy and Mirror didn't get a lot of visitors, but now there was someone at the door. Chappy opened it.

There was a man. Behind the man, dark heavy clouds scudded across the sky like fallout drifting in the days immediately following a holocaust. The air was chill and smelled of rain. But, Chappy thought, as the man stepped into the house, it might be cold enough to snow. As he closed the door behind the man, a feeling of delight floated up through his chest into his throat.

It's magic, Mirror. I understand the magic of paragraphs.

Mirror thought it would be cool to understand the magic of paragraphs. But more than that, she loved it that Chappy had said, It's magic, Mirror. Finally, after all their years together.

I like most kids in this world. I like the lost kids especially, though. In this world, where the mother is the boss, she makes herself beautiful but unavailable. Something so completely at odds. Sometimes you show up just to try to see this. It's something the mother shows you in the end. Like she owes you something, but can't find it in her pocket. So she owes it to you.

I like the lost kids, said Mirror. She looked back down at Chappy's notebook and read more: In this world, where the mother is the boss, she makes herself beautiful but unavailable. Something so completely at odds. Something she shows you in the end. Like she owes you something but can't find it in her pocket. She owes it to you. Honest.

Mirror looked up. Chappy was on the other side of the room. He'd left the chair he'd been sitting in, which was directly across from where Mirror was sitting.

Chappy was getting ready to abandon something. He was at the window, the light cutting sideways across his face, making a soft light of it.

Write, Chappy, Mirror said. Okay? She managed to make this a question, and then to make what followed a magical newness.

Somehow accommodate, she said. Make a present of yourself, of your words – that need, or reason. That jungle

prescience. Interior movement in the driver's seat. The
writer's right.

When you've figured things out as far as you can, and you
find yourself sitting in the kitchen trying to figure out whether
to have toast or a piece of that pie your mother-in-law made,
everything that's left from now on is God, said the owl-eyed
boy. The girl just looked at him. She had big eyes, almost
mirror images of the owl-eyed boy's eyes. They stared at
each other like siblings long separated, now reunited.

What are you talking about, Owl? the girl said.

The bus stopped. God got on. He stayed at the front of the
bus a moment, looking at the people on the bus. He looked
at them sadly. He looked sad when he looked at the people
on the bus. He looked distant.

Chappy went to the front of the bus and put his arms
around God. People had told Chappy you can't get your
arms around God, but that one day on the bus, Chappy was
able to get his arms all the way around God. God felt warm
and vulnerable. When Chappy looked in God's eyes, he was
surprised to find them empty. He had thought he would see
great wisdom in God's eyes, but God looked like an idiot.
Chappy half expected to see drool in God's beard. It wasn't
loneliness that Chappy saw there, but the cold emptiness of
glass. Like a machine built to look like one of us.

You don't even look at me when I talk to you, Mirror said.
Then she walked away.

Chappy thought: She's right. Should I change? No. I'm a
jerk slotted into a chair near a computer.

Mirror came back. Look at me! she said.

Fuck off.

Mirror put her hands on Chappy's shoulders and her face close to Chappy's face. She looked him in the eye, made a face, then stood up straight. What have you been eating?

Garlic.

You stink.

And cheese.

Gods.

And a potato. And a Kit Kat.

Mirror laughed. All you do is eat. Mirror's little breasts were near Chappy's face.

She had a tight little top on. She was a very small girl. One of her eyes looked broken.

You want something small and soft, said Chappy, but you find yourself huge on the couch, crying in blue light. On the TV, small pockets of soft people touch each other. You cry alone into the square room, and into the dark sky above the square room, and the sky steps up to God's clouds and God's stars and God's moon – all the huge things that belong to God, and you're so huge you wonder if maybe you belong to God, but your small tears drip onto your blouse and remind you how wet things can get and how you belong to no one.

We were having a meeting at work, said Chappy, and we were in a meeting room I've never seen and I can't remember who was at the table, except I think Michelle was running the meeting and it was going to be my turn to speak soon and I got up and walked slowly away and someone called me good-naturedly and I just kept moving away thinking, Fuck you. I was sitting on the toilet and there was a mirror in front of me and I could see three girls I knew in the mirror standing behind me and one of them said, You can't get away from us.

Mirror said nothing. She watched Chappy. When Chappy was telling a dream, it was best not to hinder him. It was like he was in the dream again. Mirror knew not to infringe. At best, he would stop telling the dream; at worst, Mirror didn't like to think.

Chappy spoke very quickly when he was like this, like he was in some kind of speed-induced trance.

I thought oh great and they came around and now there was a window in front of me and we were looking out. One of the girls wasn't Danny, but now I'm thinking someone like her. One of them might have been Katrina my friend who died of leukemia. But they were not really people I can identify although in the dream I saw them vividly – but I can't now.

Chappy sat in silence. He looked shell-shocked.

The view out the window was just some old buildings.

Chappy was slowing. His eyes were dull. He was struggling to remember.

There was an old poster, half torn off, on the wall of a side of a building, and one of the girls mentioned it. I said, Derek did a paper on that, man. Meanwhile, I was trying to wipe myself inconspicuously, but it was not going well. I was getting it on my hands, not hiding it well at all. One of the girls said, You've got the best view from here, as though I owned the cubicle. The view now was of the top of a sort of bluff and over by the poster a couple of guys – they looked like brothers – were performing tricks on stilts. You couldn't see the stilts, because they had pants over them, so I pointed out to one of the girls that I thought they were on stilts. Then one of them went right to the edge of the bluff and stuck one leg out over the edge and we could see the wood of the stilt and the guy said something and grinned and that's all of it.

Mirror was silent. She looked a bit sad and a bit happy in the face she gave to Chappy, and Chappy seemed happy to have that face given to him, but he also seemed finished, not just with the dream he had been telling, but with everything.

I was going to have to perform in front of a huge audience on my guitar and I thought I'd just explain at first that I wasn't that great and do my best. I thought I could always do Tell Me Why. I was thinking how I'd handle it as I sat in the audience and that was pretty much the entire dream. The concert was in a big place, like Maple Leaf Gardens, and I was way up in the audience with someone I can't remember now and it was this someone who told me I was slated to perform.

Chappy left Mirror a note: Take the blue books off the bookshelf, please. I'll be home by five, so try to be finished by then. Put them on the floor in a pile. Put the biggest blue book on the bottom, then the next biggest, and so on. Make more than one pile if you have to. Take frequent breaks. Stretch. Try to get some aerobic exercise while on your breaks. But limit your breaks to fifteen minutes. Use the stairs if necessary. Toast is a good quick snack. Always keep some bread around. But don't always put jam on your bread. And remember that always doing any one thing over and over again takes five years off your life.

Everyday, I have an idea that I use to carry me through the day and not despair. Yesterday, it was that something great big and wonderful was coming my way and I just had to be patient. The day before that, I was thinking all day about miracles – how little miracles occur all day long, but we don't see them because we're too caught up trying to make something happen. We all want to make our own privately constructed little miracles.

Mirror saw out the window that the sun was round like a red transport truck moving across the sky in first gear. A small bird landed in a tree outside the window.

I have tried to give up my own privately constructed miracles, Chappy said.

Mirror saw the way the snow sat on the roofs across the street.

I have tried to see the little miracles that were already there around me without me doing anything, said Chappy. Like how I can arrive at an intersection on my bicycle just as the light changes. If the light turns green, I get to keep going. This is good because my brakes are shot. If the light turns red, I get to stop, and the miracle of this will reveal itself in what I see as I stand by the curb waiting for the light to turn green so I can go again.

Mirror looked at Chappy like a mute girl trained to express what she feels through the pain that stains her silent face.

I saw how the two ideas, being patient and waiting for little miracles, might be combined, and that's a good thing for getting me through the afternoon today.

Oh, Chappy, Mirror said. She put her forearms on Chappy's shoulders and dipped her face to his chest. They were like two kittens in the kitchen, waiting to lick each other, sitting side by side at the table, but they were turned toward each other so their knees touched. They had coffee and they had a plate with coffee cake, but the coffee no longer steamed and neither had touched the coffee cake. Why do you have to have a new idea every day? Mirror said. Her lips were against Chappy's shirt and it was hard for Chappy to hear what she was saying, but he listened hard and thought he understood the vibration he felt against his chest.

An idea comes to stand outside you, like a creature with a life of its own, with desires of its own, desires that it will use to try to find you, and hurt you, and even kill you. It's so hard to placate an idea. You come to want to placate it at any cost, and so it will come to dictate how you live your life.

Chappy took Mirror's face in his hands and lifted it from where it lay against his chest. He held her small face close to his own and looked into the pools of her eyes where they shimmered and he felt himself falling. Mirror, he said. How long do you think you can hold onto an idea without losing yourself to it? Probably the moment you are given an idea, the moment it enters your head, you are lost to it and all that's left for you is to do the work to escape it.

A tear broke free from the pool that was Mirror's left eye. Her lips trembled. She couldn't understand how Chappy did this. His voice was soft.

Say there was only one single idea, Mirror, and say that idea consisted of a single difference, and say that single difference was the difference between Christmas and the ancient Greeks, and every idea a person has is just that same idea in a new suit of clothes. Can you see how the work we do with an idea is really always the work of extricating ourselves? Think of all the times people get ideas about who you are. How one action you took one time defines and haunts and hunts you down. And you no longer manage to surprise anyone. And it isn't because you aren't a constant surprise, it's because you've been identified and labelled and discarded in favour of the person you were labelled as because of something you once did and because it's easier than trying to reinvent a person every minute.

Mirror had no words, but she nodded now and kissed Chappy on his lips and Chappy felt the wet substance of Mirror's face against the skin on his cheek and nose.

What's the story called, Chappy?

It's called Wisdom of the Crowd.

Let's hear it.

Chappy read: Cowan didn't answer. He's a cow. Why was I talking to a cow? Because, I decided, it doesn't matter. When you talk, you just talk. No one cares what you say in the words you say. What they care about is what's behind the words, what gets fed to the soul.

I hate my nose, Cowan thought.

Mirror laughed. Chappy looked up. He smiled at Mirror. He liked making Mirror laugh.

And so you should, Levon, the cow said.

Chappy looked up at Mirror again. He was worried about this part of the story. About the talking cow.

Mirror smiled, but said nothing. She nodded for Chappy to go on.

Chappy looked back down at the paper. He was feeling vaguely sad. But he read on: The walkers read clouds, and trees interrupted their reverie long enough to make them understand. Put me in your story, Levon told the cow. Put my nose in there. The walkers read clouds as they passed through the boughs. God whistles wind as he pisses in trees, into hair, over water, in my ear. I heard more in that whistle than I'd heard in the words of the people who come to me every day. Walkers never came to me. They had God's whistle. Sometimes it irked me that they never came to see me. Other times I was glad. Walkers can be such a bunch of losers.

Once again, Mirror did not fully understand what Chappy was trying to get at with his story. Chappy was not sure why, even, he wrote any stories to begin with. What Chappy wrote was more than a journal, but less than an attempt to communicate.

You should send Wisdom of the Crowd to a magazine, Chappy. That's a good story.

*

Chappy smiled at Mirror. He looked at the paper he was holding. It was a crumply looking piece of paper, torn at the edges. It was from the scrap pile, Mirror understood. Paper used on one side that Chappy rescued and kept in a cubby under his desk. Chappy's penchant for making stories seemed as much about using up pieces of paper he had rescued as it was about making stories.

I want to give each piece of paper a shred of nobility, he told Mirror one night as he drifted off to sleep. The statement had come out of nowhere, with no context to give it meaning, and Mirror had understood immediately that it was about the scrap paper that was sitting under Chappy's desk, but that it had come from the other side of Chappy's consciousness and so was about something else, something she probably would never understand.

Bob says six key messages are too many. He says a good idea can fit on the back of your business card.

I was in a river. Asleep. Cowan was beside me, mooing, drinking. Happy, you'd think. But mooing never sounds happy. It's hard to tell if a cow is happy. Some farmers can tell with cows they've had a long time.

Don't beat yourself up over it, Chappy. For all you know, Cowan really was very happy.

I guess.

Don't guess.

I know.

What else?

Chappy's head pivoted slowly around, as though seeking something on the surface of the air.

Did you get that week in September off? Mirror asked suddenly.

I couldn't.

Okay. Sorry to interrupt. Can you tell the rest of the story with Cowan now?

Every time Cowan mooed, I drifted far enough out of sleep to feel sad for him, then back to sleep and dreaming and water all around us. Absolutely no wind, yet the leaves fluttered sprinkly bits of light over everything beneath them. It was such a beautiful day, and I finally awoke completely wondering what the fuck exactly was bothering Cowan. What the hell is your problem, Cowan? I said. But Cowan didn't answer. Cowan is a cow, and cows don't talk.

I'm glad to hear you say that, Chappy. It's a distinction I think is important to make. It's one thing to talk to a cow.

Yes, Chappy said, quickly, because he didn't want Mirror to continue. He didn't want Mirror to deny what he knew she must ultimately deny.

Chappy wanted to believe that certain things were possible. It wasn't so much that he wanted to believe that cows might talk in some universe he could possibly gain access to; it was more that he wanted anything to stay possible for at least a little while. He wanted everything to stay possible till the day nothing was possible anymore. He wanted the day that nothing was possible anymore to be the day he died. It seemed to Chappy that if no one denied a thing in words the possibility could remain, floating in a world yet unformulated.

The owl-eyed boy looked away from his father. After a moment, he looked back, eyes full of hurt. I'm not going to play with you anymore, he said. He got up from the table and went into the playroom. He sat on the floor in his playroom and picked up one of his toys.

It does take a huge number of years for the tears drying on your face to give it that crusty feel. The lips can feel very dry and the nose can feel terribly congested with mucus when you cry hard. In short, you don't feel particularly presentable when you have been crying hard.

You've slept quite a while, Mirror told Chappy.

Chappy blinked. How long had Mirror been standing there watching him sleep?

Would you like to wash up and come for dinner? Mirror asked.

No matter where you are in this world, you're encased.

Chappy was sitting in a chair that encased him snugly. All around him, the world was wide open. Three thin, spindley pine trees stood sentinel around the sandy path that encircled the deck. The lake rushed away to the horizon, bobbing little sailboats on its waves. Whitecaps crashed on shore. But Chappy chose this cozy chair, the squares of his glasses encasing his eyes, his book in his hands, the story he read encased in book covers, and standing between him and the vast open endless.

Chappy had the phone dangling in his hand. It was a landline phone with a cable from the keypad to the handset. Say you buy a dozen phones in your lifetime, Chappy said. Each phone breaks. It can't be fixed. So you buy a new one. Say each phone costs you a hundred bucks.

Mirror waited, but Chappy said nothing more. He hauled the handset up by its curly cord and placed it gently in its cradle.

Chappy and Mirror were living in another part of town by then, sitting in the living room, reading their books. Each sat cradled in a corner of the couch, each under a little lamp that caught them each in a cone of light.

Listen to this, said Chappy. He read from his book.

Mirror watched Chappy over the top of her reading glasses.

Chappy stopped reading. He looked at Mirror over the top of his glasses. Their eyes met for a moment, wondering each about the other. Even after all these years, they still didn't know.

Listen to this, said Mirror, and she read from her book, which was a book of poetry:

God tried to teach Crow to talk.
'Love,' said God. 'Say, Love.'
Crow gaped, and the white shark crashed into the sea
And went rolling downwards, discovering its own depth.

'No, no,' said God. 'Say Love. Now try it. LOVE.'

Crow gaped, and a bluefly, a tsetse, a mosquito

Zoomed out and down
To their sundry flesh-pots.

'A final try,' said God. 'Now, LOVE.'
Crow convulsed, gaped, retched and
Man's bodiless prodigious head
Bulbed out onto the earth, with swiveling eyes,
Jabbering protest –

And Crow retched again, before God could stop him.
And woman's vulva dropped over man's neck and
Tightened.
The two struggled together on the grass.
God struggled to part them, cursed, wept –

Crow flew guiltily off.

Vulva? said Chappy.

Mirror looked at him. Is that all you have to say about this poem, Chappy?

No. But Chappy said nothing else.

After a while, they both went back to reading their books.

The owl-eyed boy came into the living room and climbed onto the couch between his mother and father. He had a book. He set it in his lap, opened it in the middle and started reading aloud. He read for two minutes. Then he stopped reading. He looked at Chappy, then at Mirror. Waited. Chappy nodded. Sounds like a good book, he said.

It is, said the owl-eyed boy.

Mirror said nothing, only smiled. All three went back to reading.

Much later, they all got up and brushed their teeth. They went to bed. When all the lights were out, the owl-eyed boy lay on his back and stared into the dark above his bed, and wondered about Santa Claus.

After they'd been married for a few years, Chappy and Mirror went out and got a dog. The dog was there every night when they got home from work. It was a thing they could depend on, a thing they could touch after work.

The cat sat up, and in so doing brought the castle into view. The drawbridge was open. Are you the wizard? the cat asked.

No, said the man.

When the man said nothing further, the cat got to its feet. I am the cat, the cat said, extending a paw, hoping the man would take this as a cue to introduce himself.

I know who you are, said the man. Come, he said. Without another word, the man turned and led the way across the drawbridge and into the castle.

I am the person who tells people to wait here.

Wait here.

The owl-eyed boy lay on the floor in the hall. I'm too tired to get my pyjamas.

Hurry up and get your clothes off, Chappy said. He went to get the owl-eyed boy's pyjamas.

Daddy?

Yes.

Is tomorrow Mommy's birthday?

No. It's the day after tomorrow.

Oh.

Now go to sleep.

Okay.

We were in the cafeteria eating the daily salad. The daily salad had a different name each day of the week, but it always looked much the same to me: rusty lettuce, shredded carrots, unpeeled cucumber slices and a single, decorative radish on top.

*

I wanted to tell someone that he was wrong. I wanted to tell all the people that they were wrong. I wanted to tell people that I wasn't who they thought I was. I was someone else. But I didn't know who I was, so I found it hard to get involved in my life. I wanted to be involved in my life. I thought that one day I would see who I was, that all the hard work I was doing to try to see who I was would one day pay off and I would be able to be relaxed and get involved in my life. If people didn't think I was involved in my life, they were right on some level. But I was involved in my life on other levels. How could anyone who worked as hard as I did at finding out who he was not be involved in his life? My life was finding out who I was. I was involved.

When they got to Yonge Street, they waited for a green light. Okay, let's go, said Chappy. They started across. A minivan was waiting to turn left.

The owl-eyed boy rode off the curb. The woman in the minivan decided to try to make it through a break in traffic. Chappy saw her. He yelled for her to stop, but she had to keep going to keep from getting hit by oncoming traffic.

When Chappy yelled, the owl-eyed boy stopped. The van took the corner.

What, Daddy? the owl-eyed boy said.

Chappy could see that the owl-eyed boy was scared. That woman nearly hit us. Come on. It's okay. They finished crossing the street.

I was trying to think about how to tell people about the difference I was making every day. Someone started talking about some bikers they'd seen in a restaurant their dad took them to one time when they were a little kid, and I didn't get to tell anybody anything.

Chappy and the owl-eyed boy were in the parking lot of the drugstore. I'm going to get a Megamouth, Daddy.

Chappy gave the owl-eyed boy a dollar.

The owl-eyed boy went into the drugstore.

Chappy waited in the sun.

The owl-eyed boy came out of the drugstore holding a can of Mountain Dew. Yes, they still have the Megamouth, Daddy. The owl-eyed boy held the can out so his father could see it. On the can, in a red splash of letters, it said, Megamouth.

Chappy raised his eyebrows. Wow. Want me to open it?

The owl-eyed boy handed the can to his father.

Chappy opened the can and handed it back to the owl-eyed boy.

The owl-eyed boy sat beside his father on the curb.

Can I have a sip? Chappy asked.

Sure. The owl-eyed boy handed the can to his father.

Chappy took a sip.

When the owl-eyed boy was finished drinking his pop, they got back on their bikes. They took a different route home than they usually did, along May Avenue. There was less traffic.

Keep looking at precious things.

*

That lady almost hit me before.

Yes.

But I wouldn't have died.

No.

I might have broken my leg.

Maybe.

That lady might have pancaked my leg, Daddy.

Chappy looked at the owl-eyed boy as they rode their bikes along the sidewalk. He looked at the owl-eyed boy's face, trying to see if he was being funny. It was difficult to tell. He might have been smiling a little, or he might just have been thinking.

When Chappy and the owl-eyed boy got home, it was late. Mirror was in bed. She was almost asleep, but she called out when Chappy and the owl-eyed boy came in. Hi.

Hi, Mommy, said the owl-eyed boy.

Hi, honey, said Chappy. You go to sleep.

Do you have the key, Mommy? the owl-eyed boy asked.

Mirror seemed to have tears in her eyes. I'll get the key, she said.

Thank you, Mommy.

Mirror turned away.

The owl-eyed boy waited in the kitchen, listening to Mirror rummaging around in her room.

The safe gestures might save us, said Mirror.

They might, said Chappy.

Still later, Mirror said nothing still.

Still nothing, said Mirror, later still.

Sometimes I have to go back and read a sentence over to figure it out. Sometimes I forget how to put words together. Then I have to go back and keep reading those few words over and over until I see how they might go together. When that happens I am amazed. Not at the writer who wrote the words. That's not why I'm amazed. I'm not amazed at the way that writer manages to get the words together and make them work together. I'm amazed at myself for rescuing any sort of meaning from the words.

In what seemed to be a dream owned by his mother, the owl-eyed boy saw Mirror emerge from her room looking dishevelled.

Are you all right, Mother? the owl-eyed boy asked.

Yes, said Mirror. She held out a tiny silver key. It was in the top drawer all along, Mirror said.

The owl-eyed boy took the key.

Chappy saw Mike on the sidewalk where he and the owl-eyed boy were riding their bikes. He hadn't seen Mike in quite a while. He rode along beside Mike. They talked.

Walking home from work? Chappy asked.

Yes, said Mike.

The owl-eyed boy rode ahead. When he looked back, he saw his father talking to Mike. He stopped.

Mike walked along and Chappy rode slowly beside him till they got to where the owl-eyed boy was standing, straddling his bike.

We're going to the drugstore, said the owl-eyed boy.

Are you? It's a nice day to ride to the drugstore.

It's my birthday in two days.

How old will you be?

Eight.

Holy smokes.

We should all get together sometime, Mike, said Chappy.

Yes, said Mike. We should.

You and Helen could come over to our place for a barbeque.

Sounds good.

They said goodbye.

Chappy and the owl-eyed boy rode on. They came to an intersection. Chappy called out to the owl-eyed boy to be careful. The owl-eyed boy stopped and waited.

Remember that girl, Elizabeth... what was her last name? It was hyphenated. Do you remember her, Mirror. Smith-something? Laraby? No, that's not right. Chappy looked away. In order to have this conversation he and Mirror had to have known each other for five years or more. How long had they known each other? Chappy wasn't sure. More than a year, for sure. Two years? No, he didn't think so. But maybe.

*

Chappy heard a sound coming from the back of the world, a sound like his heart breaking on the shore of his fears. A sound like fear in the empty cove where his stomach acid washed ashore like waves on the beach of his mortality.

Is there someone else here? Chappy asked.

Mirror looked up. No, she said. She glanced around.

Why? Did you hear something?

Through the window, Chappy could see the tall beautiful girl at the bus stop growing blurry as water formed on the window and streaked toward the ground. Fat drops of water adhered to the window. Tiny streams of rainwater trickled down and entered the fat drops of water, making them fatter. Too fat to maintain their integrity, the fat drops burst apart, jettisoning new streams that joined other fat drops of water further down the window. The tall beautiful girl looked like a painting that got wet and was running away down the canvas. Soon the girl would be gone, her colours flowing together in rivulets running along the curb toward the storm sewers.

Chappy looked at Mirror, tried to tell her about his fear. He wanted her to console him, but the look in her eyes was one of terror.

Chappy looked around for a place to hide. There were quite a few places to hide. He saw them all immediately and realized he'd been watching for places to hide, without knowing it, the whole time they'd been living here.

Mirror looked toward the living room.

You want me to hide? Chappy asked.

Mirror looked at Chappy, her eyes bright, startled. She seldom told him anything he really didn't want to hear. Wait here, she said.

Chappy nodded off again on the couch. He suddenly looked so young. Mirror wanted to scoop him up and cuddle him. She smiled and walked toward the kitchen.

Chappy woke. He got off the couch. He sat on the floor,

cross-legged, playing with his socks. His shoes were in the front hall, by the door. It hadn't been raining when he'd come home, but the ground was wet from all the rain the night before and Chappy's shoes were muddy. He felt very afraid, like a worm that wakes up on top of a garden to realize there are birds all around and his family is gone. Chappy lay down because he thought it would make him less visible and any birds that saw him might think he was a stick.

Chappy heard Mirror's voice in the other room. He knew she wasn't talking to him. He crawled into a little space behind where the corner table met the couch.

Chappy ate his breakfast. He walked through the ravine to the bus. While he sat at his desk at work, he heard a song. When he got home in the afternoon and sat under the living room lights talking to Mirror, the song was a soundtrack. It made him feel made up.

At times Chappy thought he could almost detect a pattern. But when he thought he might put his finger on this pattern, quantify it, qualify it, even just give it a name, the pattern ceased to be a pattern. The pattern ran off in some new direction that left the empty space in Chappy even emptier than before.

Chappy heard the music of the street, punctuated by percussive rain blowing against the window that sat in the wall above where he lay. He remembered the tall girl. He remembered the triangles of the tall girl. He remembered her dress. Her hair. The space between her fingers where the webbing stretched. She was gone now. She's on a bus,

Chappy thought. She's very wet. She's dead. Washed away
into sewers. Her name is Ariana.

A new kind of music arrived and mounted the summit of
Chappy's consciousness. The earth rose up close to Chappy's
face and he saw the soft brown breast of the earth studded
with cigarette butts, stones, bottles and Styrofoam cups.
Littered here and there with maple keys and gum wrappers,
mint green and ice blue. The world was building something,
something so huge you could see only a tiny speck of it. You
knew it was there and that it was growing every day. But you
knew you'd never see the whole thing, except maybe in that
final moment before you died.

Everything was officially perfect now. Chappy thought he
might find a moment to sleep. Just as he began to fall, a
voice startled him. It was not Mirror's voice. It was the voice
of a creature Chappy couldn't name.

Mirror was in foreign territory. She was in a land not at all of
her making. She had never been here before, never visited,
never even imagined visiting. Still, it was a land of her own
making.

Mirror claimed that she and Chappy didn't make worlds,
they participated in them.

This time it was Mirror's voice. Chappy kept himself tucked
tight into the breakfast nook, the plastic bench cover sticking
to his cheek. He couldn't help thinking he was fucked. They
were going to take the owl-eyed boy away and the only way

to save him was for Chappy to leave. Chappy knew this as truly as he knew the fingers of his hand where they touched lightly the stainless steel leg of the table in the breakfast nook. Chappy had to pee. It was like someone swimming upstream frantically, splashing, drowning out the music of the rocks, the patter of waterspider feet on the surface of the still pool at the centre of the universe.

Chappy sat under a canopy of vegetable green. Alone, each of the trees above him was scraggly, dry, almost brown; but together they created a canopy. There was a new wooden fence next to the sidewalk. It was not as cold today. The snow fell in large soft flakes. There was no wind.

Chappy sat in a snowbank and leaned against the fence. He closed his eyes. The snow landed at his feet. He sat under the protection of the grand czar's canopy. A car swooshed through slush on the road. Houses sat forgotten amid four and five foot banks of snow.

Heading off in certain directions, without the slightest idea what we'll find, in the end, what we find is always the same.

What will we find, Chappy?

We'll know when we find it.

What did you find?

I don't know how to say it.

Mirror felt confused. At the same time, she realized that no amount of questions could ever help her clear up her confusion, so she stopped questioning Chappy and unlocked the box.

They rode along the sidewalk, side by side. Sometimes the owl-eyed boy drifted toward Chappy and Chappy had to cut over onto the grass.

They came to the end of their street. Go that way. Chappy pointed.

You can tell me to go right or left, Daddy, the owl-eyed boy said. I've got an L and an R on my handlebars.

Chappy had a book in his lap. He looked over his reading glasses at Mirror.

Do you think I interpret everything you do, Mirror?

You interpret everything, Chappy. Not just the things I do. You're an intrepid interpreter.

I can't help myself. Chappy shook his head. He had a stack of books beside him that he wanted to work his way through.

There are sentences in between the sentences in these books, he told Mirror. These are the sentences I am looking for, Mirror. The impossible sentences. The sentences that aren't actually there on the page. The sentences that are inferred. He looked down at the book. For a moment,

Mirror believed that Chappy had started reading again. She felt bereft. She wanted to say something just to fuck with Chappy's concentration. But then, suddenly, Chappy looked up.

I wish every sentence told of sentences that never should have been.

The owl-eyed boy stood in the middle of the street in his snowsuit. You couldn't see his face past his hood, which was cinched up tight with a drawstring. You could only see his nose poking out and the glow of his eyes if you saw him at the correct angle.

The street was covered in a packed down layer of snow and the sun was out. Banks of snow lined the road on both sides and it was cold.

The owl-eyed boy was watching the man he called Mikecar come out his front door. Mikecar was wearing a light jacket, his long black hair tied back. He had a cigarette in his mouth and he jumped into his car. No matter how cold it was, Mikecar always kept the top down on his MG Midget.

The owl-eyed boy watched exhaust shoot out of Mikecar's exhaust pipe. He watched the smoke billow up, then float silently out behind the car. Mikecar revved the engine and more exhaust billowed out. He backed his car through the cloud of exhaust.

For a moment, the owl-eyed boy couldn't see the car. But then it emerged through the smoke. It stopped in the middle of the street. Then it lurched forward, and sped away. The owl-eyed boy watched it disappear.

Chappy came out of the house and swore about how cold it was. He went into the garage. Then he came back out. The light hurt his eyes. He was carrying a toboggan. He tied the toboggan to the bumper of the car. He put the owl-eyed boy on the toboggan. Started the car. He pulled the owl-eyed boy around on the toboggan on the small streets near their house. It was early Sunday morning. Not a lot of cars were out.

The moment I first realize I'm awake, I don't even hear the lake. Chappy was looking down at his hands, focusing on remembering. His hair hung over his forehead, but it was shorter than it had ever been and did not even reach his eyebrows.

Think carefully, Chappy, said Mirror. You need to get this right.

I take a piss, says Chappy.

Chappy!

Chappy looked up at Mirror. Well I did.

Call it pee.

Okay.

Chappy looked back at his hands.

I take a pee. I look at the clock. The lake goes rolling onto the beach at the bottom of the hill. Chappy adds this last as an afterthought, as though he's afraid he's missing something important.

Below the cottage, he says, but he stops. His face looks pained, like this is hurting him. I look out the back door, he says. Sixty degrees, the thermometer says. Wind from the south. Maybe the lake will be warmer today, I think. I slip into my bathing suit. I go out. Walk around the cottage. I see the lake. There's no one else around. I feel enclosed in this space of my life that keeps repeating itself. I feel expansive. Today the air is truly warm. I smell the pine trees lined up at the top of the hill. Three of them, their tops tipped like doormen's hats. The sand still morning cool between my toes. The breeze riffling my hair. I stomp down the path, the way you have to stomp when you walk in deep, loose sand. As I come out onto open beach and get nearer the lake, the sand grows solid. It becomes easier to walk. I continue on until I'm at the edge of the water and my toes are in danger of getting wet.

Mirror lay back on the couch with her eyes closed, listening to Chappy. Her face looked composed, relaxed. She was there, on the beach, with Chappy.

Chappy continued to attempt to maintain the silence he had brought with him when he entered the room. Without reference to Mirror, he stated: We each have our own standard of what we like and don't like. Here is where we step away and allow subjectivity to claim the day.

I see what you mean, Chappy, said Mirror. But I'm not sure I care.

I began with a desire to do something, Mirror.

We all began there, Chappy.

I know. But Chappy didn't look like he knew. He looked frustrated. He gave Mirror a little boy look, pouting with his lips and raging with his eyebrows. Do you have a desire to do something for me, Mirror.

Not at the moment.

I know. Chappy's face seemed to relax. He looked out the window and Mirror fell in love with the light on the surface of his face, and she imagined that what was caught in the

light went deep, like roots struck deep into a brain after a
person is buried in the ground.

If my inclination were betrayal, Chappy said, but he didn't finish.

Mirror pulled Chappy close and held him while he cried.

My inclination, said Mirror, after they were silent for a while, is to set a standard by which we can exist together.

Mine, too, said Chappy. He hiccupped.

You're such a baby, Chappy.

I know. I'm sorry. Chappy pulled away and looked at Mirror. Chappy looked at Mirror like he wished she was his girl, but knew she never would be, even now, when they were married.

The standard needn't be an object, Mirror, Chappy said. It needn't be something we hold out as though in answer to the question. The question is still there.

He spread himself across the air, lifted himself over water. The quality of this memory made it so unlike life, so unlike living.

Memory stomps on living, Chappy said. Memory stomps on living in ways that make living seem thick, like air in the hair on your arm. Memory is rich and textured and thick, in ways life can never manage. Life can be exhilarating and frightening and joyful and heartbreaking, but it can never match memory for texture. Life is insistent. Memory resists. There was no one in the room to hear Chappy. He tried to remember what he'd just said, but already he forgot.

Mirror was laughing.
    Chappy smiled.
    Stop, Chappy, Mirror said.
    Okay, said Chappy.
    Chappy stopped.

Chappy set out to tell the story of Kerry, but so far he hadn't mentioned Kerry at all. But it was still the story of Kerry. Even though Chappy had not yet mentioned Kerry, this story was still all about Kerry. It was snowing big flakes outside in the dark, but the streetlight picked up cones of flakes and Chappy and Mirror kept the living room curtains open so they could watch. Mirror sat cradled beneath Chappy's arm.

Kerry died, Chappy said.

We all die, said Mirror.

But Kerry's already dead.

Mirror said nothing.

That makes him unique. That makes his story unique. That makes his story worth telling, don't you think, Mirror?

I'll be the judge of that, said Mirror. She tipped her head up and to the side a bit and found herself looking up Chappy's nose. It was surprisingly clean.

I see faces everywhere I look, Mirror. Straight out the core of my being, I see faces.

Or, maybe, what I see is more like a presence, a being. But when I look with my eyes, the presence is gone.

It seems that people are too busy to talk with me, Chappy said. He looked at Mirror challengingly. I embrace this busyness. I welcome it.

I know you do, Chappy.

I've become a great proponent of busyness. A practitioner. I've done it, Mirror. I've been busy like that.

Mirror tried to keep her face from moving.

Just tell them all: Chappy is busy.

Mirror looked worried.

Like all of them, I also feel very busy. Chappy didn't want her to worry. He knew that the more he went on about this

– about anything – the more she worried. But somehow he wanted to go on talking, trying to talk Mirror out of her worry.

I stay busy in order to enforce the silence for which I hunger, said Chappy. But the silence I hunger for is a kind of communion, a sharing of silence. Driving people away by staying busy obviously isn't going to lead to real spiritual communion. Is it, Mirror?

Is that really what you're looking for, Chappy? Spiritual communion?

Maybe, said Chappy, and then he sat looking at his hands in his lap. His hands were lying palms up with the backs of his fingers curled against his thighs.

If one seagull sees another seagull in a place a ways off, the one seagull thinks there must be something good over where the other seagull is, so it goes over. Then another seagull sees there are two seagulls over at the place where the one seagull thought there was something good and the third seagull thinks there must be something good enough for two seagulls to be over there, so it goes over. Then other seagulls see a bunch of seagulls all together in one place, and the other seagulls think there must be something really good over there where all those seagulls are, so they all go over, too.

That's how you get a bunch of seagulls all congregating in one place. It isn't that seagulls like to commune together. Most seagulls would rather be alone. But they can't stand to see another seagull getting good stuff that they don't have.

What are you reading, Chappy?

Chappy put his finger on a page in the book in his lap. He read aloud from the book: The letter he was holding in his hands was the last earthly communication he would ever receive from his only daughter.

That's intriguing.

I know. Chappy went back to reading.

Mirror had a book in her lap, too, but she wasn't reading it. She was looking across the living room, toward the curtains. Does he receive any unearthly communications from his daughter? she asked.

Chappy looked up from the book, trying to pull himself back to where he was. The cone of yellow light from the lamp barely reached him where he sat at the far end of the couch. I don't know yet, Mirror. He hasn't had any unearthly communications from his daughter, yet. But he just finished reading the last earthly one, and it's still early in the book.

What happened to his daughter, Chappy? Mirror asked. She looked disturbed. Her face looked slightly contracted. How did she die?

I've told you about this before, Mirror. You didn't want me to read you this book. I would have read it to you. But now I've started it and I've read a couple of chapters and it's too late. I won't start again so you can find out what happened so far.

I know, Chappy. I'm sorry.

You can read it when I'm finished.

Thank you. Mirror said nothing after that.

Chappy looked at Mirror's face, at the look on her face. Chappy knew it was too early to go back to reading. Mirror was getting ready to say something else, and he didn't want to start reading again if he was going to have to turn from the book to listen to Mirror.

It was the cover of the book, Mirror said finally. I didn't like the cover. It looked like a shallow book. Just from looking at the cover, I mean.

It is a shallow book, Mirror. You were right.

I know. I mean, I figured it had to be shallow. But right now, I could use a little shallow.

You want me to read to you starting where I am now in the book.

No. I'd just drive you crazy asking you what happened before. It wouldn't work. You know that. We've tried it before.

I know. I could just stop reading. We could talk.

Thank you, Chappy, Mirror said, but I don't think I have very much to say.

No. I don't think I have very much to say, either, said Chappy.

So let's just go on reading our books.

Mirror tucked her legs up under her on the couch and tipped her head forward to read her book.

After watching Mirror for a moment and feeling a pang of regret, Chappy went back to reading his book, too.

Mirror was laughing. She was catching Chappy up in laughter. She was trying to do Redding's voice. It didn't matter if she got it right, since Chappy didn't know what Redding sounded like anyway.

She sounds like some old school marm, said Chappy.

She is an old school marm, said Mirror.

What is an old school marm, anyway, Mirror? asked Chappy. Is marm even a real word? I should look it up.

It's a word, Chappy. You don't have to look it up.
I want to look it up.
Let me finish the story first.
I wasn't going to look it up right now.
Chappy was looking out the window.
What are you looking at? Mirror asked.

I like his voice, Mirror said. He looks sort of dumb, but his voice is like silk.

What's wrong, Mirror?
It's like... Mirror stopped. She looked so lost. It made Chappy's heart stop for a moment. He watched her standing by the kitchen sink.

The kitten pushed against Chappy's ankle. Chappy reached down and scratched the kitten's head.

*

Mirror looked up at Chappy. I'm not hungry anymore, Chappy, she said.

I was attending a concert while attempting to ascertain the speed at which you would need to throw yourself forward in order to coincide with the you you'd rather be.

Chappy and Mirror were on a campsite somewhere north of where they lived. It was late October. Chappy felt the warmth of the dying fire on his face. The back of his head was cold. He pulled down into the sleeping bag, like a lump of coal pushed to the surface of the earth. He felt like a lower case letter struggling to find a place in a world where upper case was better. Better by common decree – decree among commoners prepared to debase themselves at the foot of the great capital. Chappy slept.

I've been having two kinds of dreams lately, Mirror, Chappy said. Chappy was sitting on the edge of the bed. Mirror was in the bathroom sitting on the toilet. She had the door slightly open so she could hear Chappy. Dreams where you find my lighter in various places and I spend the rest of the dream trying to explain to you why I have a lighter; and dreams where I am dreaming about the walkie-talkies at work, and everyone is trying to call me on the walkie-talkies, but they can't get me because I've forgotten to get my walkie-talkie out of the manager's office and clip it to my belt. The toilet flushed. The water ran. Mirror came out of the bathroom pushing hair away from her face. She sat down on the bed beside Chappy and put her hand on his knee.

Diski's book looked like a good book to transport on my bicycle, said Chappy over the phone. So I borrowed it. You want to read it? I can bring it home tonight.

You think it's a good book?

I don't know. *Skating to Antarctica* was a good book. This one is small and easy to carry on my bike.

Okay. Bring it home.

There's some good reviews on the back of the book.

I thought you didn't care about those reviews.

I care about them. Chappy was silent for a moment. I find them reassuring, that's all. They never seem to have

any relation to the quality of the book. I've seen books where
the cover was absolutely covered in good reviews and I could
barely read the thing.

When Wendy's mother died, Wendy started coming into
work wearing her mother's clothes. She talked about dreams
where her mother phoned her up from a phone booth in
heaven and complained about all the pain she was having.
She complained about the weather, and about her son,
Wendy's brother.

Chappy tried not to ever say anything mean to anybody. Sometimes he said, Tell it to my dick, but he never said this to anybody's face. He worked it into speeches he imagined making as he crossed the mall parking lot at lunch.

When Chappy was twenty-four years old, he wrote poems. He wrote poems about old men standing in the rain in Greece. He wrote poems about men standing ankle deep in garbage in parking lots on the outskirts of cities that had been abandoned due to nuclear holocaust. He wrote poems about hollow trees that looked lifeless, but then suddenly sprouted insects like lava blowing out the top of a volcano. He wrote poems about turtles that, from a distance, looked alive, but from close up were dead and maggot-infested. He wrote poems about red-headed women vanishing from malls. He wrote about the sound of steam engines stuck on inclines deep in lonely mountain passes. He wrote poems about flagpoles.

Chappy mailed his poems to small magazines and waited six months for rejection letters. Once in a while, a little magazine published one of his poems and he received free copies of the issue he was in. Whenever Chappy received a magazine with one of his poems in it, he snuck it into the house and hid it in his desk so Mirror wouldn't see it.

Chappy was reading *The End of Nature*, a book about the greenhouse effect and ozone depletion. He read a chapter every Saturday morning and then came downstairs and did the dishes and drank coffee. He never talked to Mirror about what was in the book. When he finished it, he passed it on to a friend.

Chappy was working at a bookstore for a while. He was sitting in a chair on the loading dock out back when a school bus pulled up and a man he hadn't seen in years named Guthrie got out of the bus.

Chappy had *A House for Mr. Biswas* in his lap. He was at the epilogue section, a section which always made his heart sink in any book he read. The epilogue always left him feeling sad for the remainder of the day. He was sorry he had decided to read the epilogue of *A House for Mr. Biswas* on his lunch hour. He looked up at Guthrie morosely.

Hi Chappy, Guthrie said. You have any books on astrology in there. Guthrie tipped his head toward the loading dock door. He looked like he was trying to be clandestine.

Yeah, said Chappy.

Guthrie flashed his white teeth in a grin. It was so hot that the air seemed to conceal Guthrie in a curtain of clandestiny. His cheeks stretched and his eyes reshaped so they looked like two halfmoons in the dark skin of his face, but to Chappy he looked like he was behind some kind of veil, or like Chappy suddenly needed glasses. Chappy could feel the humidity in his nose. It made him tired.

Hang on a minute, said Chappy. He went into the stockroom and grabbed all the books he could find on astrology. There were eight of them and he took them out to Guthrie, stacked along his arm, the way he stacked them when he was in the store shelving books. Take as many as you want, he told Guthrie.

I only want one, said Guthrie. Guthrie took one with a yellow cover. He held it in his hands, regarding it. Okay, he said. Thanks. He got back on his bus. He set the book in a wooden box he had on the floor by his seat. He settled himself in his seat and pulled on his seatbelt. He still had the door of the bus open. He waved at Chappy before pulling on the silver handle that closed the bus door. He drove away.

Before that day behind the bookstore, Chappy hadn't seen Guthrie in over four years. He never saw him again after that.

After sitting on the couch, watching the wind blow the trees about, Chappy got up and went to wash the tears from his face. He felt suddenly very hungry, so he went out the front door.

It was spring outside. The snow was gone. A little cow stood on a far off hill. If this seemed unusual to someone who lived in the middle of a large city, Chappy showed no sign of being surprised.

The sun was shining weakly over the tops of the houses across the street. It was almost ten o'clock. Chappy went through the little gate at the front of his yard. The fence was a half-picket. It went halfway to Chappy's waist.

It looks like something from miniature world, said Mirror when she first saw it.

Chappy's shirt was purple, with a rip near his shoulder, so a little flap of shirt hung down exposing some of the skin on his chest, just above his left nipple. It was Chappy's favourite shirt. He planned on sewing it sometime. Maybe today when he got home from eating.

The old man from next door was standing on the sidewalk in front of his house, face turned toward the sun, eyes closed. He heard the gate open in Chappy's yard and he opened his eyes. He looked at Chappy. Good morning, Chappy, the old man said.

Chappy felt disoriented. He'd been alone in the house all morning. He wasn't sure where Mirror was today. He wasn't sure she even existed, really. When was the last time he had seen Mirror? The old man's voice echoed in Chappy's head. Being alone with the silence, sitting on the couch all morning, Chappy was filled with emptiness, and the old man's voice echoed in that emptiness like something let loose in a tin chamber.

Mirror sat bolt upright in bed, then went to the laundry hamper in the hall closet. She pulled the laundry hamper into the bedroom and started sorting the laundry.

Mirror came out onto the front porch of their townhouse with a can of club soda in each hand. Do you want these? she called.

No, Chappy called back.

I thought maybe you wanted them for lunch. They were out on the counter.

No. Thanks, Mirror. Chappy felt sad that he wasn't taking the cans of soda from Mirror. He felt like he was abandoning Mirror on the front porch. He closed the hatch and got in the car. He looked up through the windshield at the porch. Mirror was standing on the front porch, waving at Chappy with the can of club soda in her right hand. The can of club soda was blue.

I wanted to see a woman I'd never seen before. When I woke up that morning in January, with the sun shining in through the bedroom window onto the covers of my bed, warming my feet, I made that my goal for the day: to see a woman I'd never seen before standing barefoot in my kitchen, making coffee.

I've seen that woman, said Chappy.

Hey, Chappy, said Mirror, when snakes die, do they go rigid? Could you use them as sticks?

Who is that woman?

What woman? Mirror was holding a magazine open, but she looked up now.

That one over there. See her, in the express line.

The one in the black skirt?

Yes.

Never seen her before. Mirror went back to her magazine.

The woman in the black skirt turned and looked at Chappy. Chappy looked away. He felt like he was deceiving someone.

Wait, said Mirror. I do know her. You know her too, Chappy.

I know I know her, Mirror. That's what I'm trying to tell you. Don't tell me who she is. I want to figure it out by myself.

I don't know who she is. I only know I know her.

It's on the tip of my tongue. Don't tell me. Chappy looked at Mirror and tried to see in her face if it looked like she was taking him seriously. I'm serious, Mirror. It's going to upset me if I don't figure out who this woman is.

Mirror laughed. Who cares, she said. She went back to looking at her magazine. Chappy glanced surreptitiously at the woman, hoping she wouldn't notice him looking at her.

You want to load the groceries on the belt, or bag them? Mirror asked. She put the magazine back on the magazine rack.

Neither, said Chappy. I need to try to figure out where I've seen that woman before. If I can figure out where I've seen her before, maybe I can remember who she is. Chappy looked at Mirror. Mirror was grinning, looking like she was about to say something.

Don't even give me a hint, said Chappy. Mirror. I'm serious.

Oh, I know you're serious, Chappy. It's quite evident how serious you are. Mirror started putting items onto the grocery belt that was rolling toward the cashier. The grocieries would roll, then stop, then start rolling again as the cashier scanned the items for the person in the line in front of them. Mirror kept putting things on the end of the belt as the belt moved forward.

Chappy was watching the woman. Suddenly, without warning, the woman looked up at Chappy again. Their eyes met. The woman smiled. She waved.

Fuck, said Chappy under his breath. He didn't move his lips. Only Mirror could tell that he'd said anything. Chappy smiled back at the woman and raised his hand a little. The woman was at the express desk. She started loading her items onto the belt.

She recognized me, Mirror. Great. If I don't remember who she is by the time we get out of the store, we might have to talk to her.

She's only got a couple of items, Chappy. She'll be long gone by the time we get all our stuff checked through and bagged up.

She might wait to talk to us.

Mirror looked over at the woman, who was now paying for her items.

She might come over and say hi.

She won't.

How do you know, Mirror? You don't know.

I know, Chappy. That woman is not going to come over here to talk to us. She's not going to wait out in the parking lot. She's not going to go out of her way to say something to us.

Why? Doesn't she like us?

I don't know who she is, Chappy. I only know I've seen her somewhere before. But she isn't going to go out of her way to say hi. She probably doesn't even remember who we are either. Now, I have to bag the groceries if you're not going to do it.

I'll do it. I wish I could remember who that woman is.

Put the heavy groceries in first.

What are you reading? Mirror asked.

Chappy was sitting up in bed with coffee beside him. Mirror was standing in the doorway. It was Sunday afternoon. Chappy had been out of bed earlier, but he got back in after lunch and now he was still there. He had books and papers on the bed all around him.

It's called, I Have a Stapler, Chappy said.

Is it good?

It's kind of frightening.

Mirror waited.

There's something frightening in committing yourself to any course of action, Mirror.

What happens in the story, Chappy?

Two things happen. One: a guy buys a stapler, a random act that has no consequences and is ultimately a waste of time, as you find out later in the story, because the stapler just sits on the counter unused. Two: the guy commits himself to stapling his friend's things. He volunteers to do this, and this is no less frightening in some ways than getting up in front of a lot of people and speaking.

Are you worried about getting up in front of all those people, Chappy?

Yes.

Mirror took Chappy's head in her arms and pulled it onto her bosom. She rocked him. Chappy put his arms around Mirror. After a bit Mirror asked: So, is that all that happens in the story?

At one point, Chappy said – and he was talking in the direction of Mirror's crotch – the guy thinks: How could I have been so stupid? These doubts assail us in even the most mundane of self-conceived undertakings.

Chappy, Mirror said, continuing to rock him. I wish

I could make you stop hurting.

        I'm not hurting, Mirror.

        Yes, you are.

        I know.

I'm pretty sure it had nothing to do with Patty, Mirror. I'm
fairly certain on that score. In fact, I'd go so far as to say that
I've made my mind up that it's a forgone conclusion that it
had nothing to do with Patty. So that gets that out of the
way. I mean, I've accomplished something here, don't you
think, Mirror? Chappy looked at Mirror and Mirror looked
back. Mirror smiled She nodded, sort of meekly, Chappy
thought. This made Chappy's heart pump. He smiled back,
also meekly. He felt nervous of Mirror today.

    I've taken a step here, don't you think, Mirror? Chappy
said this more to fill the air with some words than anything
else.

    Mirror nodded. She had her hair tied back. Chappy could
see every part of her face beyond the line of her hair and
ears and beyond where her neck dropped from her chin into
shadow.

    I've made some movement, Chappy said. He'd looked
away from Mirror, back into his thoughts, to try to get a
grip on this. Not a lot of movement, he conceded. But that's
okay, he added. That's the name of the game here, right?
The idea is to make some progress, to get along a ways, but
at the same time, not go too fast.

    He looked at Mirror again, this time inquisitively. Right?
he asked.

    Mirror immediately mirrored Chappy's inquisitive look.
They searched each other a moment, tried to penetrate, to

see deeper.

Would it help if I told you something about Patty? Chappy asked.

Mirror looked like she thought about it for a second or two. No, she said.

Chappy woke up. Everyone was gone. The house was empty. There was his bedside table. There was a table lamp. He reached over to the table lamp, put the light on. There was a plate with crumbs.

Downstairs, the light was on in the kitchen. Chappy must have left it on when he went to bed. Or maybe Mirror left it on. When did Mirror leave? It could have been a long time ago. It could have been years. How long had the light been on?

Chappy fixed himself an egg. He sat at the table. Something about the table. He tried to remember. He stared. Something to do with staring at the table. He stood. He'd taken two bites of his egg while he sat at the table, before he stood up. He had not yet reached the yolk when he set the fork down and stood up from the table. He felt regret. What was he regretting? An egg yolk? No, he thought. Not an egg yolk. There was something he was regretting, though. What was it?

He went into another room. There were rooms all over the house.

He went to five different rooms in the house.

In the sixth room, it occurred to him they might all be the same room.

He came to the table with the egg, and sat down.

Something about the table.

He took the plate with the egg and put it in the sink.

He sat down again at the table.

He stared.

He heard voices.

Were they voices in the kitchen?

No.

Out in the yard?

Were they just in his head?

Have you heard those voices coming from waterfalls, water tortured on rock, falling, crashing, tortured, broken? It was the voice of tortured water falling on rock.

In the story Chappy last told Mirror, one of the brothers had to make a list. Another brother had a terrible headache. The brother with the terrible headache hadn't told the other brothers about his headache. The brother with the headache was determined to just ride out the headache. The brothers might or might not be together like this again. There was no way of knowing. There is never any way of knowing. People depended on the brothers. But it was time to move on. It was time to prove something. Even having the dad come by like that had been nice and the brothers felt a bit of a warm smile inside. It had been nice sitting on the sidewalk with all the brothers. And then the dad coming along like that.

Clive lived long and loved the baby dragon, just like everybody else, Chappy told Mirror.

But Mirror didn't care. Mirror was gone.

By baby dragon, I mean the small child, said Chappy. The small child birthed on that auspicious day. The child of the beautiful woman, Jill. But the way Clive loved the baby dragon left him feeling sad. Clive was feeling longing from having been so close to Jill's hair, and he was transforming his longing into love for the baby dragon.

The dad dumped some capsules onto the sidewalk, told the boys to go about earning their keep.

Her name was Jill, Chappy told Mirror.

Mirror listened as though her life depended on it. She listened like her hair was in her eyes, permanently, and all she had left to live for was her hearing.

Jill lived with her four blonde sisters in a house shaped like a triangle, Chappy said. The mother, he continued, had long blonde hair that spoke of longing. The mother looked a lot like Jill, especially in the facial features and in the way she moved her body. The brother who had been with the girl had seen the baby dragon. He had just come from watching the view through the back window of the beautiful girl's car. The one who arrived, Clive, was wearing a hat with earflaps. The two other brothers had stopped their fight. The one fighting brother had just finished rubbing the other brother's face in the slush. But they stopped now. The three brothers sat on the sidewalk in their hats and mitts.

Mirror saw what all this might mean. To her. To Chappy. It might mean anything. But she thought, for a brief instant, that she saw how it might mean something utterly specific, but without seeing the specifics themselves. This made Mirror feel broken.

The father arrived along the sidewalk in his postman uniform, Chappy said. Chappy was speaking fast now. Like the story was getting away from him. Like the story was a dream he was trying to remember that was turning into smoke, wisps of smoke high in the air among the tops of the trees on a cold autumn morning at a campground. You could see the wisps of smoke, smell them, but soon they would be gone.

There was a brief exchange, Chappy said, already moving into the abstract from no longer having the concrete to draw on. Including, Chappy continued, but not exclusively, but he was stammering, slowing down, losing the thread, including the possibility, he stammered, of the dad, he continued, being relieved.

Chappy, please, Mirror said, but even as she said it, she felt afraid of what was coming. Give up, she said. Mirror desperately didn't want Chappy to give up, but somehow this is what she felt had to be said. Somehow this is what she said. What she wound up saying.

What are you saying, Mirror? Chappy asked.

Nothing, Chappy. Go on, please. Finish the story. I want you to finish the story.

Chappy looked hesitant. But he went on, finally, slowly, trying to rebuild. But there was no one they knew, those brothers, no one in the cold thin air of winter whose authority could accomplish the relief of duty they sensed imminent in their dad. And then the dad saw his boys, his kind, soft-hearted boys and he bowed his head a moment and gave thanks.

Don't let them talk you out of it, Chappy, Mirror said. Maintain that you've been to see the king. Say, Hi, I've been to see the king. Call Hiroko. You read his other story, right? About what a little fucker he was. He'd hardly seen you. Who knew? He turned out to be such a little guy. Remember how you first read his stories. How you met him once. Mention how you met him once.

Chappy caught his breath.

What happened early in the life of McFarlane? Mirror asked.

Chappy now saw that there was going to be trouble.

What were McFarlane's inspirations? Mirror asked. What was his single biggest triumph? What changed McFarlane? Why did he change? Did anything in McFarlane's life suggest McFarlane would make such a legacy?

Chappy wrote each word beside the one before it, never fearing, never going back to see what came before, until he no longer knew where he'd been and only that next word not yet written existed. He would not retread, he told himself. He was not writing a love story. He was writing for the love of story.

Mirror was on her side on the bed looking at a book with pictures in it. Currently, she was looking at a picture of a concrete bridge in Amsterdam, with Dutch people crossing.

Chappy lost his train of thought. He stopped writing to look over at the picture of the Dutch people crossing the concrete bridge. He looked at each of the Dutch people. He formed a small impression about each of the Dutch people. Each impression was the actual size of one of the Dutch people in the picture.

Chappy remembered immediately this time to pull the door to make it open. A lady in pink tights smiled at him as they passed each other near the cockpit. The tags were confusing, though. It took Chappy a while to understand that he had to keep moving. The batteries were on special, but it wasn't a good special. Chappy pulled the door open and walked out. It was one of those doors where you have to pull on it to make it open. Chappy was waiting for a door to open. He felt like God.

Outside, some heavy white clouds, shaped like cotton balls glued together by a child in kindergarten, cut the sun. The father had gone. Now they all looked up to see what the clouds were doing.

The clouds were doing what clouds were always doing, what they'd always done. They were shifting and morphing and slightly diminishing until they were completely gone. They were disappeared from view.

By this time, they were far, the clouds, far away from the boys, over a town many, many miles away.

Mirror especially loved Chappy's stories about clouds. Even if the clouds never seemed to be the main characters in the story, they always seemed to matter the most to Chappy and this made his storytelling about clouds very endearing to Mirror, breaking her heart and making her hopeful all at the same time. She wished she could put her head in Chappy's amazing clouds.

Chappy was in a room with bookshelves. Bookshelves and filing cabinets. Chappy had never seen this room before. It was a room at the bottom of a set of stairs. Chappy climbed back up the stairs. The stairs were enclosed in a number of walls and railings and a ceiling, and there was no light. Chappy could find no light.

There was a light switch. The light switch was on the wall by the door. You opened the door and there were the stairs. Chappy went through the door and he was in his house. He closed the door. The furnace was going. He felt warm air. He could see through to the kitchen. Beyond that, he could see through to the yard. There was a man in the yard. Chappy checked his e-mail.

One message said: Yes.

Chappy checked the subject line. It said: re.

The message was from himself. It was a message from Chappy. He had answered his own e-mail message: Yes.

Another message said this: Some questions I wanted to ask you, Chappy:
– if you start off pretending you like someone, will you naturally and organically start really liking them for real?
– if you fake it for a while, will it eventually become real?
– were you ever afraid of escalators?
– if I start off penetrating you, will I wind up penetrating everyone?

The new man was far off down the hill. The woman, who was a woman only in the sense that we are all women, was a moment ago standing in the sun. Before that she was standing with the man. But now she was sitting in the sand.

Chappy looked at Mirror. She might be sleeping, he thought. She had her eyes closed. Sometimes she liked to close her eyes and listen to Chappy tell stories. But sometimes she was just asleep. You'd think her head would tip over if she were asleep. But her head didn't seem ever to tip over. Chappy could never really know for sure if Mirror was sleeping, or listening with her eyes closed, so he stopped trying to figure it out and continued to tell his story.

The woman might have been laughing along with the man, or she might have been drying her hands in the sand, it was hard to tell. The man's breath steamed out into cold air.

Chappy looked outside. It wasn't a cold day at all. It was humid and dark, giving him the feeling he was in a darkened state, waiting for the show in his heart to start.

And the new guy is laughing, Chappy said. And there are streaks of blue sky where the sun could come out again any minute now. Only minutes ago, the sun was out. But now it's gone. Gone behind clouds. Shining. The sun is still shining. But now it shines behind some clouds.

Mirror had her eyes closed, but now she smiled a little, with her lips, with her eyes. Her eyes were closed, but they crinkled. Just a little. The smile was like a pair of spiders playing love games under the skin of Mirror's face, playing on her lips and under her cheeks and in the skin around her eyes.

Maybe Mirror is dreaming, Chappy thought.

Silver angels fell, sizzling on the atmosphere. They had screamed, and they had broken away. There was something in what I said that they didn't hear, and I said it. I thought by telling their story I might capture something elusive and put it on display. They didn't hear what I talked about when they heard me talk. Something hidden in me didn't get said. Angels didn't want to hear me talk. Their story was something in me that I couldn't seem to say.

When I was young, I wanted to capture sleep the way a cowboy wrassles a cow to the ground. I became a writer. I felt I had something to say. I felt I might have something to say. I felt that if I wanted to say something, what I wanted to say would be in the oil on my skin. I felt that what I wanted to say was sparkling like sun on water. I was totally deluded. When I said there was something jewel-like about the morning, I was wrong. I was whacked. I had encountered something I had never encountered before. That was back when there was something conclusive about the end of each day.

Chappy was pushing too hard. Mirror opened her eyes. The smile still played on her lips. When she spoke, she rose out of the sentence like something fucked. She wanted to pinch the little cheeks of her sentences, but she held herself back, and she held back the tears. Come over here, she said. Chappy got off the couch. He crossed the room, sat beside Mirror. He sat up straight, with his hands in his lap, like someone waiting for an interview. Mirror pulled his head into her lap.

I can tell the story of this planet, Chappy said. But I'd rather go to sleep. I like to go to sleep, Mirror. I'd like to go to sleep.

Go to sleep, Chappy.

Goodnight, Mirror.

Goodnight, Chappy.

It was around this time that Chappy got out of bed and went to the window. There was snow on the cars in the parking lot. It's too late for snow, Chappy thought.

A man with black hair was brushing snow off his car. Chappy could see the man's breath as the man moved around the car, fanning his brush across windows. Then the man got in the car and drove away. Exhaust hung in the air where the car had been parked.

Let's go into the house and get some lemonade, Chappy told the owl-eyed boy.

Chappy was looking out through the window over the kitchen sink at the yard next door. Mirror was at the breakfast nook in her blue cotton bathrobe. The man from the house is coming out, said Chappy. He is standing beside the little boy. They are both looking over the back fence onto the busy street behind the house. The boy is less than half the height of the man. The man is saying something to the boy. The boy is running away.

Chappy looks back over his shoulder at Mirror. My wife, he thinks. Mirror is still asleep.

Chappy goes out the door and along the hall to apartment 207. He knocks on the door of apartment 207. It seems he has to wait awhile. He thinks he hears padding, like slippers, inside apartment 207. But then he doesn't hear anything. He stands at the door a long while before going back along the hall, back to his own apartment.

Mirror is still asleep.

Chappy thinks about looking out the window again. He's been looking at snow for months now. The floor in the front hall is gaining something. It has a grainy feel. This comes from Chappy and Mirror and the owl-eyed boy tracking in the sand that they put on the sidewalks.

Chappy looks out the peephole of the door. He does this every ten minutes. He never sees anyone.

I stare across the naked shoulder of the sun. We drink coffee and someone laughs. But I don't think it's me. There is no sense of joy. Then she closes the sun. There is no more light. Windows in here stay dark. She nuzzles my throat.

The time when Chappy knocks on 207 for a second time, he definitely hears slippers padding. The padding stops. Rhonda is looking at Chappy through the peephole. She opens the door. She is wearing a long green nightie. Her hair is out of place. She has no pants. In the sun, the wolf understands the language of shadow.

Chappy sits in the living room watching birds fly across the sky. To be a bird, Chappy thinks, you need to be brave. You need to be able to just fly out as far as you want. You need to aim at the horizon and just keep going. You could go anywhere you wanted if you were a bird. You wouldn't have to ask anyone. You could just fly away.

I'm going down the street to buy a paper, Chappy tells Mirror. He goes down the hall and knocks on 207. Rhonda opens the door right away. She's in the same green nightie.

The upstairs apartment from Chappy and Mirror's apartment is a part of the building that has light coming through sheer curtains. The sun is so bright, the man upstairs has to close his eyes and sit on the side of the bed to keep his head from reeling. The canopy on the bed is of sheer curtain. The bed is covered in metallic brown. The bedside table is well appointed.

Do you have a paper? Chappy says to Rhonda. Rhonda goes out and buys a paper. She comes back and gives it to Chappy. Best of luck, Chappy, she says. Chappy tucks the paper under his arm.

Mirror is frying mushrooms when Chappy gets back. When Chappy steps through the door, Mirror looks up from where she's standing in the kitchen in her bare feet with her nightie coming down below her knees. She smiles. Chappy sits at the dining room table with the paper in his hands, not looking at anything. Out in the parking lot, a child screams.

Part Three

Chappy's got a book about Hemingway, *The Paris Years*. It's checked out on Mirror's library card. This is what Mirror has been able to do for Chappy this week, as though they are still at the start of their relationship, living in separate places, each with their own library card.

The one story Chappy told this week was a terrible story about a guy shaped like a bucket. Chappy has given nothing to Mirror this week. He feels he owes her something. He's had this feeling before, at other points in the marriage. So far this week Chappy has consumed coffee, and he gave some books to Goodwill.

No one had ever called Chappy at work before.

Hello, he said. The phone hung on the wall above the manager's desk. Chappy was rubbing his hand on his apron, trying to get the grease off.

Hi.

It was Rikki.

I don't know how to tell you this, Rikki said.

Chappy thought she was going to ask him out. It was the

middle of the summer. He hadn't seen Rikki for a month. Years before, Chappy had had a crush on Rikki. He had decided to ask her to go steady with him. He remembered sitting down in his bedroom in the basement of his house in the dark.

Chappy held the phone against his ear and waited.

Terrence is dead, Rikki said.

Chappy looked at the manager's desk. He picked up a pencil that was lying there. He tried to imagine Rikki, standing at a phone in her house, maybe the phone on the table by that curving staircase in the front hall. But she probably had her own phone in her bedroom on the table by her bed. He tried to picture Rikki lying on her bed.

There was one sad tune they played whenever Spock did the Vulcan mindmeld that Chappy was trying to hum. He could hum most of it. But he couldn't get the ending right. But he kept trying, till Mirror asked him to please stop.

Chappy could hear his father's voice. He could hear his father's words floating above him in the dark. He had no idea what his father's words were saying. Instead, he cared about the light pressure of his father's hand on his back. He smelled his father's warmth. He stopped crying. Lay quietly.

*

Mirror was sleeping by the time Chappy stopped trying to hum the Vulcan mindmeld. Chappy went into the bathroom to take a shower. He put some cream rinse in his hair. He wanted to look his best.

You have to try to get really specific in a way that specifies nothing, Mirror, said Chappy. I realized today that I need everyone. And I need that realization that I need everyone. And I even need the people I don't need. And I need the thought that I don't need the people I don't need. I need the people I don't need just so I can have the thought that I don't need them. Does that make sense, Mirror? And I need that girl over there. I need that girl's hair. I need that girl's hair to plane out on the wind. And I need the woman whose tired eyes stand as lines I don't even see, lines I feel as a wave of age and fatigue. And I need to go back to work now.

Okay, Chappy, Mirror said. I'll see you tonight after work.

Okay.

The streets were empty, except for the odd early shadow stalking a worker at a bus stop, or scaling a wall behind the bus stop, or standing in a driveway next to a car.

The doughnut shop was three minutes from where Chappy and Mirror lived. It was at an awkward place to get into because of traffic. There were always pickup trucks idling in the parking lot.

They are making coffee in the back room, Chappy told Mirror. Maybe everything isn't going to go just right today. Maybe lies will be told and the vibes will be slightly off.

Maybe we should go home now, Mirror.

Chappy read a poem to Mirror. They were in the bathroom together. Mirror was at the mirror doing something to her

eyes. Chappy sat on the edge of the tub with his notebook
in his lap.

It's called Boy on a Rock, Chappy said. It's a true story.
It's by me:

> He rode the cloud
> That horse-faced boy
> Lost everything
> His scarf. The newspaper
> His shovel with the girl's
> Face imprinted on the blade
> The bull ran back
> sad-faced men rippling behind.
> Someone thought the morning might finally come.
> But Mother said no.
> If anyone had a claim to the mountains
> it would be that bear we saw
> in the summer after
> the weather turned.

That's a really beautiful poem, Chappy, Mirror said. She
daubed makeup pencil near her eye. But it's not really a
poem, she said.

It's not? said Chappy.

No. It's more of a story. She turned and looked at Chappy.
One of her eyes was made up dark and blackened the way
she liked. The other was not. She had her hair pinned back
to keep it off her face. She looked like Two-Face.

Chappy felt something sharp in his chest and throat.

Really, though, it hardly does it justice to call it a poem.

You don't really like poetry, though, right, Mirror?

Not really. She was back to blacking her eyes into boring tunnels of light from a source of intelligence Chappy still couldn't even begin to guess at.

Harvey prayed mightily that the wind would let up. And sometimes, yes, the trees stopped falling, and the members of the tribe would gather together in the calm, amid the carnage, shiny-eyed and hungry. Lem, Harvey's dog, would live long enough to see the river again. Harvey loaded things into his wagon. Whenever he got the chance, he put in bits of lumber he'd saved, trinkets he'd stolen. He filled the wagon and pulled it out onto the road. Harvey's pa stood on the porch and screamed hisself hoarse at Harvey to get his sorry ass back home, but the wind took his words and tossed them over the roof of the house and Harvey never heard a word nor even the sound of his father's voice.

Did you just say hisself, Chappy?

Yes. Chappy waited to see what Mirror's reaction would be. He had been unsure of that one word in the middle of his story and he was glad she called him on it. He wanted to be sure of everything, and Mirror had the capacity to loan him her surety on matters such as this.

I just wanted to make sure I'd heard right.

Chappy took this as consent. He went on.

Harvey turned only once, Chappy said. And when he did, he saw his pa with his mouth wide open but silent. That's the last he ever saw of his pa.

By then, his ma had gone back to the straw hut she built when Gil was born. Little Lou Anne was destined to die before she finished preschool.

Harvey kept on pulling the wagon down the muddy road,

lifting it over trees, marching through waist-deep water that
covered the road in places where the river had burst her
banks.

Chappy stopped. He was silent for a time. Neither he nor
Mirror said a word.

Now that's a poem, Chappy, Mirror said, finally, into the
silence.

I think you're a very confused person, Mirror.

Not at all, Chappy.

Maybe not.

Dad saw something in me he wanted and couldn't have. So
he decided I couldn't have it either. He took it away.

It was heart that Dad took away. I had Dad's heart.
I saw into Dad's heart. Dad couldn't see into his own heart
anymore, and he couldn't stand to see me seeing into it, so
the fucker just left me there.

I hate that bastard, Mirror. The worst part is, beyond this
terrible rage, I have no love at all for him. Sometimes you
hope that under all the rage is a deep and abiding foundation
of love. But there's no love.

After a while, I wanted Dad's heart in the same way he
wanted it. I wanted his heart in a way that gave me nothing,
it was just a simple ugly theft, a way of getting back at him
for not caring about me, and it made me as false as he, as
false as us all.

All that you hear will surely break your heart, Mirror said.
You'll know the sheen of automobile metal in sun. You'll hear
the lost volcanoes of God smoking in His endless fucking
garden. Gnomes walk miles, lost, never even spotting the

walls at the edge of everything. Only lightening can kill, and, even then, you often come out of it blackened but alive. Wake up! Wake the fuck up! It's time. Wake up and love. Do not be afraid.

Coffee is just cream sometimes, Chappy thought. And a chocolate éclair is just a girl at a counter, a girl who wears a white top. The white tops of the girl's breasts are white like doughnut dough before it's cooked.

I knew you were going to order an éclair, the girl told Chappy. Chappy thought he detected a look of regret in the girl's eye. The girl was chewing gum.

Make it triple cream, Chappy said. He couldn't think of any other subject to broach with the doughnut girl. What else, really, was there to say?

There was a show window under the cash register, and Chappy turned when he heard the sound of water running at the back of the shop. He felt disoriented for a moment. He kept his hand wrapped around his coffee. He wished he hadn't ordered a to-go, because he would have rather held a warm ceramic mug.

Three construction workers seemed to notice something flying in the air above their table, for they were all staring up into the near distant space directly above their table.

For the first time in his life, Chappy felt he could possibly put himself into a book.

He's a nice guy, Chappy thought. Why do I hate nice guys so much? This beautiful world is getting away from me, man.

Chappy slowed his bike down and got off at the curb. He put his bike on its side and sat in the grass in front of somebody's house. He was in a residential area, somewhere out near the shopping mall. Trees waved at one another, green and flat against a washed out sky. Cars cruised by with sweaty men coming home from work, and the vital organ of humanity sang in the buzz of the insects that flew by Chappy, caught forever in wind, going straight on forever to the ocean, then out over the ocean, dropping eventually, floating – then gone. Eaten, maybe, by fish. Or maybe just floating away.

I want to tell you a quick story about what happened to me yesterday, Chappy said.

How quick? Mirror asked. I have to go to work.

I was trying to tell Belle Johnson something, Chappy said. But Benson and Johannsen were listening in.

Is this the story, Chappy? Because I don't have a lot of time here. Is this the actual story, or some kind of prelude?

You mean preface.

Chappy.

I'm just saying, Mirror, a prelude is usually a music thing. A least, I think it is. I'm never certain of these things when I get started thinking about them. I think about things too much, Mirror. Why couldn't a story have a prelude? I should look it up. Maybe you can use prelude for a story. I'm never really sure of these things. I need to carry a dictionary wherever I go.

I have to go, said Mirror.

No, wait. I'll be good. I'll tell the story properly.

We've talked about this before, Chappy. If you don't tell a story properly, no one is going to listen.

I know.

Well, then, go ahead, tell the story. I'm going to make some toast while you tell it. Is that okay with you?

Absolutely, Mirror. Thanks. I love you.

And I love you, Chappy. Just don't make me late for work. I hate being late for work.

I know. Make your toast. I'll tell the story.

Mirror went to the cupboard with the bread. She tried not to crinkle the bread bag too much because Chappy was telling his story, and Mirror generally didn't like to do anything extra when she was listening to one of Chappy's stories. Secretly, she loved his little preludes, or prefaces, or whatever they were. She loved Chappy's asides and the way he wandered off topic and disappeared to look up words in the dictionary. Her favourite times were weekends before the owl-eyed boy was born and Chappy would tell her a story that lasted all day. Not because it was a long story, but because Chappy told it in a way that spread it out in all directions, including up and down and north and south and east and west and even, sometimes, it seemed to Mirror, through slits in the air that led to other dimensions.

I was trying to find the right words to tell Belle Johnson something, but without allowing Benson and Johannsen to muscle in on the saying of it. I wanted a sound that wouldn't be repressed by words. A sound that couldn't be expressed in words. Or torn by meaning. I wanted a deep primal sound. I think I was maybe trying for the harsh toneless silence of God whispering in your ear at night in that moment between sleeping and waking.

Chappy, I told you about trying to get that sound. You can go for it with me. The toaster oven dung, and Mirror took out the toast and put it on a plate and scraped some butter across it. But you can't subject other people, especially a couple of brutes like Benson and Johannsen.

I know. But I couldn't resist. They seemed so resistant. Particularly resistant at that moment, standing by the dumpster behind the building.

My new project, Chappy told Benson and Johanssen, is to run out of things.

He looked to see if Benson and Johanssen were paying attention. It was hard to tell. They had faces that never seemed to change.

Like milk, for instance, Chappy told them. Or cat litter.

You have a cat? Benson asked. His voice boomed. I have a cat.

Really? said Chappy. I never imagined you as a cat person.

It's my wife's cat, really.

Oh. Well, anyway, said Chappy, I was a bit worried about this project, this effort I was making to run out of things, till it came clear how obvious it was. I wanted to practice. The thing I'm most afraid of running out of is time, and I wanted to practice running out of things so that when it came time for me to run out of time, I would be ready for it.

Benson and Johanssen both nodded at this. They seemed to get it. Each had a solemn look on his face, although the solemnity took on a different character for Benson than it did for Johanssen. For Benson, the solemnity was present in his mouth, which turned down on both ends. For Johanssen, it was more like a change of light in his eyes and something in the tilt of his head that made him look so solemn.

Neither Benson nor Johanssen said anything. Chappy

himself was out of things to say. They all stood in silence, and Chappy tried to see his own breath, but it wasn't quite cold enough. He remembered yesterday morning. His breath had steamed yesterday morning. He wished there was some steam between him and Benson and Johanssen now. But there wasn't.

I was the stranger in their lives, Mirror, Chappy said. The man with the aroma.

You mean aura, Chappy. You were the man with the aura.

I was Chappy, said Chappy. The man who ran out of things.

Gravity pulled Mirror down and made her wonder why she kept getting back up. Her life was going nowhere, she knew. Her happiest moments were on the couch. She was happiest deep into the evening, sunk into the couch, when the owl-eyed boy was in bed, and she and Chappy were on the couch, and Chappy was telling her stories. Mirror knew she could publish her life and let the entire world see it, but she also knew it wouldn't do her any good. She knew it wouldn't do anyone any good. Mirror could push her life in a certain direction. She understood this was possible, for she had done it. All it required was to see a place out ahead that she could head toward. Then, just find a way to ignore the fact that, no matter which way she headed, no matter what she saw up ahead, she was always headed for death.

I keep changing my mind, said the piano. I can't make up my mind anymore. I used to be able to make up my mind.

Chappy changed his clothes while he listened to the piano. I can't see without my glasses now, he thought. He looked more comfortable in his new clothes. He sat in the chair he loved and fell asleep. Then he died.

If you don't get what you want in life, Chappy told Mirror just before she died, it's only because you made the mistake of wanting.

Mirror laughed. She was on the bed, wasting slowly away. Chappy saw that she was different from what she was a few months before. But he couldn't see how the idea of wasting away was apt. He couldn't see her changing from moment to moment, the way you would expect to if you heard a person was wasting away. He only knew she was different from what she once was because of memories he had of what she might have been if she hadn't been wasting away. But even this wasn't a sure thing for Chappy.

Chappy remembers Mirror telling him stories.

Mirror told Chappy the story of her sister-in-law. She told Chappy about her sister-in-law's recipe for spaghetti. Chappy doesn't want to hear this story, Mirror thought. So she told Chappy a story she'd read in the newspaper. Chappy asked to hear more stories about the sister-in-law. She never cleans herself, Mirror said. Whenever I go to visit, she cleans herself a little, but you can tell she's just doing it because someone is coming to see her. I have to clean her myself sometimes.

*

What I've learned so far in this life, Mirror confessed to Chappy one day, is that people don't clean anything they don't have to clean if they think they can get away with it.

Elsa Curry threw herself from the seventh floor. It was easy as stepping over a fence. She whistled a lot. There was a lot of air inside her. She whistled to get the air out. She wasn't a very good whistler, yet she always whistled. But she whistled more than usual the week before she killed herself.

Every morning, Lydia ate scrambled eggs and she was afraid it was going to kill her one day.

I write because I read, Chappy said. He was sitting at Mirror's feet, playing with the ears on her slippers. He wasn't talking to her so much as he was talking to the creatures on her feet. My best reading experiences involve a lot of communication where silence imparts meaning, he said.

Mirror wondered how she could compete.

There is a lot of silence in the act of reading to oneself, Chappy said.

Tell me about it, Mirror thought. She looked out the window. She could see the world through the window, but she couldn't hear it. There were clouds and wind and the tops of trees. Mirror decided she didn't have to compete.

Sometimes when I read, what I'm reading feels noisy.

Mirror decided she would just listen. Something inside her broke, then settled, and she felt her shoulders loosen.

Chappy looked at Mirror. It seemed to Mirror he had seen. He knew.

There be anger in your eyes, Chappy, Mirror said. But it was too late for Mirror, and Chappy saw that she had stopped trying.

Did you just say, there be? Chappy asked.

Yes, said Mirror.

Chappy felt there was more to be said. He determined, despite the stone in his stomach, that he would say what had to be said.

But Mirror didn't hear what he said. She heard wind. She heard the hum of Chappy's voice. She determined that Chappy's voice was modulating at a frequency of B flat.

My best experiences reading, Mirror heard Chappy say... but she heard no more, and it all made perfect sense to Mirror, in the way something that has no words can make perfect sense to someone.

Chappy seemed desperate now. Although, Mirror had to admit, his voice was dead calm.

Mirror felt tired. When Chappy was done, she would go to bed. She would skim the surface of the world for now, till Chappy finished what he was saying. She would flit. But when Chappy was finished what he was saying, she would ask him to go away, and she would go to sleep here on the couch. Chappy would respect her wishes. He would put a blanket over her and respect her wishes and leave. This was beyond doubt, as far as Mirror was concerned.

Chappy stood. He eased Mirror down onto one end of the couch. He lifted her legs, set them on the other end of the couch. He got the blanket that was folded under the couch and spread it over Mirror. He kissed the top of her head, and went upstairs to get ready for bed.

Mirror wandered through the nursing home, stepping slowly. Dancing, but very slowly. She'd learned to hear the music. She heard the music in her head. She almost heard it. She was trying to the hear the music in her head. She felt she should choreograph her steps to music. To some kind of music. She felt it was her duty to hear music. Like when she'd first been pregnant with the owl-eyed boy. Swollen and happy, she heard the music. And then, at some point she could no longer remember, she stopped hearing it. Her hair fell forward, straight, dark, like rivers of night. She slid her feet along the hardwood. She smiled to herself. Sat cross-legged on the floor. Looked at her Christmas tree. It was beautiful. It wasn't as big as she'd hoped. But it was beautiful. It was hers. She'd made it hers.

I wanted to whittle the world down to one word, said Chappy. I wanted to write that one word down. I wanted to fold it up. Put it in my pocket. Be done with it. There would be no more words after that. I'd be done with words.

If there was just one word left, Mirror, what would that one word be? What would it be, Mirror?

I don't know, Mirror said. She knew Chappy wasn't really talking to her. He was settling up with himself.

That is the problem, of course, said Chappy.

Of course, said Mirror.

What would this one word be? And what would I be once I found this word? What does a person look like when he has no words?

I don't know, Chappy. I've never seen a person who has no words.

I don't know either, Mirror. A dead person, maybe?

It was one of those dark places where the trees make tunnels. Moss on rocks. Dampness. Moisture. Darkness. I could see it. I could almost smell it. It was a place I wanted to go, but it was also a place I only wanted to look at. I could only look at it inside my head, for I knew it didn't exist.

*

I lay in bed and saw the forest. The forest was a tunnel. I knew, suddenly, that the forest was a woman and that I was in grave trouble. I knew that I was facing a great power and I wanted to turn away, but I couldn't. I could imagine a path of escape. I could imagine such a path any way I wanted, and the endless possibilities presented by women were like the endless permutations available in a path you make up in your head. If you write down what you've seen, the possibilities get flattened out and a real path emerges, like something in Tolkien, or Lewis. But if you allow the path a place in your head beyond all expression, it maintains its essence as pure possibility. I'd denied myself the rambling

possibility of this imagined path a long time, and now I felt
trouble coming for me the other way along the path, and it
seemed there was no way out. The path now seemed set and
I rued the end of imagination.

This must be why we collect things, Chappy said, it somehow
makes us feel happier. We each collect things for a while.
I collect words. You collect something else. Stones, maybe.
Betty collects antique bottles. Honour collects butterflies.
One person collects one thing, another another.

The longer Mirror pushed herself toward that nowhere that
was always her destination, the freer she felt, until finally
she crashed, slept a few hours, then woke in the middle of
the night, her eyes the only bright spots in the blackened
bedroom.

Chappy struggled to remove the car keys from his pocket. He
dropped his éclair in a puddle. He looked at the éclair.
He watched it for a while, sitting in the puddle. You fucker,
he said. He thought about picking it up. He could see puddle
water seeping into the brown paper bag. He knew he should
never have parked in a puddle.

He looked back into the doughnut shop, expecting to see
people laughing. No one even noticed Chappy, or Chappy's
fallen éclair.

They said, don't worry, we'll make you assistant, but the
main boss kept showing up at the beginning of the day,
saying he couldn't stay because he was in the middle of a
messy divorce. He'd talk for a few minutes about the divorce.

He told Chappy how much it was costing him, this divorce. The other guys were all starting to get to work, sipping at coffee, turning on computers, sifting through papers on their desks.

Chappy looked about the office. It was a mess of cubicles. One big open floor on the fourth floor of a seven-story building. Chappy could see heads rising above cubicles, then disappearing as people sat down at computers. Most of the people who worked in this office were guys. There was a woman in the far corner who Chappy had a little crush on.

Finally, the main boss would leave. The other people in the office hated Chappy, because he wasn't the boss they had been hoping for.

Chappy got in his car. He drove back past his apartment, toward the sunrise.

*

Chappy wanted to stay home. Everyone else seemed to be leaving home. But Chappy wanted to stay home. Everyone else was going to work, or going shopping, quietly placing themselves in the corners of other people's lives, like pillows pushed into hollows in trees where squirrels left their nuts.

At the library, Chappy looked at leaves falling off trees. He sat at his desk by the window and watched. Leaves drifted. Chappy went out and gathered up some of the leaves.

When we are young, Chappy thought, we do those things that young people do. We gather. We turn around. We see.

The stream of things we see blowing by is endless. Till the snow falls and puts a stop to all that.

There were too many leaves. Chappy got a bag. He put the leaves in the bag. He tried not to smush the leaves. But there were just too many leaves.

Mirror seemed so serene when she was pregnant. It was like the kid inside Mirror had a knowledge all his own and he was sharing it with Mirror, like some secret joke. Sometimes someone will know a thing nobody else can know.

Chappy swore. But then he decided to lay down and go to sleep. But then he got back up to put his pjs on. He went back to bed and lay his head on the pillow. At midnight, he got back up to brush his teeth. He looked at the toilet beside the sink as he brushed his teeth. He decided to pee. Then he went back to his bed. But he stood beside the bed for a while, thinking. Finally, he got into bed and stayed there. But he didn't go to sleep right away. Instead, he touched the things on his bedside table in the dark, trying to identify everything that was there.

Chappy was past the city limits. He drove past farm fields and passed through small towns. He drove for three hours and then stopped at a restaurant in a little town. He decided he would have lunch.

Are you quieter now? Chappy asked softly. Mirror lay in the bed and looked at Chappy as though she were packed in a small suitcase. She looked limp, like someone moving out after thinking for a long, long time about moving out. She had a rag in her hand. She must have been dusting before she fell onto the bed.

Are you like the sound of being busy, Chappy? Mirror asked. Do you walk like the sound of someone moving? Mirror didn't move, but her face changed. Her eyes seemed to spark beneath her crumpled eyebrows. She looked frightened, and then more frightened. She's lost something, Chappy thought, but she hasn't given up quite yet.

Do you move with your own sound, Mirror? Chappy asked. Are you everything sounding like a kind of fun? And, are you, finally, Chinelle, cooking?

Who the hell is Chinelle? Mirror asked. Her eyebrows relaxed, and though her eyes were still laced with fear, overall she looked more relaxed. She even let out a little laugh. Chappy smiled.

The substance of the wind touched the windshield like a lover touching a loved one. The windshield was a tiny patch of something that Mirror didn't get. She wound up standing beside the car with a putty knife in her hand, crying. She lay her head down on the hood of the car and wept.

Mirror remembered when she was small and her father went to the restaurant with the gas station in front of it for breakfast every Sunday morning. It was an epic way to begin the day. The restaurant was well north of the city, but you could see the city from the restaurant, because the restaurant was at the top of a long rise that rose out of the city like a long, wide waterslide, and headed north till it

reached the restaurant and sat with it at the top of the hill.
From the restaurant, the city rose out of a kind of haze, and looked like blocks scattered by a giant child passing through on his way to the lake.

Chappy began to gain something. It was something like confidence maybe. Chappy couldn't put a name to it. People around him seemed happy enough to eat burgers and make small talk.

Chappy ate his burger and watched the girl across the table from him. There was a highway outside the restaurant, a highway that headed north. Outside of town, no one seemed to ever need to know about Chappy. Chappy decided north was a good direction for when he left the town. After lunch, he would go north.

I'm always gone, Mirror said. Somehow they convinced me the coach was gone, too. I'm always Riley, or I'm some name I can't pronounce properly.

How the hell did he get the onion chopped up so fast and without crying?

Chappy got back from the dry cleaner with Mirror's dress that was cut low down the back and held her breasts like small gifts.

Put it on, Mirror, Chappy said. He held the dress out to her.

No, Chappy, Mirror said. Not now.

You could just wear it around the house for a while.

I just got it dry cleaned. I don't want to wear it around the house.

Mirror was standing at the counter, talking. She was talking to someone named Riley who Chappy couldn't see. And someone called Coach. Riley and some other people convinced Coach that I knew nothing most of the time, Mirror said as she chopped the onion. She ran her hands under cold water every ten seconds. Just give up and stay home, they tell me. So I miss all the fighting.

I realized that no matter who I thought about, Chappy said, even if it was someone I'd never thought about before – even if it was people whose existence I never even suspected until I thought them up in my head – they all seemed to know secret things about me, things I'd told no one.

Everyone goes to the library, I thought. By library, I meant any place where they kept books on a shelf. But then, almost immediately, I knew it wasn't true. There are people who never go to the library.

I wanted to go on, to progress through the book, to read the next sentence and then the next.
    When was this, Chappy?
    Last night.
    Before you went to sleep?
    Yes.
    When you were reading to me?
    Yes.
    I remember.
    Instead of progressing through the book, I found myself progressing through something inside me, some process, something partially physical, partially ephemeral that you

could never prove. I was rereading the same passage in the book over and over again. After the fifth time of rereading the same passage, I closed the book, but I held it in my hand a moment, my lips resting lightly on your neck.

You read the same passage over and over. I remember that. I thought for a while that was how the book was written. One passage, over and over. It seemed possible. Those are the kind of books you sometimes read to me. Books where it sounds like the same passage is getting said over and over. But after the third or fourth time, it no longer seemed possible that this was how the book was written. I wondered what was happening to you. To us. It felt like we'd gotten stuck somehow.

Then I moved my head down to your sex and put my mouth on it. You tasted of salt and urine. I licked.

What did you do with the book?

I set the book on the low bedside table. I lifted my head to look at you. You were exactly as I had pictured you. Head thrown back, eyes closed. Looking at you like that, I couldn't move. I couldn't breathe.

The cat came into the room and jumped up on the bed. Mirror opened her eyes. She touched the cat and looked at Chappy. Mirror saw something in Chappy's eyes. Chappy looked away.

Chappy was sitting in the chair by the writing desk. He watched the cat. He watched Mirror's hand stroking the cat. God, Chappy realized, is in the static gap between Mirror's hand and the cat. If you hear yourself in the moment, it's already too late, Chappy thought. Eyes must read the space between time.

Mirror's hair lay spread out, a dark river on the bed, flowing over the edge of the bed in a waterfall that Chappy had to navigate. But it stopped short of the floor, and Chappy finally crawled under the bed and curled up into a ball.

Chappy felt Mirror roll about above him, her sleeping body searching for his. His eyes wide open, inches from the metal bed frame. Chappy imagined Mirror, because he couldn't see her.

When Chappy got to the next town, which was nothing but a general store and a farm machinery place, he stopped at a pay phone. He called Mirror.

Spooky Man was a friend of mine, Chappy said to Mirror over the phone. Between his mouth and the phone mouthpiece was cold air that made his lips feel something that wasn't exactly Mirror, but was close to the breath he felt when Mirror held her face close to his and breathed. Spooky Man told me to be smart, Chappy said. Spooky Man used to say, Get loosed in a river of play.

Is that what you're doing, Chappy? Mirror asked. Getting loosed in a river of play? Because, you know, you were supposed to take me shopping today.

I'll be home tonight, Chappy said, and he hung up the phone.

Chappy kept driving north. The towns grew further and further apart. The bush grew denser. At five o'clock, Chappy turned around. By the time he got back home, he had begun to think that the world was a lonely place, that it didn't matter where you were, in the city or the country, most people were bastards.

Chappy put his lips to Mirror's neck. He put his lips beneath the edge of her thick dark hair and read to her from *Housekeeping*. He imagined – because he could not see her face – that her eyes were closed as he read the words, his lips brushing against her neck, brushing their sibilance onto her skin, like basting a turkey. Chappy imagined that Mirror had her head tipped back slightly, as if to listen for some far off sound, not the sound of words, but a sound inside herself that the words aroused, a sound that couldn't be represented in words, but could be called forth by words. A sound like wind in trees outside the window on a cold winter day.

Maybe it makes me feel like I'm incoherent, Chappy said. Maybe it makes me feel like I'm just mortal. Maybe it makes me feel like I'm more in control. I don't like to be out of control, Mirror.

Nobody likes to be out of control, Chappy, Mirror said.

It's not control like when you feel in control of your body, but more like you feel like you are having control continuously wrested away by some idea of yourself that people give you and you take to heart without seeing that you're becoming something you were never meant to be. Chappy looked at Mirror. He must have decided something about what he saw when he looked at her. Or else he decided the likelihood that she was listening was good enough for him to take the risk of carrying on speaking. He knew he often carried on too much, as when Mirror said, Oh, how you like to carry on, Chappy, which made Chappy feel like he was discussing something with his grandmother. Like when you're in a car, Mirror,

Chappy said. You're driving, and you're getting where you need to be, and you're getting there faster than you could by any other means of transportation, but, somehow, when you get there, you feel like you've been hijacked.

*

Chappy put some ketchup on his grilled cheese and took it out to the car. He ate standing beside the car. He didn't want to get ketchup on the seats.

Bits of you must rust, Spooky Man once told me, Chappy said. Your search stops here, little dude, Spooky Man said. You broke the loosened circuit.

How did Spooky Man get his name? Mirror asked.

From his parents.

His parents called him Spooky Man?

No. His parents called him Ralph. He was Spooky Man from a story he once told: Water sneaked out past the forest and there was nothing any of the trees could do to stop it. Oh sure, the trees could suck up a bit of the water through their roots, but the majority of it got away and ran down through the meadow, laughing over rocks and splashing off mud embankments, pulling down soil, slowly, like death arriving in ultramarine ultra-slow motion. It was spooky, man. After he told that story, we always called him Spooky Man.

Why did Spooky Man tell so many sad stories, Mirror asked?

You think his stories are sad?

All the ones I've heard. At least, the endings always seem
very sad.

It was because we were so fond of sad endings, Chappy said.

Deftly, Chappy washed himself. Under his arms. Between his legs. He was maybe just a little under-washed. The real smell was getting out from under the soap.

Just that morning Chappy had seen through something. He didn't smell bad, exactly. He had trouble breathing. The smell of him filled Mirror's chest. Mirror was a cashier at nights and on weekends. She wanted nothing to do with this boy and his smell.

Chappy was very skinny. His pants didn't seem to ever fit him. He made riding the bike look so easy as he rode out of the grocery store parking lot. At night, after being a cashier all day, Mirror cooked for both her parents.

When Chappy got back to the apartment, Mirror was up watching TV. She came over to the door and gave Chappy a long hug. She repeated a joke she'd heard on Johnny Carson.

I thought there had been some kind of mistake, Chappy told Mirror. I thought that I was witnessing some kind of miracle. I thought that the Dewey Decimal system, in all its splendiferous beauty, could never count its way into the place I found myself that day in the library.

What have we done already? Chappy said into the phone. It was not clear who he was.

It was not clear who Chappy was talking to anymore. It was not clear that he was talking to anyone.

Return tomorrow, after three rings. I'll wake Mirror with a kiss on the cheek. Suddenly, it's seven p.m. The lights go out. The curtains are open, but it's dark outside already. We fall asleep together in a fleshy web of light and love. A firefly smells the moment and arrives to tell us stories. Lighted moments punctuated by frightening spells of sudden darkness.

I have a question? Mirror said. She was excited. She rarely

had a question for Chappy. When Chappy was telling a story he always told Mirror: If you have any questions, Mirror, just ask.

So Mirror asked a question.

But Chappy didn't seem to hear.

Before Christmas, Chappy said, the light sparkled in a special way. Two-watt light bulbs ate the night in tiny increments. Nowadays, we sit outside and watch our breath make great strides toward living lives independent of our own.

What is it that Padua is talking about? Her eyebrows capture sunlight. The baker shuffles by outside on the sidewalk, his breath a steamy soup, his head the ball of matzah. Shot dead on the bed, Mirror said. Fred died, she said. Fred was dead. Then they had bran flakes, bacon, toast and coffee. To wake us up, Mirror said. To get us started.

Chappy felt the hurt in his stomach and then in his legs and chest and neck and then his arms went weak. He thought he just wanted to be deeply loved, but this didn't seem right. He wanted to keep his family safe. He wanted to be touched. These were the things he wanted, he thought. Maybe these were the things he wanted. But he couldn't be sure. He couldn't be sure if these were all the things he wanted. He couldn't even be sure that these were some of the things he wanted.

*

Chappy and Mirror had a meeting. They met in the kitchen. Neither Chappy nor Mirror liked meetings. Their goal for the meeting was to make it a good meeting. Chappy had some amorphous ideas about content for the meeting, but mostly he wanted to prove that he and Mirror could make a good meeting.

They wore their bathrobes to the meeting. Chappy made coffee. They could get food at any point during the meeting if they wanted, because the meeting was in the kitchen and either of them could get up in the middle of a discussion, or presentation, without causing much disruption.

We should be allowed to interject or ask questions at any point, Chappy said.

Mirror nodded agreement.

They had the meeting first thing in the morning. Mirror didn't want to talk. The night before she said, My part in the meeting will be more of a physical presence, Chappy. It's going to be too early for me to be doing any actual talking. I'll be awake, but that's about the full extent of it. For the meeting, Chappy sat at the wall end of the wooden bench in the breakfast nook and Mirror lay on the bench with her head in Chappy's lap.

It was Chappy who first broached the idea of having a meeting. He had some papers he brought to the meeting. But when they were settled into the breakfast nook and Chappy had his papers spread out in front of him, he found he couldn't focus. He took a sip of coffee. His coffee was cooling and tasted very good. Chappy let out a little sigh from the taste of the coffee, but that was the only sound either of them made. Chappy couldn't quite face interjecting his voice into the silence.

The silence of the kitchen was actually a series of small sounds. The hum of the fridge. The tick of the white clock over the sink. Some unidentifiable sounds from out in the yard that came muted through glass. Chappy felt, on a purely theoretical level, that the voice of the meeting should consist of something musical. He imagined a sentence he might say – or even just a single word he might say. He started to hum a little, trying to work up to some words. Mirror closed her eyes and listened to Chappy hum. She had no idea what tune Chappy was humming. Chappy listened to much different music than Mirror. Often, Chappy's music didn't even sound like music to Mirror. Chappy liked singers who seemed to Mirror to be some of the world's worst singers in popular music today.

The tune Chappy was humming was quiet and windy. It whispered its extensive existence tentatively, touching the air beyond Chappy's mouth like a creature full of fear in a pond, creating waves in the air that rippled out across the kitchen making Mirror feel warm and asleep. To have the room full of something so full of fear made her feel utterly safe and utterly tired. She must have gone to sleep, a place she liked to go, because she seemed to have just woken up to hear Chappy say: Well, I guess that's it. I guess the meeting is over. Meeting adjourned. Mirror looked at the clock. It had been about a twenty minute meeting. Was it just the humming, then, Chappy? Was that the whole meeting? I think I fell asleep.

Yes, that was the whole meeting, Mirror. It was just me humming you to sleep.

*

As soon as he finished speaking, the man touched his lips, almost as if he were wondering why his lips had opened in the first place. Why had they shaped the words he had just uttered? He looked utterly devoid of hope. But a moment later, he was speaking again. He must, he believed, direct the motion of the people who worked for him. He must influence the people who worked for him. But subtly, not through directives but through persuasion. There was a level of detail the man was going for in his talk, a density of verbiage he seemed all but incapable of excavating. But he continued to dig. He sniffed now as his words collapsed into silence. He rubbed his nose. Spoke again. His hands moved, held the world together, opened spaces, lured. He stopped. Sniffed. What am I doing? he thought. He was doing nothing. Building up a tower of nothing and watching it collapse again into nothing, forcing him to try again to make nothing into something.

A god had been in this room, the woman knew. She could tell right away by the thickness of the god's presence, and she immediately mourned the absence of that god now that he was gone. The god was gone. The woman turned off the light and closed the door. She would never return to this room, she knew, and nor would her god.

I think the world is ending, Patty told Chappy. She said it with a level of intensity that bedevilled her usual devil-may-care attitude. The lilt in her voice said: Chappy, try to figure out if I am happy about this. Chappy would not hold it against her if she were happy about this. He sometimes wondered if it would be better if everyone died the day he died and no one went on without him.

The cap off my pen disappeared, Chappy told Mirror. I thought, so what? I'm not the type to worry about the cap off my pen. I went over to one of the other desks, the desk of a guy named Oliver, a guy who I don't dislike, nor do I really like him, and I stole the cap off his pen. I put it on my pen. It fit okay. There was no way you could identify it as the cap off Oliver's pen. No one saw me steal it. We all use the same pens at the office. You can't tell one pen from another. I would never be caught.

Chappy sees a man step into the horn of a bus. The bus turns over like a beast bearing its throat in preparation to die. Like an animal turning the corner of knowledge. Down the street from the bus, two young girls caress and smile. Cameras click and light the night like posters. The girls go home to their mothers.

My daytimer keeps beeping at me in Japanese, said Chappy. He was on the phone from work to Mirror. It's like a little whimper. It's hurt, Mirror. My daytimer is hurting. It's reminding me that it wants a rematch. It's upset because it got beaten by a Radio Shack product.

You know those sudden surprises that limp out of a story? Chappy asked Mirror.

Mirror nodded.

What's it like for you when that happens?

I'm not sure I know what you mean, exactly? Mirror said. She looked over her glasses. She had the knitted brown blanket over her knees. She had gained weight recently, and Chappy found her ravishing.

I mean, when there's an obvious surprise in a story and it hits you like a damp rag weakly thrown at you by a preschooler.

Oh, that. It feels disappointing. What about for you?

It makes me really angry. Do you think that's unhealthy?

I don't know, Chappy. It's probably okay if you know that it's happening to you and it isn't just taking you over.

That's a great word, said Chappy. Sublimated. What does it even mean?

You don't know?

I do. Kind of. But, no. Not really. I know what it's supposed to mean. But don't you think it actually means so much more than it's supposed to mean?

A lot of words mean more than what they're supposed to mean.

What do you think about the loss we feel when something we have done has been gauged by others as successful?

This is a whole different question, Chappy.

Is it? Chappy was trying to be dramatic, but his hair was too messy and he wasn't really dressed for drama.

Mirror laughed. Yes, you moron, it is.

Chappy had a silly grin on his face. He laughed. They closed their books and Chappy leaned away from his couch to kiss Mirror. She kissed him back. Their books fell to the floor.

Wait, said Chappy, pulling away from Mirror, licking his lips. I dropped my book.

Me too.

They laughed. They picked up their books.

I lost my place, Mirror said.

Me too, said Chappy.

They went back to reading.

Chappy fell asleep on the couch. He was snoring lightly,
making it hard for Mirror to concentrate. She held her book
open in her lap and stared at the wall across the room.

It's called, Nothing Can Be Fixed.
    I'm not sure I want to hear it.
    No, you'll like it, Mirror. I wrote it for you.
    Does this mean I can't be fixed, Chappy?
    Maybe. But that's okay. It's the things about you that
can't be fixed that make me love you.
    I know that, Chappy. You do need help, little boy.
    Chappy read:

Nothing Can Be Fixed

We pass tomorrow
running in the other direction
with its hair flying out in all directions
so now everything is ruined
and there's no way to fix anything
and nothing can be fixed
everyday there are more and more people
showing up at the complex where I live
and at the beach
blowing sand kisses
the windshield reminding the windshield
of its origins
this isn't *Romeo and Juliet*
not quite
we run the wipers
even though no rain falls
the windshield is shedding tears.

Mirror took the paper Chappy was holding and looked at it. She read the poem over several times. She looked up at Chappy. Chappy thought there might be tears in her eyes.

There are no tears in my eyes, Chappy. I like this poem. Can I have this?

Yes.

Mirror came back the next day and read her poem to Chappy.

We pass tomorrow
running in the other direction

everyday there are more and more people
showing up at the complex where I live

at the beach
blowing sand kisses
the windshield
remaining the windshield of its origins

this isn't *Romeo and Juliet*
not quite

we run the wipers
even though there is no rain
the windshield is shedding tears.

Chappy picked up his book and turned to page forty-seven. For some reason he believed this was the page he'd left off at when he was reading the book on the subway on Wednesday. Chappy was succumbing silently to a kind of mysticism that denied his inability to remember things like the page he was on in a book. He chose to believe everything was stored somewhere in his brain and that sometimes by not paying attention he could access knowledge that wasn't available to him consciously.

...had known as a child, it said on page forty-seven of the book, and Chappy had no idea what was going on here. She was now where she had longed for so long to be, it said in the book.

This was the end of a section. Chappy resisted the urge to turn back. Don't do it, he told himself. He employed some willpower and was able to resist. He began the next section:

Everyone who rode that bus knew that Milly got on at John Street and then off again one block south at Centre Street. The bus was a green monster that swallowed people. It swallowed them, then spit them out in another place. While people were in the belly of the monster, it was as though they had lost track of something and, because of this losing track of something, they couldn't quite manage to stay awake.

What are you reading about? Mirror asked. She had just come from the kitchen. She was standing in the entrance to the living room, not far from the entertainment centre.

Milly, Chappy said.

Who's Milly?

She's the hero of my book. She gets on at one bus stop and then gets off at the next one, a block away. She does this every day.

How does that make her a hero?

I guess it doesn't.

Sounds like a fascinating book.

Yes, said Chappy. It is.

Milly came onto the bus like a character entering another person's dreams. Some dreamed of a secret lover, an old gentleman who couldn't leave his house for some reason. Some dreamed of a woman on her way to the corner store to buy a bag of milk. One man dreamed of a love that left Milly spent and weak, her back against his chest. The man dreamed this dream so many times that he began to believe he knew exactly how Milly would feel, naked against him, how firmly she would push back against him, the smell of her hair. Milly never turned to face the back of the bus. She stood at the front each day, beside the driver, and stared out the front windshield as though she had never seen any of this before. No one knew her name was Milly. She was an anonymous shadow on the edge of a thought.

Morning barking like a dog. The moon a round white television. Slithering. Squirming. Trying to poke her head at us. I'm not sure if I'm smack on the conk on this one, but it seems to me there was a chance for something, once upon a time.

Mirror had her theories, like anybody else, on linguistic consciousness. But Chappy didn't take her seriously. Chappy was always making fun of her. Fuck you, Chappy, Mirror said, but she smiled. She was doing the dishes. She kept her face to the window so that Chappy couldn't see if she was smiling. It didn't do to encourage the bastard. But Chappy

could see Mirror's reflection in the window, with the light
around her hair like a halo, and he thought she looked like an
angel and that any theory she might have must be divine.

The mayor walked out onto the civic square and cut the
ribbon.

Nothing that leaves ever enters, said Chappy.
    You make me sad, Chappy, said Mirror.
    Things leak out, Mirror.
    I know.
    They culminate. Years later, you recognize everything
that has been left behind.
    Chappy would not leave again, Mirror knew. But he
would die. And she would die. And it made parts of her
body ache to think of this.

The sun is shining, Chappy. It's gorgeous out. Let's go wash
the car.
    Let's drive the car off a cliff.
    Mirror laughed, but she didn't feel light or bubbly. It was
the sort of nervous laugh she used for when Chappy made
her feel nervous. He got in the corner of the living room like
that, with the light on over him and the curtains closed and
he got a book and she wouldn't see him all day, unless she
went to the living room to look at him. She might call to him
from the kitchen while she made herself something to eat, or
while she did the dishes, and Chappy might answer her. Or
she'd go into the living room and he'd have books piled up
beside him and some music going and maybe the TV on. Or
he'd have nothing. He'd sit on the couch and stare. If Mirror

talked to him he talked back, but in a monotone that Mirror could tell was meant to tell her something Chappy's words could never say.

Chappy called Borden's office. It was Borden himself who answered the phone. I can't possibly talk to you right now, said Borden, but he stayed on the phone, talking. Chappy listened, afraid to interrupt and say what he'd called for. He could hear a woman talking in the background and every so often Borden would interrupt his conversation with Chappy to speak to the woman.

That's my sister, Borden said. God love her. I don't deserve so much goodness. Then Borden dropped the phone. Chappy heard the clattering, then silence, then more clattering as Borden tried to get the phone up off the floor.

During the time the phone was down on the floor, Chappy had some time to think about things. Some things came to Chappy and other things slipped away. Chappy would have liked to think that the things that came to him while the phone was on the floor were things of great significance, but the truth is, they were merely a group of extra things to think about.

Chappy was thinking in specifics. Numbers of things and so forth. But what held this group of thoughts together was the feeling Chappy got being down on the floor with the owl-eyed boy while Mirror scrambled eggs in the kitchen.

*

There was a guy living near where Chappy and Mirror lived who played loud music. When Chappy and Mirror sat outside evenings, they could hear his music. They could hear the pounding of the bass guitar and drums.

I'd like to go over there and kill that guy, Chappy said.

Me too, said Mirror.

I'm not talking about a cold, calculated murder here, Mirror.

Me either.

I'm talking about going over there and taking a bat to the guy's head.

Yes.

And not just batting his head once. I'm talking about beating his head to a bloody pulp.

Exactly.

Really? said Chappy.

Or just grabbing his face in your hands and pushing your thumbs into his eye sockets. Or jabbing something sharp into his ear so he can't hear anymore and playing that stupid crap he calls music won't do him any good anymore.

Maybe he'll turn it off soon, Chappy said.

Maybe.

We could probably wait it out.

If I don't convince one of these bastards,
   pretty soon,
   that he is living in a cave
   I'm going over the edge
   baby.

Alone.

Chappy and his father were in a cave. Chappy's father hadn't worked for years. There were other men in the cave. Friends of Chappy's father. They were trying to get the feeling of being in India, meditating in the tradition of the great Swami Mahavishnu. Chappy had gone along with his father, thinking they were going for a steak at a restaurant near where he lived. Now they were in this cave with these slightly verdant men.

A man from Neighbourhood Watch came to the community centre and everyone in the neighbourhood went over and sat in the meeting room to listen to the man talk. The man was talking about crime. He showed everyone some things and told them they could only get these things from a locksmith. You can't get these things from Home Depot, he said. He showed them long striker plates with silver screws designed to be driven deep into a door frame. He told everyone that if they didn't put the right type of deadbolt on their doors, they might as well leave their doors unlocked. You might as well leave them wide open, he said. Leave them swinging in the wind.

Chappy wrote this in his notebook: Leave them swinging in the wind, he wrote. He looked at this sentence.

When Chappy got home from the meeting, he read the sentence to Mirror.

What is that? Mirror said. A poem? What were you doing over there? Listening to poetry? I thought you were seeing a guy from the Neighbourhood Watch.

We were, said Chappy. That's one of the things he said.

He said, Leave them swinging in the wind? I wish I went, said Mirror.

Most of it wasn't that poetic.

What else did he say?

I didn't listen. I couldn't concentrate. The meeting room over there has the smell of a classroom, Mirror. The smell of years of children being frightened into submission.

Were you frightened, Chappy?

No, Chappy said. Yes. Maybe a little.

Mirror put her arms around Chappy and held his head against her chest.

They say the deadbolts are there to keep the bad guys out, Mirror, Chappy said. But I believe that what makes us afraid is the cacophony of everything inside us hiding from the people we love.

It was really snowing out. Sitting at the kitchen table, seeing all that snow outside the window, Chappy felt his heart sinking. He picked up the phone. It was Borden himself who picked up the phone. Chappy could hear lots of people talking in the background. Talking and laughing. It made Chappy feel sadder.

Who is this? Borden said, because Chappy had said nothing since he heard Borden say hello, and then all the laughter and glasses clinking in the background. Was Borden having a party? Was it snowing where he was? Was the lonely child inside Borden gone into hiding for now? It was that lonely child that Chappy wanted to talk to right now. He was afraid that the lonely child in Borden would not come out during a party, which is what Borden must be having, because girls were screaming and giggling in the background.

Chappy tried to remember what number he had dialed. Was this actually Borden's office number? Was he having a party in his office? Chappy had seen Borden's office just once. It was a small office. Chappy didn't think Borden's office was big enough for the kind of party he heard going on in the background of the phone.

Mirror came in, came up the steps from the front hall, kissed Chappy on the cheek, then went the rest of the way upstairs to the bedroom. There were some clumping sounds, then the bathroom door closed and some water started running.

There were a very few poems that Chappy kept in a binder and he could read these anytime he wanted and this would cheer him up.

Chappy lay down on his bed and moved some of his pillows around. He lay on his stomach. He moved some more pillows around. All his friends were close by, standing in a circle, encircling his bed. He felt safe. Protected.

*

Chappy splayed his hands. He looked really closely at his fingers. Mirror thought he seemed pretty upset.

God's lawn is endless, Mirror told Chappy. If you follow God's lawn to its outer edge, you will follow it forever. Chappy nodded a little when Mirror stopped talking. He didn't want to encourage Mirror, but he did want to see what would happen next, even if it meant Mirror went on talking about God's infinite lawn.

Mirror said, Jesus once said: Those who follow my lawn to its outer perimeter are in hell already. Hell is the outer perimeter of my lawn.

Jesus never said that, Chappy told Mirror. They were in the kitchen. Mirror was standing by the stove, stirring something in a pot.

How do you know? Mirror asked Chappy. You don't know everything Jesus said.

That's true.

Mirror went on stirring.

Chappy sat quietly in the breakfast nook looking at the mole on the back of his hand.

Chappy was at home in the kitchen when the refrigerator stopped working. He heard it stop. It ground to a halt. In the silence after the fridge stopped working, Chappy remembered the guy from the Neighbourhood Watch Association saying, No one is safe. He heard the voice of the guy from the Neighbourhood Watch in his ear like a small wind. Chappy wondered if refrigerators would be something no one was safe from. Certainly, Chappy felt he was not safe from refrigerators.

Chappy was reading a cookbook when the librarian known as The Weeder walked by. Chappy hadn't seen The Weeder in weeks. He had begun to think The Weeder no longer worked at the library. He wanted to go after The Weeder and talk to him, but there was nothing he could think of to say. Chappy put the cookbook back on the shelf and started to move away when a guy came up to him and said, Do you work here?

Yes, Chappy told the guy. I work here.

I'm looking for a manual to fix my truck, the guy told Chappy. I have to fix my truck, he said. He squinted. He rubbed his hands together. Can you help?

Chappy wanted to go home and see Mirror.

Did you try the computer? Chappy asked.

I can't work computers, the guy said. He seemed nice enough, but he needed a bath. He needed to wash his hair. He was wearing a white t-shirt that was so worn you could see his nipples. Chappy tried not to look at the man's nipples. The man was in good shape. He had good nipples, embedded in strong looking pecks. He had strong arms. He needed to buy some new shirts, though. And he smelled a little.

Chappy took the guy by the arm and led him over to the automotive section.

Chappy and Mirror were at a church picnic when Chappy's sister, Jewel, came over a hill. Then Jewel's entire family came over the hill behind Jewel.

A guy dressed as Jesus was addressing the crowd. Chappy felt like he and Mirror were sitting on kitchen chairs under a sky full of clock hands – reaching, grasping, foraging clock hands. Chappy looked back over his shoulder. There were people as far back as he could see. Surely the people at the back could not even hear what Jesus was saying.

Chappy thought of all the coffee he'd had in the last two months. Cup after cup. He was thinking also about his sister and how happy she must be now. He remembered yesterday, too.

Chappy remembered the two cats climbing up the hill together toward the pile of tires at the top of the hill. The cats were doing that thing they do when they get down and knead at something. Tell them I saw those cats again, Chappy told Mirror.

Mirror was on the phone. She was standing by the window

with light on her face. It wasn't sunny outside, but it was bright. It would be sunny soon, Chappy could see. Something in the weather was just now burning off and something new was beginning. Soon it would be revealed. Meanwhile, Mirror's face was already bright in the light by the window as she was talking on the phone. Mirror looked at Chappy now when he spoke to her.

Tell them it's eight-thirty in the morning here, Chappy told Mirror.

Mirror put her finger to her lips, trying to shush Chappy.

Chappy and Mirror were going to the drive-in, but then it got cloudy.

It's going to rain, Mirror said. They were in the car in the parking lot of their apartment. They had paper towels and window cleaner for doing the front windshield before the movie started.

It might clear, Chappy said.

It won't clear, Mirror said. She looked at Chappy. Look out there. She leaned forward and looked up through the front windshield. Chappy leaned forward, too, but the steering wheel got in the way. Still, he could see enough to see it wasn't probably going to clear.

You're right, Mirror. It probably isn't going to clear. Chappy sounded thoroughly defeated. Like it was his fault it wasn't going to clear. Mirror took Chappy's hand. They sat in the car, looking out the front windshield, holding hands, not saying anything. Let's bring the window cleaner anyway, Chappy said. He started the car. They drove over to the mall to get money.

Before they had been planning to go to the drive-in, they

had been planning to go dancing. Mirror vetoed that. I'd have to fix my hair, she said.

Chappy was glad. He would have had to put on good pants and a shirt to go dancing. This way, with the drive-in, he could basically just go in his pjs.

Let's look at bras while we're here, Mirror said when they got to the mall.

After Mirror found a bra they went back outside. It still hadn't rained.

We could still make it to the drive-in, Mirror said.

Chappy looked at his watch. What if the movie's already started?

It's still too light out, Mirror said.

Okay, Chappy said, but let's hurry.

Yes, let's. Saying this made Mirror feel like a little kid.

Sometimes I can sit right there in the same room as them and they don't even know I'm there. They must be... what? People who stay in rooms not noticing they're being watched, like animals in the wild when National Geographic arrives quietly and sets up in the bluff overlooking the waterhole? They'll be working away, talking amongst themselves and they don't even notice me.

Is that a good thing, Chappy?

It's great.

Really?

Listen, Mirror, I don't want to be noticed. The less I'm noticed, the better.

Don't you want me to notice you?

Not really.

Chappy and Mirror went into the bra section in K-Mart.
Chappy said to Mirror, You won't get a bra in here.

Why not? Mirror asked.

They have lousy selection.

How would you know? Mirror had a look of utter bemusement on her face.

Don't give me the look of bemusement, Mirror, Chappy said. They have a lousy selection of everything in this godforsaken store. It only stands to reason they'll have a lousy selection of bras.

If you behave and help me find a bra, said Mirror, I'll buy you breakfast after.

It was early Saturday morning and Chappy very badly wanted breakfast. And Mirror knew this. And Chappy knew Mirror knew. He felt manipulated.

Okay, he said, but he was starting to pout.

Don't pout, said Mirror. She walked away from Chappy, toward a rack of bras. Pouting is not behaving. I need a sports bra, she said. Look for pictures of ladies doing exercise. Mirror held up a box with a picture of a lady in a bra. The lady was holding a tennis racket. Chappy could see the lady's nipples through the bra. It looked to Chappy like the lady had sweated up the cups and now you could see right through them.

Don't show me that, said Chappy. He looked away, trying to get a look of disgust to stay on his face. But then he looked back. He looked at the nipples of the lady on the box. He wondered if Mirror thought that he was looking at the nipples, or just the whole general box with the picture of the exercising lady with the tennis racket. He felt he'd better say something soon.

That bra doesn't look like it would give much support, he said. I thought you wanted support. You can see right through that bra.

I do want support, said Mirror.

Chappy was standing in the middle of one of the main aisles in K-Mart. He was getting in everyone's way.

Get out of the aisle, Chappy, Mirror said. You're blocking the way.

Chappy got out of the way. He put his hands in his pockets. He stood still, looked at Mirror.

Mirror looked up, saw Chappy watching her. She shook her head in mock disgust. Chappy was pretty sure it was mock. Mirror was smiling a sort of crooked smile, but not really in her mouth, more in her eyes, and Chappy wondered if a crooked smile could show up in the eyes, or if he was just hoping for the best in this particular situation. He hated to think of himself as someone who hoped for the best in even the worst of situations.

Look for bras that look like this, Mirror said. She held up that same box with the tennis lady on it.

There was another man in the bra section, also with his wife, or his girlfriend. Or his sister, Chappy supposed, but he didn't think so. Who goes to the bra section with their sister? But these two were definitely together, however they were related to one another. The woman was holding up undergarments and waiting to see what the man would say. The man was saying nothing. He nodded sometimes. Other times he just stared. Chappy couldn't really see the man's face because of the angle. He could see the woman's face. She looked young. Chappy looked at her breasts. Because of the bra she was wearing, her breasts looked like lumpy mounds of clay. That bra has support, Chappy thought. He was tempted to tell Mirror to ask that woman what kind of bra she was wearing, but he didn't want Mirror to think he was looking at the woman's breasts.

What's the instrument, Chappy?

What instrument?

The instrument that has no desire to uncover the roots of itself.

What did I just say?

You said, It has no strong desire to uncover the roots of the instrument and follow a path through its most successful practitioners.

How do you remember that, word for word, Mirror? I can't even remember it and I just said it.

Maybe the instrument is a guitar, said Mirror.

Chappy looked blank.

Maybe guitar was the instrument you were talking about.

Yes, said Chappy. Maybe it was guitar. That's right. It was a guitar. Yes, said Chappy again. He looked at his hands, as though he was consulting notes he was holding, but he was holding nothing. He was holding the air. He managed to hold the air the way he might hold the tail of a cat he was trying to get hold of, knowing this was not a good way to get hold of a cat.

In the course of developing our history, Chappy said, we will stumble across some of the greats. Chappy made air quotes around greats.

Mirror settled back on the couch. She listened quietly to

what Chappy was saying.

Chappy stared into space. It was the saddest thing Mirror had ever seen. It hurt her to be forgotten this way, forgotten by a man directly across the room from her, sitting in the warm pool of light cast by the living room lamp on its first setting of the tri-light bulb.

But Chappy would remember her again later.

There was a cycle of remembrance, and, on some rare occasions, Chappy and Mirror remembered each other at the same instant, and there was warmth. It was a warmth that rivaled the lamp light in the living room on a cozy evening in the winter when the furnace was blowing.

There were times when Mirror had to imagine the air quotes in her mind; they were in Chappy's voice, but he did not always create them with his hands. Mirror saw this as a challenge and a way to make herself pay strict attention when Chappy was talking to her.

We will hear about those already well-known practitioners who are exemplars of change; we will meet them through a newer incarnation of players who, in some cases, will worship the greats that came before; in most cases respect them; in some cases despise them; but who will, in all cases, seek to subvert them, to reinvent the history they have thrown themselves into.

Don't buy any mushrooms, said Mirror. There's a mushroom scare.

I don't even like mushrooms, said Chappy.

I know.

Okay.

Are you going to work now?

Yes.

Okay.

What is a mushroom scare, anyway?

People are dying. The mushrooms are killing them.

But what's killing them? Chappy asked. Are the mushrooms going bad? What's wrong with the mushrooms?

Chappy's mother was in the United Kingdom somewhere, on a trip. She went on a trip every summer. One summer, she cashed in her retirement savings plan to pay for her trip. When tax time came, and it was time to pay the government, she called Chappy, crying on the phone.

How am I going to pay them? she asked Chappy.

Chappy said nothing, just listened to his mother for a long time as he sat at the kitchen table pushing the salt shaker back and forth across the table.

I'm going to go to jail, Chappy's mother concluded.

Chappy had no idea how she paid for her trip to the United Kingdom this year. He didn't ask.

The room where Mirror and Chappy were sleeping was Chappy's mother's bedroom. Whenever Mirror came up the stairs to the upper level of the unit where they lived, she said, Fuck.

Mirror was sleeping on the pullout couch with the owl-eyed boy. She kept pulling the sheet up over the owl-eyed boy's body, and the owl-eyed boy kept kicking it off. It was eleven o seven according to the digital clock at the end of the bed.

What did the man look like?

I don't know, Mirror.

I was just wondering.

I didn't really look at him.

Did you talk to him?

Yes.

How could you talk to him and not know what he looks like?

I don't know. He had very full lips.

See, you do know what he looks like. You just don't want to tell me. You have some reason for not wanting to tell me what the man looked like. You should try to work this out for yourself, Chappy. You need to figure out what you're hiding from me. More important, you need to figure out why you're hiding it from me. Why do you want to hide things from me, Chappy?

Look, Mirror, I know what the man's lips looked like, but that's it. I swear to you, that's all I remember.

Why were you looking at the man's lips?

Because we were talking and that's where the words were coming from.

I just wish I could picture the man when you talk about him.

Part Four

Chappy remains at the centre of some life he'd never imagined. Everyday he wakes up at the centre of this life.

The owl-eyed boy is talking to himself as he plays with his plastic action figures, trying to get something to happen that won't ever happen. There is something in the owl-eyed boy's head that is trying to get out.

Chappy will hear the owl-eyed boy throughout his life.

As it has been said in various introductions to various books, both scholarly and not so scholarly, the history of life ends with the owl-eyed boy playing quietly in his room. In the morning, when Chappy rises to revise his history of the owl-eyed boy, so too will the owl-eyed boy rise to revise the history of his world.

The history of the world lies in the last note the owl-eyed boy sings. And what note gets sung after that will not be determined until after it has sprung.

Music is the decision to determine the next note, and so free us of history, which always seeks to determine us. Singing is play.

Chappy had seen her on the subway, standing in the slant light from the station when the lights in the train failed momentarily. She was a poem, leavened with blush. Word one was deep red lipstick; the second stanza framed by black lines drawn around her eyes. The final, breathtaking line in the air about her head, revised as it was in cooperation with her hairdresser.

For a moment Mirror was silent, staring with her big, bug eyes. Chappy held his breath.

The people who found her dead body saw her ankle bones first. They were sticking out from under the blankets she was lying under when she died. And when these people saw her ankle bones sticking out, they fell in love with her. She was on her stomach on the bed and the first thing the people who found her saw were her perfect ankle bones. Then they turned her over and they wanted to make love to her, she was so beautiful. They were teenagers, a boy and a girl. Instead of making love to the dead woman, they went off and made love to each other.

How do you know all this, Chappy? Mirror asked.

It was in the e-mail they sent, Chappy told her.

But Mirror wasn't all that convinced that anyone would send an e-mail with that much detail after a woman in the office died.

Chappy began describing people he worked with. He tried to do this very methodically, starting with the woman whose cubicle was nearest his.

She stood on her legs like a piece of artwork, Chappy told Mirror.

He wanted to make his description of the woman a work of art. He wanted to start very slowly, very carefully, and catalogue everything there was to catalogue and not miss anything, and not rush past what was most important, whatever that might be.

And when she died, said Chappy, but he stopped when he realized that he'd bypassed everything that might have mattered. Death was suddenly the thing that mattered most, and Chappy hesitated.

When she died, said Chappy, everything in the woman's workspace was very neat.

She died? Mirror said.

Yes, last month, Chappy said. He waited, but Mirror said nothing more.

There wasn't a lot of clutter in her space, Chappy said. Somehow this failed to capture what Chappy was aiming at. He had a definite goal here. He could feel this goal inside him like an unformed lump of clay. She'd been wearing white socks every day in the weeks before she died. He felt the utter futility of it now. These socks she wore were very short – ankle socks you might call them. This was a departure for her, and many people in the office commented on this new form of sock she was wearing and wondered at the significance of it. Some argued that there was no significance, but these were the same people who argue that nothing has any real significance – the existentialists of the office, so to speak, who do their job with no conviction.

The weather was iffy, so Chappy and Mirror decided to have a meeting. The meeting took place in the room at the front of the cottage. They could see out the window to the lake, choppy with whitecaps pushing onto the beach. Gulls wheeled. Dark clouds scudded. Chappy and Mirror sat across from each other on the bed. The bed took up almost the entire room. There was only a narrow aisle between the bed and the wall with the door in it. Chappy and Mirror sat sideways to the window, so they could both look out. Chappy didn't like to feel that they were at the cottage and not taking every advantage to see the lake, or to be in the lake. They would go in the lake later, if the lightening held off. The bed wasn't made, because they'd slept in it that night – or tried to sleep. Most of the night the wind kept them awake, and they lay in each other's arms listening to the weather. Sometime deep in the night the sky cleared. Through their window they saw stars over the lake. The sky was bright with moonlight. The few clouds that still drifted past now were lit like billboards near a highway. Now Chappy and Mirror sat on the rumpled bed with their legs crossed. Mirror was having trouble focusing on the business of the meeting. She was looking out the window, her attention drawn away to the world outside. Down on the beach, a pretty, young woman was sitting on a rock. She wore a billowy skirt and a loose muscle shirt over a bathing suit.

That looks like a man's shirt, Mirror said.

The woman had a brown paper bag in her lap with an apple on top. Mirror could see that the man on the beach was terrified. She sat in her little meeting with Chappy in the bedroom that was all bed and watched the man while Chappy discussed whatever he had called the meeting to discuss.

Maybe we could just play a game of crazy eights.

What?

You're not really paying attention, said Chappy. Maybe this isn't the best time for a meeting.

The sky was dark and windy. Clouds raced by too fast to shed any precipitation. The woman on the beach kept pushing back her long hair, trying to keep her hair away from her face, and the wind kept picking it up and flinging it ruthlessly. The woman reached out tentatively. Her hand hovered near the man's lap for a time, like a butterfly drying its wings. Then she scooped up his hand and held it loosely. The man did not move. He might have been speaking, for the girl seemed to shift her head a bit closer, but Mirror could not see the man's face. His head was tipped down. He might have been looking at his lap, or the beach directly in front of him. Perhaps the man was just feeling shy and nervous in the presence of such a beautiful girl.

For the girl was, Mirror now saw, terribly beautiful, in the same way the sky was terribly beautiful today. Terrible and beautiful.

The girl seemed to be wearing very little makeup, but her complexion looked creamy, almost white. It might just be the light, Mirror thought. There was no way of being sure of anything in this light. She looked at Chappy and saw that he was also watching the couple on the beach.

Mirror looked back through the window. Even from here, it was clear that the girl's eyes were her most luminous feature. Large and dark and luminous. Besides her eyes, nothing of her features really stood out, but there was such a lively, sly animation about the girl's movements that Mirror found it hard to draw her attention away. The girl laughed suddenly, her body moving to the rhythm of her mirth. The man looked sideways at the girl, and Mirror saw part of his face. He was smiling and he did not look frightened at all.

Mirror imagined the sound of the girl's laughter. She thought it would be liquid, like water bubbling over rocks. The man reached over and took the girl's other hand into his. Now he had both her hands in his.

Chappy read to Mirror: After we had the twins, life got really strange. I would ride the bus. I liked riding the bus. It was like having my own office. Only none of the people in the other offices knew me, so they left me alone. I liked being left alone.

How is that being punctuated? Mirror asked.

What do you mean? asked Chappy.

I mean, where are the periods? I can't tell what's a period and what's a comma. The way you're reading, it sounds like there are periods where it seems like I would put a comma.

Chappy held the book out to Mirror. You want to look?

No. Keep reading.

Chappy pulled the book back. Adjusted his glasses. The house was quiet. The place they lived now was far from anything busy. It was fifteen minutes to the nearest place you might call busy, and that place was not really busy, except for a brief hour or two each week on Saturday.

Chappy looked at Mirror over the tops of his glasses, to see if she seemed settled and ready to listen. Even though she was more than fifty now, Mirror sometimes still seemed like an impatient little girl. Right now, however, she showed no signs of agitation, so Chappy lowered his eyes to the book and began to read: The decisions you got to make on the bus were totally irrelevant to anything going on in the world. Whereas, when you took the car, everything you did had to be calculated to fuck over the guys in the other cars.

Mirror laughed. Does it really say that? That sounds like something you would say. Are you making this up? Is there really even anything written in that book? It sounds like that idea you had, remember, Chappy, you sell an empty book and people read it to each other and they just make up the stories as they go along.

I remember, said Chappy. But this is a real book. This is what the author really wrote. You want to see? This time, Chappy didn't hold the book out. He could see Mirror was getting tired. He knew she would stop listening soon. Her face would lose that animated look she got when she thought Chappy was fucking with her. Chappy never fucked with Mirror, but he didn't mind occasionally encouraging her delusions that he was fucking with her. He wanted to go across the room now and kiss her. But he stayed where he was, with the book in his lap.

Read, said Mirror. She looked toward the window. Outside, the willow tree was dusting the sky in the relentlessly pallid wind.

Chappy read: You had to always try, for instance, to be the first car at the intersection for a red light. If you didn't try, what was the use? After the twins came, Milly started telling me I had to take the car to work. I didn't get this.

Who is Milly?

Chappy looked up, surprised by the sound of Mirror's voice. He had thought himself alone in the room with the body of Mirror, but apparently he had her mind still, if not her soul.

I guess it's the guy's wife.

And this is the beginning of the book? You didn't skip anything? Everything I know from listening to you is everything you know, also?

Yes.

Okay. Mirror looked back to the window. Chappy went back to reading.

The girl at the bus terminal chewed the bit of apple in her mouth thoughtfully. It must have been a very small piece of apple she had bitten off, because she chewed so daintily. Chappy thought of how Mirror ate an apple; then he thought of how he himself ate an apple; then he tried to remember how his dad or his mom ate their apples; then he thought of everyone he could think of and how they ate an apple and he couldn't quite imagine any of them eating an apple the way this girl did.

The man who was with the girl did not touch the sun. The sun was smiling, but it did not seem to punctuate the man at all, despite all the windows in the bus station. The windows had iron cross pieces and looked old and dirty and tall. The man and the woman were full of sun, and when the man looked at the woman, he had to shade his eyes.

*

Chappy said: A bunch of people spent the entire morning talking about four empty Listerine bottles someone found in one of the bathroom stalls in the public washroom upstairs.

Women's or men's? Mirror asked.

Men's.

Okay.

Every time I turned a corner, I heard someone talking about these Listerine bottles.

What were they saying? Mirror asked.

Um, they were mostly trying to figure out who drank the Listerine.

They think somebody drank four bottles of Listerine? They must have bad breath if they did.

Listerine is full of alcohol.

Really? Mirror sounded quite incredulous over the phone. Chappy took the opportunity to put some sandwich in his mouth, but he didn't bite down till he could tell if Mirror was going to say anything more. It was a pretty sure thing she would say something more, but you never could tell with Mirror. That was really the joy – and the hell – of living with Mirror.

Chappy's mouth began to water, so he bit down, but he kept the bite small, just in case.

I didn't know that, Mirror said.

There was some silence across the phone lines while Chappy chewed quietly and Mirror thought about people drinking Listerine. Mirror wondered how much other stuff like this she didn't know that other people probably knew. She felt quite inadequate and small.

Chappy could feel her sense of smallness over the phone, if that was at all possible, which Chappy doubted, even as he felt it as surely as he felt the peanut butter in his mouth.

So, who do they think was drinking the Listerine? Mirror asked.

There seems to be a general consensus that it would have to be one of the regulars, said Chappy.

Like, a customer?

We call them patrons.

Do people think they know which patron it was?

Some of the supervisors eventually settled on this one old guy who always comes into the library, but never borrows anything. This old guy always carries a box with him wherever he goes. I've seen him at the mall as well as in the library, and he always has that box with him. One of the supervisors thinks this old guy uses the box to steal books. One of the other supervisors says the old man pees in his pants. Which is true. I've smelt it. He generally smells like pee and his pants are stained in the correct area for a person who pees their pants a lot.

*

I know that woman, Mirror whispered to Chappy. Who is she? I can't think who she is. I know who she is. She's that woman from the camera shop, isn't she? Chappy? Isn't that the woman from the camera shop?

Chappy looked at the woman.

Mirror had her head tipped toward Chappy for clandestine consultation. Chappy could smell her hair and it was distracting him. One wisp of her hair was brushing over his eyelash.

I'm not sure, Mirror. It could be her. He squinted. I can't tell.

Look how nicely she's dressed, said Mirror. That bitch. She treats her employees like a real bitch. Remember that time that guy came in. She's a really shitty business woman.

That guy was an asshole. You are always going to get assholes wherever you work. Everybody's an asshole, really. You have to treat assholes the same as you treat everybody else. If you treat the assholes bad, you're never going to get any business. I have to get off the bus at the next stop, Chappy. The next stop is my stop.

This is your stop? Where are you going, anyway?

To see Evelyn. Then we might do some shopping. Evelyn might drive us to the mall later for some shopping. First, we'll have to have a coffee and talk. All Evelyn's kids have moved out now, and it's just her and Reggy. Who's that guy that just got on the bus, Chappy? That one over there. Mirror had her head close to Chappy's again. He's the guy who owns the coffee shop, isn't he? Jesus Christ. What's going on here? He's not the guy who owns the coffee shop. He can't be. That would be just too ridiculous. He just looks like the guy who owns the coffee shop. Still, that was pretty weird, don't you think, Chappy? Wouldn't it be weird if all the guys who owned the shops at the mall had to ride the bus to work?

Maybe they ride the bus because they want to ride the bus.

I don't think so, Chappy. Only an asshole would ride the bus because they wanted to ride the bus.

Chappy raised an eyebrow and twisted his cheek up to show Mirror he guessed she was probably right, but whatever.

The bus stopped at the next stop. Mirror got off.

Chappy kept on going till the bus got him to the corner near his work, and then he got off and went to work.

The owl-eyed boy sat on the edge of his bed with his guitar. He was waiting. He felt a certain nothing, like he had nothing left. His right hand opened slightly, poised, as if to strike, but then his wrist gave way and his hand hung limp. No sound came from the guitar.

For a long while, the owl-eyed boy sat hunched over, staring at his knees overtop the edge of his guitar. Beneath the silence of his room he could hear his father's voice, and then his mother's, and then footsteps, and then nothing.

The owl-eyed boy stood now, holding his guitar by the neck. As he had learned, every day brings new sorrows. He leaned over and lay the guitar in its case. The guitar emitted a muted thunk.

*

There was a time, eons ago, when mind was all. The directors of the universe observed the scintillations in the ionosphere like they were talking directly to the sparrows again, completely invalidating any authority they had managed to achieve thus far. The idea that mind is all is directly obverse to what the scientists today are telling us. The scientists are wrong, though. The scientists have always been wrong. It is their strength to be wrong, and to stand within their wrongness, and to continue to be wrong long enough to glimpse what the poets see when they turn away completely from the physical world the scientists make possible for them.

And so, in her mind, Mirror lived in a land far distant from the one Chappy's mind lived in. The physical space between them on any given day hardly mattered, for it was in their minds that they met, and so the landscape of this story is a place in the mind. Or a place between two minds, if that's even possible. Chappy lived for it to be possible, to the day he died, and he spent his life trying to convince Mirror to believe in this possibility. But Mirror remained skeptical. She was willing to entertain Chappy's arguments – to humour him. But for Chappy, their relationship was a lingering hash of moments clothed in words that hung tenuously, briefly, only to fall away into the quiet breathy swell of the ocean of distance that held them apart. But what held them apart truly held them together.

A sheet of blue sky slapped against the window. A scar of airplane fog and a crystal of sunlight draped in slouching curtains. There isn't any reason for it, Chappy thought, or for me to see it. It doesn't see me.

Chappy leaves the office. Walks past a bus shelter. Crosses University Avenue. Sits in a park and cries. A lone figure enters into the light of his imagination to do something communal. Alone, Chappy lives in the living room in his mind, under the tree in the park. With silver frames and high technology, with TVs and stereos, and with the isolated pools of light, here on one side of the room, there on the other, and the many pools of light scattered over the carpet hardly knowing each other at all.

Games can also help you structure your thinking. Games can help you concentrate. When playing games, you must concentrate to complete levels or tasks required by the game. This may increase your concentration for a number of other things, including work or school. It can also increase your creative thinking. It can help you with story ideas, or drawings that you might want to make. If you ever get a job as a cartoonist, it can help you to think of new ideas for cartoon characters. It can also help you with other careers. Game designing, police officer, athlete, wrestler and psychopath.

Chappy and Mirror get in the car. At a stoplight, they get beside another car and Chappy sees that his lane ends ahead. When the light goes green, Chappy tromps on the gas, goes to ram it into second and misses. The gears grind and the car comes to a stop at the end of the lane.

Later, at the drive-in, Chappy gets popcorn. Mirror stays in the car. They watch both movies. Halfway through the second movie, Chappy has to turn the car on so he can run the wipers.

When both movies are over, Chappy and Mirror go home.

Mirror decided to eat ice cream. But thinking about it was doing her in. She couldn't eat ice cream without thinking about eating ice cream. She got a bowl. She wished Chappy were here. Mirror ran her hand around in a circle over her stomach. Her stomach felt warm through her pjs. Mirror wasn't feeling too good today.

The first thing you have to do is to starve yourself all day, Chappy told Mirror. Mirror never believed Chappy about this. For the longest time she just failed to believe him. But then one day she tried it. One day, Mirror stopped eating. And it helped. It seemed to help to starve yourself all day. If you were going to find the true meaning in a bowl of ice cream, it seemed to help to starve yourself all day before you ate it.

All that's left after starving yourself, Chappy told her, is to savour every bite. You have to keep your mind on the ice cream. You have to believe that the ice cream matters. It matters, Mirror. More than anything has ever mattered in your entire life.

More even than you, Chappy? Mirror asked when Chappy told her this, but she was giggling. Chappy was such an idiot. He was funny because he was so stupid. But he seemed deadly serious when he told Mirror about the ice cream. It was making Mirror giggle. You have to make yourself believe it matters, Mirror, Chappy told her. Making believe is the same as making anything else. It takes hard work and dedication. And it takes a plan, Mirror.

I hate the part of the day after the morning gets stale, Mirror tells Chappy. It's like you go around the rest of the day missing buses and kicking walls.

You don't kick walls, Mirror.

No, I don't. Metaphorically, though, I sometimes kick a wall.

I've kicked walls. I've hurt myself kicking walls.

I know.

I know a guy who broke his toe kicking a wall.

Stupid.

I know.

Knowing that Mirror was heading into the stale part of the day was making Chappy sad. He needed something to say. Something to correct this gross injustice. He wanted to counteract the sadness by saying something, but he knew that anything he said would only become a vessel for transmitting the sadness that was coming out of him like a bodily fluid. It was like the sadness was coming out of his pores, like he was sweating sadness. He wanted to hide this sweaty sadness from Mirror, but his face was transmitting the sadness anyway. Chappy knew that his face was a vessel for transmitting sadness. Maybe not to a stranger. Maybe a stranger would never perceive his face as a vessel for transmitting sadness. But for Mirror, she would know he was sad, so he spoke. Nothing that leaves me ever enters directly to the core of improbability, he said. He was making no effort at all to counteract the sadness. He was looking for the improbable place where word meets sadness and dances away into oblivion. Nothing touches the soul of my improbability, Mirror. Mirror was wearing her glasses. But she took them off now. She looked at Chappy. She held the glasses in her hand, far enough away from her that there seemed no real danger she would put them back on. But she kept them in her hand. Mirror was far enough away from Chappy that he didn't go blurry when she took her glasses off. Things leak out, Chappy said. Things culminate. Chappy had no idea what he was trying to get at, only that he was trying to get at it with words, and, for the most part, words were hopelessly beneath the task of getting at anything. Years later, Chappy told Mirror, I recognize everything that's been left behind.

In a way, Mirror felt like she was one of the things that was getting left behind. In another way, she felt light-years ahead of Chappy. She didn't think this, but it was extant in the silence she held so gracefully. It made Chappy swoon now to see how gracefully Mirror held herself in silence, and he grew silent, and in the silence he felt something like an intensity attempting to rip through skin. It hurt. Chappy thought he should go off and write something. One thing about typewritten words, so perfect and groomed, is that it makes the messages come out sad and not able to measure up.

When a thing gets good, Chappy told Mirror, I'm not even sure if it gets good because it truly is getting good, or because I'm suddenly, temporarily deluded enough, or horny enough, to think it's good, when really it sucks.

Saturday morning Chappy arose with his doubts, bought into them lock stock and barrel, and brought them into the kitchen where he sat at the breakfast nook with sleepy Mirror, drinking his coffee. Things that made him sad in the kitchen were the sound of Mirror eating cereal, as well as other things, but particularly the sound of Mirror eating cereal. In the silence that arose in the steam from his coffee to sting his lips into action, Chappy spoke: In some cultures in the world, Chappy told Mirror, when a woman stops loving a man, she leaves him. Chappy held his mug aloft, but did not bring it to his lips. He continued: In some cultures, the woman is expected to break something of the man's before she leaves him. She might break a variety of things. Chappy was riffing. Mirror loved Chappy best when he improvised spontaneously on a theme. The woman might break a variety of things, Chappy repeated to buy himself some time. She might even come back and break things a second time, he suddenly said, and he looked up at Mirror and smiled. He finally took a sip of his coffee, but Mirror knew he was not finished. She knew he would finish on an unexpected chord,

something with a half-tone interval buried in it. Something
that would churn her heart to ribbons.

Mirror came around the table. She took Chappy's mug from
his hands and set it on the table. She pulled Chappy's knees
so they swung out from under the table and he was sitting
sideways in the nook and she lowered herself down onto
his lap and she put her lips onto his lips and she kept them
there.

It is in the turning away, Chappy read, that the poet sees.
But it is always the scientist who makes the turning away
possible. The scientist makes the turning away possible
by being so utterly wrong, and by willing himself to hold
tenaciously to what is so utterly wrong. It is the tenaciousness
of the hold that is wrong, not what each scientist chooses to
hold onto. Chappy looked up. Mirror looked into his eyes.
She wondered what Chappy chose to hold onto and whether
or not he held onto it tenaciously.

Are you the poet or the scientist, do you think, Chappy?
Chappy said nothing. He gazed at Mirror. Shook his head
almost imperceptibly. I don't know for sure. Then he didn't
speak for a while.
What about you, Mirror? he said when finally he spoke
again. Which are you?
I asked you first.
I want to say poet, Chappy said, but, to tell the truth,
I'm not at all sure.
Me either, Chappy, Mirror said brightly. And she felt quite
bright, despite Chappy's gloomy mood. She took Chappy's

hands in hers. They were sitting sideways toward each other on the couch. She might have thought she could transmit her happy feeling through her hands into Chappy. Chappy might have felt the happiness penetrate the layers of his skin. He might have felt a little better. Go on reading, Mirror said, everything on her face smiling.

The poet locks horns with the scientist, Chappy read, and is in constant danger of adopting the scientist's tenacious hold. It is only when the poet lets go and falls through the floor of his convictions that he becomes truly poet.

Maybe we're both, Chappy, Mirror said. Poet and scientist.

That's what I'm thinking, said Chappy.

Maybe there's a bit of both in all of us.

Of course, said Chappy. It seems so obvious. But it must be stated. He laughed at the pomposity of this statement. The pomposity of his tenacious hold. He gripped Mirror's hands more tightly.

This death, Chappy read, in the physical sense, is death. So the poet must fall metaphorically, before falling finally back to the beginning, which is beyond us now, for we are only beginning and are, thus, deep in the end of things and only distantly, vaguely aware of the beginnings for which we hunger.

It was his hunger that drove him to send forth the wan, sterile physician, Juan Sterling. And it was his hunger that drove him to send forth into the world the physical presence his mind was able to muster. It was his hunger – a hunger stretched so thin as to be constantly on the verge of breaking, constantly in need of bolstering, or repair, constantly in need of being sewn back up – it was the force of his terrible hunger that brought him past the borders of the territory his own mind occupied onto the brink of the fertile land the woman inhabited. He was like a tourist, and there was nothing she disliked more than a tourist. But somehow his coming back again and again convinced her.

Mirror was silent. She knew exactly what this writer was saying. She had seen Chappy come across the great wide blue of the lake wearing a boater's hat and floppy shoes.

Press alt L and the layout menu appears, Chappy read. Press T to choose tables. Press F to choose create floating cell. The edit floating cell dialogue box appears. Name the floating cell. Chappy stopped. He looked up to see if Mirror was listening. She might be listening, he thought. But she might also have a sort of vacant look on her face. Chappy wasn't sure. He thought she might be half-listening. What do you want to call the floating cell, Mirror? he asked.

I kind of like Floating Cell. Couldn't we just call it Floating Cell?

I guess we could. It says here if you want to change the name, you press 1. Then you can type a different name for the floating cell.

Let's just call it Floating Cell. If we think up a better name later, we can name it something else. Although, I can't imagine a better name. If we ever have a baby, let's name it Floating Cell.

Chappy laughed. Floating Cell. It does have a certain poetry to it.

It's lovely, isn't it?

It really is.

I'm not sure we should name a baby that, though. It might be a bad thing to saddle a baby with a name like that. We should just name it Cindy, or Linda, or Mark, or Stephen, something common, so the baby doesn't suffer when it goes to school. People would probably do mental torture on someone named Floating Cell.

That's true.

Are we finished here?

Not quite. There's a bit more.

Well, go on, then. I need to get some coffee soon and get dressed for work.

Me, too. Maybe I should get us some coffee now. You can get dressed. Then we'll meet back here in the kitchen to finish this up before we go to work.

Deal.

When they had their coffee, and Mirror was dressed in her black sweater and pants, they met back in the kitchen. They sat kitty corner at the table and Mirror held Chappy's hand while he read.

Press 3 for number type. The number type formats dialogue box appears. Specify a format.

Do we need to pick a format?

Yes, but it's a drop down menu. I can choose a format when I actually go in and do it.

Okay. If you need help deciding, though, I can help. What are the different formats available, anyway?

It doesn't say here.

Okay, go on.

Chappy disengaged his hand from Mirror's momentarily and took a sip of coffee. He was afraid to take his other hand away from the book because it would close up and it would be hard to find his place. It was a fat book. He took a sip of coffee, then put his mug down and held Mirror's hand again. Mirror's eyes were shining in the light from the kitchen window. Chappy's face was a bit in shadow because he was sitting with his back mostly to the window. One of the cats came in. Press enter to choose OK. Press to choose a formula. The table formula dialogue box appears.

Who wrote this book?

Chappy kept his thumb in the book and closed it to look at the cover. He looked at the cover for a while. It doesn't say who wrote it, he said.

Mirror tipped her head to try to see if there was a name of an author on the cover. There didn't seem to be.

It's well written, Mirror said.

Chappy tumbled out the door, pale, grey, the sky so dark and overcast that he could hardly see himself. If there had been sunshine, it might have bored right through him, making him even harder to see. As it was, he was shadow. He moved across the green. The green was lawn. The lawn sat in front of brightly painted houses. Chappy stopped near a mailbox. He heard a sound. Something happy. Something that reminded him of some past time. Something he'd heard before. Something along the lines of something he'd long forgotten. He tried to remember. In his mind, he saw Mirror in a haze.

The sound was distant when Chappy first heard it. It grew more distant, the source of the sound moving away, until he could hear it no more. The silence that had preceded the sound returned and Chappy felt oppressed. He wanted the sound back. He wanted to remember where he'd heard it before. He tried to reconjure the sound in his mind. He moved away from the mailbox. Light grimaced behind closed curtains. Chappy moved slowly in the direction of the ocean.

*

The ocean was very far away – a very far way off – and Chappy felt so small and grey. He felt like he was nothing but a tiny project: to move across the land to get to the ocean and then to get across the ocean. He knew he wouldn't make it. He knew that when he started out. He knew also that when he came back Mirror would hold him close and love him, but that neither of them would ever get over it completely.

He hadn't gotten two blocks, moving very slowly, hobbled as he was by his utter lack of substance, when he heard the sound again, this time very close.

Yes, he whispered into the gloom, I hear you.

Chappy woke up, but he didn't open his eyes. I'm on the couch, he thought. He was sitting up. He could feel a book in his hands. He thought the light must be on because there was a brightness he could feel through his eyelids. Mirror might be on the other couch. She might be asleep.

Someone came through a door.

You forget that you are no longer connected by a cord, Chappy thought, that you no longer need to be connected by a cord. Fifty years old and I'm still nursing. It's like trying to find where the paragraph breaks.

Chappy walked down to the beach and stood in the sun. The air was cold, but the sun warmed him. A woman was further down the beach, but other than that, Chappy was alone. The waves were small, but they still crashed on the beach enough to hear them over the wind in the poplar trees that lined the top of the bluff. The woman wore a red sweatshirt and shorts and Chappy felt a terrible longing watching his need recede along with her along the beach.

A door burst open and light spilled onto a lawn. It was growing darker as night came on, crowding out the grey of overcast skies with a more pronounced grey, threatening black.

I am the distance, Chappy thought.

The black moved like a train over the tracks of horizon. Into the light from the house fell a group of laughing men, their foreheads and noses shining, their laughter like the bark of beasts. They were the bards of the beast world. They spoke low growls, but their growls were garbed in garble – or else Chappy had no facility to understand.

Chappy moved away. He was afraid. Afraid of the commotion, wanting only to continue the project, not really understanding the magnitude of what he was taking on, not knowing that this commotion was really not a big deal in the grand scheme of things.

Chappy understood the grand scheme, the idea of it, but he didn't feel it. The pain in the moment seemed to overwhelm anything that tried to enter any idea he might have of his world from the future. But when Chappy fell away from the house, slinking low to try to remain unseen, he stepped onto a road. Lights loomed out of the black and a blaring single-tone song erupted. A car flew by, hovering over the road, its tires hidden by the coming dark.

Chappy stumbled back onto the lawn, toward the house, where the men stood, silenced now, motionless.

*

The owl-eyed boy asked Chappy if he wanted to come in and see his place. He turned and went in, as if he knew that Chappy would follow.

The owl-eyed boy's window looked over the town – four church steeples, a handful of other apartment buildings, the rooftops of houses, and the waving, leafy branches at the tops of nearby trees that shot up like devil sticks poking the bum of God's blue sky, like school kids torturing someone in the school yard.

For a brief, startled moment, Chappy felt he might reach out and touch everything beyond the window.

I live in one of the squares, the owl-eyed boy told Chappy. He pointed at the yellow painted wall above his bed. A series of squares were hand drawn in black magic marker, the squares connected one to the next by lines. We're each stuck in our own little square, the owl-eyed boy explained, and Chappy thought his eyes were even wider and rounder than usual. The rest of the owl-eyed boy's face looked small with those large round eyes set there. It's like an org chart, the owl-eyed boy said. We're joined together tenuously by little threads, like these lines here, but mostly we're alone in our own little boxes.

Chappy said nothing. He didn't believe the owl-eyed boy would even hear him if he spoke.

I've found a way to move from one box to another, the owl-eyed boy said, and Chappy believed him. But we can't be in the same box with any other, the owl-eyed boy said, and he looked at Chappy now, and Chappy could see he was almost through. The owl-eyed boy looked at Chappy in an ancient way that seemed pretty unusual for a boy so young. We can't be in the same box with anyone, ever, no matter how close we get.

Chappy nodded vaguely. This seemed correct to him. Nothing really extraordinary. The boy must have heard some adult talking.

You want something to eat? the boy asked.

The owl-eyed boy is like some guy who wants to come over and hang out with me and I want badly for him to keep liking me, Chappy told Mirror.

Mirror almost said something. She already knew this about Chappy. She wanted to let him know this was no revelation to her. But she stayed silent.

He's not like a son, Chappy said, but like some guy who just wants to come over and do shit with me. He's like some guy who I love and who I want to love me back. Other times, he's like an extension of me that goes out into the world and checks things out and comes back and then is just a silent part of me again and I'm a silent part of him.

It's amazing how different we are, Mirror said. Mirror felt she was being quite wise in saying this. This seemed like the best thing ever to say.

Chappy didn't seem to notice that Mirror had spoken. He walks out of nowhere, Chappy said, and arrives moment after moment during his stay.

Well, said Chappy. I hate you.

Fine, said Mirror. You go ahead and hate me. Hate me all you want. It doesn't matter to me, said Mirror. You can hate me all you want. You're so full of hate, Chappy. But I can handle your hate. Give it to me. Give me your hate. Stick it in me. Give me everything you've got. I know what it means to hate. The hate inside me is a big, awful bag of fucking hate. My hate is a big cock stuck so deep in my cunt it's coming back out my mouth. No hate you feel for me could ever come close to the big cock of hate I feel inside myself. So go ahead and hate me with all the power you can muster, buster.

It was the muster buster that made Chappy laugh. He laughed out loud. He'd been laughing a bit inside. He'd felt a kind of nervous laughter building up inside him that he might have let out a little at a time, or not at all, if Mirror hadn't said the muster buster thing. Chappy was afraid partly because he'd told Mirror, for the first time in his life, that he hated her. Partly, though, he was afraid of what she was saying.

Chappy took the bus to the library. Wind blew in through the bus window. There were seventeen people on the bus. No one said a word. It was early. The sun wasn't even up. People stared out the window and the growing light shone on their faces like angel's breath. It took out the lines and wrinkles and returned them to another time. A timeless time. A space outside of time. A space trapped between the brackets of time. A space leading away from time and returning again to time. It was only a matter of time, Chappy knew. It was only ever entirely a matter of time. It was only a moment of time. It was only a moment. Only a moment. Only a lonely moment of time.

Chappy blew away. Chappy blew everything. He blew everything away, and then he just blew. If he were light enough, Chappy knew, if he were just the slightest bit of nothing, just the slightest breath could blow him away, and he'd float on someone's breath and drift high up in the sky and see beyond the horizon and he'd be so light he'd float back to the ground like a feather, but he'd never make it to the ground, he'd get blown by someone else's breath and drift again and maybe one day he'd get on some kind of natural updraft and just keep floating up till God's breath took him over completely and breathed him away forever and no one would ever see him again and he would only be a memory, and then not even that, just a last word, a breath, the final blow, the last time some ancestor said his name, and then no one remembered him ever again and the universe collapsed and he was the secret code at the core of the collapsing universe.

Chappy felt so sad. The owl-eyed boy was just pictures in a book now. And this woman...

Chappy understood the desire, not just to kill, but to hurt. To be a man. To contain this power, but to yearn for the silent love.

We can find each other, he said so quietly, not even Mirror heard. We can never find each other.

What are you today, Chappy?

I am an ongoing awareness session.

Of all the photographs, I love best the photograph of the three women in white – two of them really just little girls – waving goodbye to the steamer.

Is that your mother and your sister waving you off as you travel away to your new life, Chappy? Mirror held the photo album in her lap, cradled it like an open child. The blue cover stuck a little to her bare legs. Is this the picture of where you travel off to a new life where you live still with your mother and sister? A life that no longer includes your father? Mirror looked at Chappy. He was looking at his hands, which were folded in his lap. He was very quiet, not just on a verbal level, Mirror thought, but profoundly silent in a carnal sense, with his body motionless, his breathing very slow, or very controlled, Mirror wasn't sure which. Or are you the other girl in white, Chappy? Watching your life, as you know it, sailing off. Leaving you. Was your father that ship, Chappy? Was he wearing his black suit? And you dressed in white. Is this the beginning of good and evil?

We need new dresses, Mirror told the saleslady. Sybil looked at Mirror. They were under cold fluorescent light. There were mirrors nearby waiting to reflect new dresses back at them. They were cold in their summer dresses in the air conditioned store, their skinny legs and arms shooting out of holes in their clothing. But they needed new dresses.

It's hopeless, you know, said the saleslady. Some pieces of the saleslady's hair were sticking out in odd directions. Mirror could see that the saleslady was going down. The saleslady marched away in search of more dresses. Mirror leaned close to Sybil. She's beginning to despair, Mirror whispered. She put her lips right onto Sybil's ear, to feel the warmth, to smell the smell of Sybil.

Sybil giggled.

Mirror looked at Sybil. I've seen it before, Sybil, she said. She pulled her face away from Sybil's ear.

I know, said Sybil. We should go to another store before we defeat her completely. It's only early in the morning. She doesn't need this headache. Let's just go home. Let's get coffee. And sticky buns.

The saleslady was back. She lined them up, Mirror on the left, Sybil on the right. They had their backs to the mirrors.

Wear your dresses with dignity, the saleslady told Mirror and Sybil in a carefully measured tone of voice. She looked at the two girls in their sundresses. You're too skinny, she said. The both of you.

We need new dresses, Mirror said.

It was true.

Chappy was reading a Bruce Iserman report to Mirror for hope of a romantic moment. Mirror generally loved Iserman's reports.

Although, in truth, Chappy didn't exactly understand this as an opportunity to get romantic with Mirror. He wanted to see Mirror happy, that was all. But he knew in an abstract sense that wanting her to be happy might look like something very romantic. Poetry, music, flowers, the sea.

It's called Some Broken Thread, Chappy told Mirror. And it's more of a poem than a report. It's an early report, before Iserman understood that he was doing reports, not poems.

For a moment, Chappy looked down at the book. But then he looked up at Mirror to gauge her reaction. Did she want to hear this poem?

It's by Bruce Iserman, Chappy reiterated. Someone neither of us knows, but he's written us this poem.

It was after ten in the night. The sky was dark outside the window. Mirror got up and pulled the curtains closed. The light was on in its new place beside the entertainment unit. Chappy and Mirror sat at the other end of the room, bathed in a warm light. The new carpet was under Chappy's bare feet. Mirror had her legs tucked up under her on the couch.

Read it, Mirror said.

Chappy turned the book to catch a bit of the light coming from the lamp. He read:

A knot
that buds on a rope

can tighten
or undo
the hangman's art.

The knot is however
secondary;
the horse
the condemned man straddles
is more important

A horse is an animal
big enough
to kill you.

Chappy tried to work the line breaks into the reading, so
that when he said, A horse is an animal, the words stood
momentarily alone before becoming big enough, and then,
again, a pause, until, finally, the moment grew big enough
to kill you.

What a breathtaking moment, Mirror breathed into the
silence Chappy left for her at the end of the poem. The book
sat still open in Chappy's lap, a silent testament to what
had been and gone. It was a silence bordered by the light in
the room, by the curtains, by Mirror's feet tucked up under
her on the couch, by the hum of the fridge in the kitchen.
I hadn't thought of a horse as an animal big enough to kill
you, Mirror said. But it is.

Chappy nodded. Iserman is himself a hangman, he said.
He's a hangman whose noose is knotted from threads of
word; whose horse stands restless in the space beneath the
poem, waiting to gallop off and leave the reader dangling.

Oh Chappy, said Mirror. That's so sad.

Sad is a place, Mirror. It's just a place I go sometimes.

What do you see when you go there?

Little ripples of stone leading down to water. Below that, the blue, blue sea. The speckled fish blow bubbles, like tiny pockets of prayer floating to the surface and popping uselessly in the air.

A bunch of these little birds landed on the deck, three or four of them, turning their tiny heads at an alarmingly fast rate, little head twitches, the way of birds. I'd seen one of the birds before. She'd come to see me a couple days before. She'd hopped around the deck, pecking at things, looking for food, and, at one point, she'd hopped very close to my foot and it scared me. I had no shoes on.

There was this time when there were a bunch of little birds, really cute little birds, and these little birds were turning their heads really fast, really like mad, each looking at me from one side of their head. I thought, if one of those things lands on my chair, I'm not going to be scared.

Did you have your laptop?

Yes.

Did one of the birds land on your chair?

Yes, one of them landed right on my chair. It looked at me for a minute, then flew away. Then all the little birds flew away, and I never saw any of them again.

Did it scare you when that bird landed on your chair, Chappy? It would have scared me. I don't care how much I decided ahead of time I wasn't going to be scared.

It kind of scared me, Mirror. But since I told myself
I wasn't going to be scared, it didn't scare me too much. I was able to control myself.

What did you do?

I just said, Hello.

And then the bird flew away?

Yes.

I was on a stairway. I realized there was a question to ask. Or maybe more than one question.

Am I studying individuals or aggregates? Chappy asked.

Mirror waited.

I ask myself questions, Mirror, as I climb the stairs to our apartment. Every day. I have these questions.

This didn't surprise Mirror.

I ask myself again and again.

Two individuals came down the stairs toward Chappy and Mirror.

An aggregate! whispered Mirror. She was very excited. She had a glow in her eyes.

Chappy raised his eyes to Mirror's. He looked lost.

I had to stop on the stairway because I couldn't get by, Chappy told Mirror. Chappy seemed very emphatic today. Mirror thought about this. About stairways. About stopping on stairways. There was no disputing it. Chappy's tone of voice held no opening for Mirror. She stood squeezed into Chappy's deliberation, unable to move.

I stood still, by the rail, squeezed close to the wall, said Chappy. Mirror felt concern. She felt concern for Chappy, and she felt concern for the outcome of this moment by the rail. Chappy was here in front of her now, and he looked okay, but Mirror didn't know what psychic damage was about to occur in the story and do things to Chappy that Mirror would not ever be able to heal.

It was a boy and a girl, said Chappy, but the girl was on the other side. The boy was on one side and the girl was on the other. But, then, the girl moved to the other side of the boy and the boy was on the other side now. At the last minute, they both swerved and did a weave that left the boy on the side other to the one he was on before and the girl, same thing, so that now they were both on the side they had been on when they first approached, when I first saw the boy and the girl for the very first time.

I could see the individual hairs on the beard on his face. He was so close to me, Mirror, and he seemed to be saying to me, You don't know your place on this stairway, little man.

Do you really think he was really saying little man with his eyes? asked Mirror.

Chappy looked directly into Mirror. Mirror thought she might be seeing. She thought she might be really seeing. For the first time, she thought she might have seen just what she was dealing with here when she saw what she saw in Chappy. She felt she was spinning. She felt she was out of control. The situation was out of control. There was nothing for her to do about any of this. So she looked away from

Chappy. When she looked back, Chappy was looking down at the ground, like a lost little boy.

All my life, Mirror, Chappy said, I've never known my place on the stairway. And, yet, I keep going up.

Beings whisper, Chappy said.
    Beings whisper their being, Mirror said.
    Being whispers, Chappy said.
    Mirror said nothing. She had nothing left to say.

I'm not asking you to believe in the things I believe in, Mirror said.
    Mirror knew she and Chappy were struggling with some issues.
    For the brief time we are together in this house, Chappy said, and Mirror saw him saying it, saw his face, what it held, and it made her feel sick.
    The sad truth of it, Mirror said, is that I am simply asking you to believe in the strength of my convictions. That is all there is to it.
    Chappy was quiet in a way that told Mirror she should have more to say. She'd been planning to stop for the time being, maybe begin again later – or wait till tomorrow.

Measure each word to determine which word will be the last for now.

I was looking at a spider on my computer. It looked so 3-D I had to look closer, and then I saw that it was actually a real spider walking across my computer screen.

The writer's ally is silence.

Silence comes. As waves on shore. As leaves in wind. As moon-shift on star-pebbled sky.

*

A woman's strength, read Mirror, is deep inside her. Deep inside her cunt. But even deeper. A woman's power is in the roots that spread out from her cunt, roots that spread throughout her body, and only show themselves where her tits poke out. A woman's tits are little power outlets where all children find nourishment, and where some select men find nourishment, also.

I hate that word, said Mirror.

Cunt?

Yes. Don't say it.

You said it.

I read it.

That's different?

Yes.

It's a powerful word.

I know.

Sometimes you need a powerful word, Mirror. A word that stirs.

Sometimes.

This time?

Yes.

Cunt.

They were at the beach. On the front deck of the cottage, at the top of the bluff that overlooked the lake.

When the child is weak, said the owl-eyed boy, the mother is strong.

Mirror only knew right now she didn't feel very strong.

And, said the owl-eyed boy, when the mother is weak, the child is strong.

Mirror turned her head to hide her tears.

For a long while there was nothing but the sound of waves and wind.

I feel like one of those domino structures, Chappy told Mirror, where you set them all up, then tip the first one to knock them all down. They sat together on the couch, by the fire, in the cottage. Chappy felt the heat from the fire touch his face and arms.

I know where each of the dominos needs to be placed. One of these days, I'll tip the first one.

I have doubts sometimes, Mirror. But I try not to follow them too far in.

But you do follow them, don't you?

A little bit. I feel I must, or why else would I have these doubts.

But doubts are like lies.

Yes. Small lies. Doubts are exactly like small lies.

Then is certainty truth? asked Mirror.

No, said Chappy. Certainty is the biggest lie of all.

Then what is truth, Chappy?

Chappy said nothing for a long time.

The fire crackled. Something in it popped.

Truth floats, Mirror.

When Chappy returned to the cottage, Mirror was sitting, still, beside the fire. But the fire had died to nothing but orangey coals.

I've saved up some possibility, Mirror.

I hate you, Chappy, Mirror whispered. I hate it when you leave like that. Why do you leave like that?

You don't understand.

No, I don't. I don't understand at all.

I saved up some possibility. I've brought it back for you. It's like a gift. That's why I go away. To save up possibility so I can give it to you for a gift.

Mirror wavered, like heat over asphalt.

Unfortunately, Chappy, I might be wasting your time. I can't promise you I won't be wasting your time. All I can ask you to do is believe I don't want to waste your time.

Chappy nodded. I believe, he said.

Me too you, Chappy, Mirror said.

She felt finished. Not just with this, but with everything, like her days were over. She would go to sleep and start again tomorrow.

They sat quietly for a time, with the sun coming in through the living room window, lighting their faces, warming their arms.

When the owl-eyed boy came home from school, the door opened and the world rushed back into the house in a mad whorl.

Trying to hear the secret meaning is the same as trying to be a better person. I believe this, but I don't know if it's true. If I and Mirror spend our time together in this world trying to find a way of hearing the secret meaning of each other, it might help us or it might not. I believe it will help us, but it might not.

Chappy wanted to get up out of his chair. He was sick of sitting in his chair. He wanted his chair to be gone. He wanted to throw his chair out the window. He wanted to stand. But he wanted to do more than just stand. He wanted to walk. Or run! He wanted to run really fast!! Or jump around like some demented bunny on a commercial for batteries.

But now he felt funny and self-conscious just wanting to get out of his chair. He saw himself throwing the chair out the window. It seemed stupid. He felt like a little baby who suddenly understands for the first time just how dumb and stupid he really is.

Chappy didn't feel like eating something fried. He felt he'd raised Mirror's expectations. He felt he had no choice now but to take the fried thing she was holding out to him. He took the fried thing. Thanks, he said.

It was Saturday. Mirror had her little black purse hanging over her shoulder. She was thinning out her thoughts of Lake Ontario, her summer ferns, her white lilies. Her white legs came out of her cone-shaped dress and made their way down to her bare feet where they hit the floor.

*

Chappy sat in his chair. He heard cupboards and drawers opening, then closing.

You got any gum, Chappy? Mirror called.

Chappy never had any gum. He hated gum.

Chappy hated the sound of Mirror chewing gum. He hated how his mouth hurt when he himself chewed gum.

Mirror came into the living room. She looked at Chappy in his chair. She had her hands on her hips. Chappy saw her eyes fill with something black. Her eyes fell closed.

Mirror watched Chappy through her black eyes. She kept her hands on her hips, but she shifted her weight, making her look even more disgusted, if that was even possible.

Chappy looked out the window. Clouds rushed over the world like they had some place to go.

Chappy looked at Mirror. He was figuring something out.

What would it be like to be like Mirror? Chappy wondered. To inhabit Mirror the way Mirror inhabited herself. The way Mirror sat inside her skin. To not just touch Mirror's skin, to not just touch her breasts, her knees, the crease of skin where her bum folded onto her leg – but to be that skin. To be inside that skin. To feel that skin stretch. To feel that skin stretch over the whole space of whoever it was that Mirror was inside that skin.

When it comes, Chappy thought, it sucks you in, like a revolution.

Chappy felt a kind of revulsion and, in his revulsion, he

felt that terrible power that flew out of him as soon as it
gathered, leaving him weak and frightened.

After the phone had been silent for a long, long time and
no one had come through the door, and he was alone and
nearing the end of his life, Chappy swept the floor. He put
his hands on some of the objects in his house. He dusted.
When he was finished, everything was stored neatly, either
in the refrigerator or in a cupboard. Goodbye, Chappy said,
although there was no one there to hear him.

Chappy opened the magazine to an ad that showed a woman
in a light summer setting. The woman looked competent,
feminine, freed of herself by a paper product. She looked
clean. Her carefree smile obscured something crude that
Chappy tried hard but could not descry entirely.

I was going to call you this morning. I was reading this book
I found on your bookshelf. It's called *Emma's Head*.
    Is it any good?
    You haven't read it?
    No. That's such a weird title, though. I bought it for the
title.
    When did you get it?
    A long time ago. Just a minute, I have to get the other line.
    Chappy listened to soft music that he remembered from
when he was younger. He didn't hate this song. He just hated
the idea of a radio station that played this song. He had the
book, *Emma's Head*, in his lap. He was in the kitchen, at the
kitchen table, with a bowl of cereal and this book. He was
sitting sideways to the table with his feet up on the owl-eyed

boy's chair and the book on the tops of his thighs.

Emma could tip her head back so you could see down her neck, he read. He read out loud, but very softly, as though he were afraid someone might hear him, although he was home alone with only the cats.

There were lights inside Emma, and translucent bits of something floating around that looked like fly wings moving in a gentle wind, Chappy read.

The soft music stopped and Mirror's voice came on. Hi, I'm back.

This is a weird book, Chappy said. Who could do a whole book like this?

What's it about? Mirror asked.

Emma's head.

The whole book is about Emma's head?

I think so. I've only read a few chapters, but they're all about Emma's head.

Weird.

I know. But the weirdest thing is, I read the first chapter three times. Every time I read it, it was different. But it was something in my head that was different, not something in the book. The book is the same set of words every time. Like any book. What's different is not like something you could describe in words. At the back of the book, on the back cover, it says that this is a book of non-fiction.

A non-fiction book about Emma's head?

I know.

I have to go. The phone is ringing off the hook.

Okay, see you tonight.

See you tonight.

Mirror hung up.

Chappy sat at the table with the book in his lap and lifted a spoonful of cereal to his mouth.

On the other side of the solar system, a planet melts hopelessly.

The girl was young. She had brown eyes. Mirror was two sinks over. The girl smudged lipstick on the mirror with her thumb. She took her time. She stopped. Twisted the gold lipstick tube in her left hand. Smudged more lipstick onto her thumb. When she was finished, it looked like she had kissed the mirror. She stepped back. Tipped her head. Stepped forward. Cleaned up the edges of the lip marks she'd drawn. She stepped back again, nodded, twisted the gold stick of lipstick closed and stuck the cap on. She dropped the lipstick into her purse. She looked at Mirror and winked. Mirror felt something like love rise up inside her, and then the girl was gone.

The killer is the cream in your coffee, Gwendolyn told Mirror. But Mirror didn't believe Gwendolyn. Mirror believed the killer was Gwendolyn's eyes peering over the top of her computer all day. And Mirror believed the killer was Gwendolyn's curly orange hair. And Mirror believed the killer was the way Gwendolyn had her hair clamped down by those clamps Mirror admired because they seemed like something only a little kid would wear, yet here was a grown adult named Gwendolyn wearing them. And, finally, Mirror believed the killer was Gwendolyn's tongue.

The killer was Gwendolyn's tongue and her ears where they stuck out from her hair being clamped down, and her eyes, and the black makeup Gwendolyn wore on her eyes. You could see right into Gwendolyn through her eyes. It was as if Gwendolyn was translucent in her eyes.

And the killer, Mirror believed, was Gwendolyn's eyebrows. What was so incredible to Mirror was how Gwendolyn could pluck her eyebrows so ruthlessly, yet still have it be the eyebrows that were the killers, along with the eyes and the hair and the chin and the ears and the clamps in her hair.

Mirror found a scrap of paper on the kitchen table after Chappy left for work. It said:
  – read more books
  – do laundry
  – eat food from other countries
Mirror called Chappy. What is this list that says eat more food from other countries on it? she asked when Chappy answered the phone.

There was some silence, then Chappy's voice. I thought I put that in my pocket. That's my to-do list I'm making, Mirror. I just got it started this morning. I was going to add to it over the course of the day.

Mirror loved that Chappy said, over the course of the day. It was like poetry when Chappy said over the course of the day.

Mirror loved Chappy's voice. It was a calm, quiet voice. Very professional, with nothing of the edge that crept into the voices of so many other people Mirror listened to talking every day.

Okay, Mirror said. I gotta go get ready for work.

Are you dressed?

No.

Did you do your hair yet?

Not doing it today.

Excellent.

Not so excellent. But I still have to go.

They said their goodbyes. Mirror did a kissy sound into the phone and Chappy did it back. It was still early. His office would be pretty empty of other staff as of yet.

I never pretended to be smart, Chappy told Mirror.

Well that's okay, Chappy, 'cause you're not that smart anyway.

Why thank you, Mirror. Thank you very much. Chappy looked in his coffee. Like he was looking for clues. Clues to what, though, Mirror wondered. She had no idea. Chappy actually was pretty smart, Mirror knew. He was just clueless about certain things.

I don't know what I've done, Mirror. I never pretended I wouldn't hurt. I don't try to hurt. I don't pretend to know the answers of why I hurt.

Mirror smiled and touched Chappy on his upper arm. He felt warm and his t-shirt was soft. It was the t-shirt he wore at night. He took it off before he got in bed, to feel the sheets on his skin, he told Mirror.

I am not afraid, Mirror. I am not afraid of anything I know about, but I don't pretend to know everything. And I'm not afraid of what I don't know about.

This is what I want, said Chappy. First, I want to thank you very much.

How much?

Very much.

Okay.

And this is what I drive you crazy to have, said Chappy. I want your ears. I love you with your face wet and you begging me to help you and I can.

Mirror's face was wet. She looked away. She felt vulnerable and cold. She hugged herself. Her hair needed brushing.

I can hold you in my words and calm you, said Chappy. But Chappy seemed to Mirror to be hiding whatever was real behind the words he wanted to calm her with. Sit here in these words, said Chappy. I feel very calm now, Mirror. I don't need you to cry. Just look at my words and be calm.

I don't feel calm, Chappy, Mirror said. Maybe you feel calm. But you sound frantic, and you're scaring me. I have to go.

We're not trapped like birds, said Chappy. We're free like birds. There was a silence in the kitchen while these words floated out between Chappy and Mirror. It was the weekend, still pretty early in the morning. Sun was in the kitchen, touching Mirror and giving her highlights. Chappy was beyond the reach of the sun, on the other side of the table.

What are you talking about, Chappy?

Mirror was trying to get something sewn on her sewing machine. It seemed to Chappy she was having a bit of trouble. She had her face down close to the machine and her head twisted sideways to see under the vertical arm of the machine, around where the thread threaded through. She lifted her head away from the machine when Chappy said the thing about birds. She could look at him with her hands still resting on the machine. She looked like she was trying to remember something, and Chappy understood that she was going over in her head the words he had just spoken, trying to remember the precise order that Chappy had ordered them in, and trying then to make order of them herself. She giggled. You're an idiot, she said. What exactly are you trying to say to me here? She shook her head, looked back at her sewing machine, but didn't do anything with it yet, just looked at it.

I'll fly today for all of us if I have to, Chappy said. But come along if you can.

What do you want, Chappy? I don't have time for this. I have some things I need to sew.

I want to be the secret ingredient in something beautiful. I want my life to be a poem about the love I feel. That's all I want.

Mirror looked at Chappy. Oh, okay. I see. She went back to fiddling with her sewing machine.

Chappy knew in his head that he was only really trapped in his head. He felt pretty lucky. He couldn't remember why he'd trapped himself this way. He couldn't bring himself to care about any of this anymore.

After a time, the sun no longer shone through the kitchen window. Then it was shining in the living room for a couple of hours. Then it went behind the townhouses across the way and, eventually, it got dark. The weekend was gone.

Chappy left his rubber boots on the porch and sat down at the wooden table in the middle of his cabin. There was a woman outside on the meadow, trying to reason with her two children. On the far side of the field men worked and waited for the light to fail. It was beginning to fail when Chappy got up and went to see about making himself some dinner.

Men walked by the cabin on their way home from work. Chappy could see the woman with the children through the little window over his kitchen sink. She seemed preoccupied. She'd lost interest in the children. Chappy tried to see the men's faces as they passed by the cabin. Someone on the other side of the settlement was baking pie. Chappy could smell it. The woman looked up. Chappy wasn't sure if she could see him inside the cabin. She seemed to be looking at him. The children were aware of Chappy, as they were aware of the sky and the ground underneath them and the wind taking their hair on its short trip away from their scalps. They were aware of Chappy in the same way they were aware of everything, like fish feeling the pulse of water from a motor boat far away on top of their lake. The woman stood, walked to the door of Chappy's cabin. Chappy opened the door before the woman could knock. The woman said nothing. Her dress looked ragged, but clean. She nodded to Chappy. As though acknowledging something she had heard inside Chappy of which he was not aware. The children are under the trees, the woman said. They love no one and no one loves them.

Chappy didn't know what to say.

They are very sad, said the woman.

What is it you like so much about that photograph, Chappy? Is that you in the picture?

Chappy said nothing.

It's you. Isn't it? said Mirror.

No.

Fuck you, Chappy. Don't mess with me. Mirror pulled at the hem of her dress. Let me see your feet, she said. Take off your shoes.

Why? What are you going to do to my feet?

The boy in the picture has bare feet. I want to see your feet. I'll be able to tell if that boy is you if I see your bare feet.

Chappy looked at Mirror. He loved that she thought she could I.D. him by seeing his bare feet. He bent down and untied his shoe laces. He pulled his shoes off, and then his socks. He stood on the kitchen linoleum. The light over the sink was on, but not the overhead light. Mirror went to the wall and switched on the overhead light. She went back to where Chappy was standing and got down on her hands and knees and peered at Chappy's feet. She beckoned to him to give her the picture. Chappy handed her the picture. She held it beside Chappy's feet. They're yours, she said. This boy is you. Look how he has his fingers in his mouth. Just like you.

I don't have my fingers in my mouth, Mirror.

Mirror grabbed Chappy's hand and pulled it close to her face. She was kneeling in front of him. She held the picture close to his hand. They're your fingers, she said with some vehemence. Aren't they? The fringe of blond hair peeking out from under the cap of the boy in the picture broke Mirror's heart.

Who will lead us to salvation? Chappy asked. Anyone? He looked at Mirror. Mirror somehow felt she was being accused of not leading the people to salvation. She knew that this wasn't what Chappy meant. But it might be a subconscious thing. Weren't boys always trying to get girls to save them, and weren't girls always trying to save boys.

Somehow I doubt it, Chappy said. No one is going to lead us to salvation.

What about an ongoing awareness session? Mirror said. It was one of the tactics they'd developed and had been using at the sporadic meetings they held at the kitchen table.

They called this tactic ongoing awareness sessions, but neither really knew the origin of that term or what it could possibly mean, beyond a vague notion of what an awareness session might be and how it might go on and thus become ongoing. They'd tried having meetings every Sunday morning, but they were generally too tired, and happy to stay quiet, and it didn't seem like much of a meeting if everyone in the meeting stayed quiet and just drank coffee.

We could go out. On a day-by-day basis. There's been some discussion, right? Is this the right approach? Christ, we wasted time. We found new and incredibly innovative ways to waste our time. Then, they paid us back. They talked and they wouldn't stop talking. So what do you do in a case like that? You kill them. You fucking kill them. Dead. That will shut them up. Yet, they are so nice when they aren't talking.

The lake was small. It stood at the end of a long field that seemed, from high in the air, utterly devoid of life. As the plane drew closer to the ground, the owl-eyed boy could see the tops of the trees, densely packed, like a layer of bright green cloud below him. There were clouds rolling on the blue sky, and the painfully bright sun angling forward, attacking the horizon, pushing shadows over the lake. I'll bring it down on the lake, the pilot said. The owl-eyed boy barely heard the pilot's words. He leaned forward and saw the lake. It's a small lake, said the owl-eyed boy. And then he said nothing.

At the far end of the lake, a wall of rock rose forever into the sky, the plane a small insect in the face of the giant cliff. The plane was still well above the ground when it crossed over the shoreline and headed out over the lake, toward the wall of rock. The owl-eyed boy wanted to keep track of his life. He had a notebook open in his lap, a pen in his hand. The plane continued on toward the wall of rock. The owl-eyed boy wanted to use only special words in his notebook. He wanted to join words together in a way that kept them safe. When the owl-eyed boy looked up from his notebook, the wall looked close. The owl-eyed boy felt he wanted to stop words from spiraling away out of his control. He wanted to stop them losing all meaning. He wanted to end this desperate insistence on story.

The plane banked. I'll bring it around, said the pilot, so we won't be headed toward the cliff when we hit the lake.

The pontoons touched. Water sprayed. The owl-eyed boy felt his body lurch. The plane slowed as the pontoons cut into the dark choppy water of the lake. Clouds tangled in the sky, throwing darkness over the place on the lake where the plane was juddering into the questionable substance that made up the top few feet of the lake.

The plane stopped fifty feet from shore. The engine died.

The lake gets shallow here, the pilot said. I can't get any

closer. Water lapped against the pontoons, making a bumping sound. The plane rocked. The owl-eyed boy felt cold air seep into the cabin. It smelled of oily water and pine. The pilot disconnected his seatbelt. The strap retracted. The shoreline was moving. The plane was drifting. The pilot looked to where the owl-eyed boy was looking. When the owl-eyed boy looked back, the pilot smiled. But, to the owl-eyed boy, the pilot looked sad.

To the pilot, it seemed certain there would be trouble. Whether it would be trouble for the owl-eyed boy, or for the pilot himself, he wasn't clear. It would be a complicated sort of trouble. The plane might go down in the woods. The pilot would have to hike back toward the lake and find the owl-eyed boy. The boy doesn't look afraid, the pilot thought. He looks quite sure of himself. I'm the one who is in trouble here. Can you swim? the pilot asked.

Years later, in a dream, the pilot ran down the lake. The owl-eyed boy was gone. The pilot ran until the dream ended.

Did you see, Chappy? Did you even see?

Mirror was writing in her journal. She felt deeply alone on the couch, sinking down into the cone of light shed by the lamp above her. Chappy was reading on the other couch. The fridge was humming. Otherwise, the house was silent. It wasn't a bad house, Mirror knew. Don't misunderstand, she wrote. I'm reduced to something so raw, it hurts to walk. She put the end of the pen to her lips and thought. I have made me like this, she wrote. I see that the me that made me like this can pull me back out, and the me that pulls me back out can make me stumble and crawl. I walk and I almost stop. I speak and I move again. I want to fall and fall and stop and be held. I don't care if I feel frantic or happy or savage. I just want to lie safe somewhere and die safe there for a while and stop being alone, speaking such loneliness as words always speak. I want to speak wounds and feel them on my tongue.

I came home early yesterday, Chappy told Mirror. I took a long hot bath and read till my eyes started closing. Then I put on a most gorgeous Avro Part symphony. I never knew how beautiful his music can be.

It can be beautiful, can't it, said Mirror.

Chappy smiled. Yes, he said. It can. Chappy smiled a bit more. It seemed as though Chappy looked serene, although Mirror couldn't be sure. Mirror wanted to hear his voice again, coming out of that serene look he had.

Then what did you do, Chappy? After your bath and the Avro Part.

Chappy looked at Mirror, focussed suddenly, and the thing that Mirror had seen in his face and loved so much was gone.

I sat at the kitchen window, said Chappy. He looked away from Mirror. I was waiting for the owl-eyed boy to come home. When he got home, he looked up and saw me in the window and his face lit up.

When my kid calls and gets my machine, Chappy told Ingrid, he always says: Where are you, Daddy? Don't you ever do any work there? All you ever do is buy coffee.

It's true, said Ingrid. She laughed. You've got a smart kid.

I know, said Chappy. They laughed together, then Ingrid

went back to work and Chappy went to buy some coffee.

Chappy took the owl-eyed boy camping.

a.m. 11:50-12:15
Dear Mommy
Today is Monday! Were not at the camp site yet. I'm doing a great job on navigating! It's raining. Me and daddy saw cows standing up! We saw this baby cow. It looked so, so cute! After that, we saw this car crash! One only had a bad crash and another had a giant dent in the door, wires sticking out of the roof and a lot of wirers cut off and the hood cut off and the cut off wires were in the trunk.
Sincerely, O.

P.S. We saw a mini pony and a cow together!

3:05-3:15 p.m.
Dear Mommy
We have arrived at Port Burwell. We have an excellent campsite with shade and privacy and the owl-eyed boy says he will probably go pee in the trees. Right now the owl-eyed boy is roasting marshmallows. It is now 3:05 in the afternoon, July 7. The owl-eyed boy is an excellent help setting up a campsite. It was the easiest time I've ever had putting up our tent. It just popped up the first time. He helped put up the kitchen and move the picnic table (you know how hard it is to move those things). The owl-eyed boy pumped up the air mattress by himself and then loaded in all the sleeping bags and pillows. It poured just before we got to Woodstock – I could hardly see out the windshield – but by

the time we got to highway 19, the rain had stopped. Right
now the sun is just breaking through so we are thinking of
heading to the beach.
Love, Daddy

P.S. today is still Monday.

Mr. Dude
by Owl

I came from this weird place and it looks funny. I like the
place I came from. It's fun! I like those silver and gold circles
you call money. Once I got some and went to the big M!
I like to sleep in my mush. Once I went up this thing that
moved. I went into the thing. I pressed the top button on the
little pad thingy (I ran away because I don't like that thing
anymore) I felt a cool breeze (whatever that is) then I looked
over the side of the huge thing that I was on and something
almost came out of my mouth! I was so scared I jumped off
the tall thingy. You should try it, it's fun! Then I spread out
the wings I got from Toys R Us (whatever that is) I looked
on the side of them and it said "caution, not for skydiving"
then, just that second I landed on some white fluffy things.
I think they were in a truck (I know that much about your
planet). I ended up getting kicked out and back into my pile
of mush. I got two of those white fluffy things. They're fun!

Chappy slipped out of the tent when the owl-eyed boy
was asleep. He came out into dark and wind. Four lights
lit the long lanes along the lake. Beyond that: deep dark,
spoiled, depression-framed chicanery. Kids on bikes on the

beach, visible under lights momentarily, then gone, popping wheelies and screeching: I will never surrender!

I will never surrender, Chappy thought. He felt himself sway in wind. There were no trees, no buildings to stop the wind, just fields of short-cut grass and the lake on the end of everything. White sailcloth lifted. Wind. Popping. Stuttering. Loud. The wind died. The sailcloth sank. Silence.

You will die! Perry winked.

Are you nuts? said Chappy. But no one heard. The loudness of the wind tunnel they lived in incapacitated words.

From the cupboard: God saw the end. But he kept it to himself. No use alarming people, he thought. I'm tired, he thought. I'll be glad when it's over. Without the people, God was nothing. Unnamed. Unloved. Un-hated.

I've got a hole in my chin, Chappy said.

What are you talking about? Mirror put her hands on her hips. You need sleep, Chappy.

I need to investigate the possibilities, Chappy said.

No, said Mirror. Definitely not. I refuse to allow it. You cannot investigate everything, Chappy. You could investigate for the rest of your life, but eventually you have to give up. You have to stop investigating and go to sleep. Then you can get up refreshed and go out. You need to stop investigating and get out into the world. You won't die.

I will die.

No, Chappy. You won't.

Everybody dies.

Okay, yes. Eventually, yes, everybody dies. But you won't die from giving up investigating and getting some sleep. You might die if you don't get some sleep. You will die, actually, if you don't get enough sleep.

Hello, my name is Little Boy.

Who are you talking to? Mirror laughed. She thought it was funny when Chappy made up new names for himself. Chappy had the phone on his ear. It looked like a little ornament stuck to the side of his head. There was a sore spot on Chappy's scalp and he kept rubbing at it.

Goldie? God? Chappy shook his head and pulled the phone away from his ear. He looked at it like he would maybe kill it, or maybe it would kill him. He looked a bit disgusted, and a bit afraid, and Mirror thought he was going to drop the phone and stomp on it, but he merely flicked a button with his thumb to end the connection.

Who was that, Chappy?

Goldie.

Who's Goldie?

Goldie is Stan's wife.

Mirror had no idea who Stan was, but she knew better than to press the issue. Where did you meet Goldie and Stan, Chappy?

On the phone.

No, I mean, where did you meet them originally?

Oh. I don't know.

What did they want?

I'm not sure. I hope they don't call back. That was confusing.

You're confusing.

I know. I'm sorry, Mirror.

Don't be. I have to go out in half an hour. Mom is picking me up.

Okay.

This is my way of saying, fuck you, I don't need you.

Sometimes I feel afraid. Sometimes I feel defiant. Sometimes I can even relax and be alone in peace. But I am always alone.

When I met you, I felt I'd met someone who saw what loneliness really is. Saw it, and wanted it.

All I've ever wanted, Chappy, is to say, Fuck you, I want to be alone, and for there to be no repercussions. For you to go on loving me when I say fuck you and for you to come back so I can say fuck you again, until one day, maybe I don't say fuck you anymore.

Doesn't everybody want to be alone, and they lie to themselves, and to everybody else, lie so deep they don't believe themselves anymore and they think they really want to be with other people all the time.

When you tell me a story, do you feel that you are simply saying what you want to say? How does a person just say what he wants to say? What if a person wants to say something that isn't something that can be said? What if what a person wants to say isn't something he knows how to say without saying it some way that isn't just saying what he wants to say? What if he wants to fuck around and try to say things in ways that the things he wants to say can't seem to be said, ways indifferent to what he's been saying all along?

It is very cold here today, Chappy, Mirror wrote in her notebook.

*

Chappy was at the heavy wooden table in the middle of his cabin. He'd just finished making the table out of wood he got in the forest. He was trying the table out. He wanted to try it out in a way that seemed appropriate. Chappy thought about having a big meal at the table. Having a big meal seemed like an okay way to try out the table.

I have no idea how to respond to the things you prove to me, Chappy wrote. With your theories and proofs. I have to ride home in the icy cold wind. Tomorrow, I go to court. Hope all is well in la la land. My best to the Zee folks. Ta ta. He was in a bad way. Chappy knew this. He knew he had nothing. He knew that nothing mattered. Even right now, sitting on the pot, shitting, Chappy knew he had nothing.

At his new table, a table he'd made himself from wood he'd gone out and got from the forest, Chappy saw that he had nothing. There was no meeting. There were no doughnuts. You couldn't even get doughnuts in the village. Chappy no longer drank coffee, mostly because this was something else you couldn't get in the village. You had to cross the river to get coffee, and Chappy knew that if he crossed the river he might never come back. It wasn't that he loved this place so much. He couldn't even bring himself to love this table, a table he'd formed with his own hands. It was basically inertia that kept him from going over the river. He was too tired to find out if he needed to continue this endless journey.

Why should you care about me? Chappy asked Mirror. Mirror was sitting by the fire. She said nothing for a moment. She stared at the fire, watched it writhe. She looked at Chappy.

Because you do something important, Chappy.

Chappy looked at Mirror. His face was knotted up in concentration. Why didn't you care before? he asked.

I did, Chappy. I always cared. You just didn't get that.

Why should I care that you care? said Chappy. Who are you? I don't even know you. Why should you matter to me? Why am I suddenly so important to you? Am I just an opportunity for you, Mirror? Why are you so eager to turn me into something other than what I am? I am a man at a table that I made in a cabin that I discovered in a village where music falls from the sky once a year on a cold night in the middle of winter. What do you want to turn me into, Mirror? Why does reinterpreting who I am seem like a good idea to you?

It doesn't.

Mirror was asleep on the only bed in the cabin, with the owl-eyed boy tucked up close beside her. Chappy was talking to himself over near his table. I'll talk to her nicely, he whispered. He didn't want to wake Mirror. It wasn't a matter of being considerate. Chappy needed this time alone to talk to himself.

Chappy was putting on new underwear. He ripped the cellophane pack the underwear came in. He extracted the underwear. It was black underwear. Chappy put the cellophane on the edge of the bed. He pulled the underwear up over his wiener and bum. Mirror was sitting on the bed in the soft light from the bedside lamp, which was the only light in the room. The curtains were blackout curtains and they shut out all light from outside.

Will you give me love? Chappy asked.

Mirror had coffee on the bedside table beside her. The steam from the coffee wisped up from its surface.

Will you give me God? Chappy asked.

Mirror picked up her coffee. She sipped. She was in her nighty, but she wasn't cold.

Will you give me a comprehensive list? What will you give me, Mirror?

God?

Will you give me God?

I'll give you God.

Will you give me Kate?

Who's Kate? Mirror set her coffee down on the bedside table.

Will you give me funding? Will you fund my project, Mirror? Chappy stood up in just his underwear and looked at Mirror.

Yes, Mirror said. She lifted her feet from the floor, turned onto the bed, tucked her knees up under her chin, and tucked her toes under the edge of the blanket. She pulled the blanket over her body, up to her chin. She slipped down a little in the bed, but stayed sitting up a little so she could drink her coffee. She looked at her coffee, but did not yet pick it up.

The black blank sun of God pursues me, Chappy said.

Are you composing? Mirror asked. Do I even need to be here this morning, Chappy? Could you maybe go into the bathroom and do this. I think I might go back to sleep now.

I helped shine the green! Chappy exclaimed. He had his clothes on now, everything but his socks. He was pulling one sock on, but his other foot was still bare. He was trying to get his socks on while standing up.

Renew the western hills, Caroline, Chappy said. He had the sock on and his foot back down safely on the floor and Mirror felt relief that he hadn't fallen.

Get ye to a haberdashery, Chappy said. Glow on nor we fly.

Who's Caroline? Mirror asked. Who were all these women Chappy kept mentioning in the mornings?

Chappy's tie was knotted but still loose, lying on his shirt, like a noose just after the hangman drops it over a man's head but hasn't cinched it up yet. Why was Chappy wearing a tie today? Did it have something to do with Caroline or Kate?

God is next to cleanliness, Chappy said. Holy cows.

Do you mean holy vows?

Mid-sized cars, Chappy said. Little brains. Do the fucking math. Do a fucking meeting. Big ideas. Workbooks. The hearts of staff today. The long fields we walk in. Let us know what you think. Hate us. Love us. Don't care. You suck. You rock.

You have a meeting today, don't you? Mirror asked.

Yes, said Chappy. He had his other sock on now, but both socks were not pulled up properly and little flaps of sock stuck out ahead of his toes and flopped onto the floor as he walked out of the bedroom.

Mirror pulled her knees up, still under the blankets, and hugged them to her chest. She looked at her coffee.

Don't snore, Daddy, said the owl-eyed boy.

Chappy lifted his head a little from the pillow and looked down at himself. He was still in his work clothes. He was lying on the side of the owl-eyed boy's bed, one foot on the floor, the shoe still on it.

Don't whisper words of wisdom, Daddy.

Let it be, Chappy mumbled. He was falling asleep again.

Chappy was somewhere else, the owl-eyed boy knew. Daddy was in bed beside him, but he was somewhere else at the same time and this confused and excited the owl-eyed boy. It seemed that a person could be two places at once and it made the owl-eyed boy excited just to think about it.

Times of trouble, Chappy said. Don't cry for me, Argentina.

Who is Argentina? the owl-eyed boy asked.

What do I do when I'm feeling sad or alone, said Chappy. I have this pool in my mind, with really blue water, only it isn't water, it's acid.

Mirror wasn't sure she was ready for this.

I try to feel the depth of that pool. I swim down and try to touch bottom while still knowing I can make it back up without running out of breath.

Do you ever touch bottom, Chappy?

It's impossibly deep, Mirror.

I know, said Mirror. She knew Chappy was making this up as he went along and that it was coming out of a place she didn't want to know about.

Mirror heard Chappy, but chose to continue with her letter.

Bring it, she wrote.

She would never send this letter.

Run in the wind, she wrote.

But who was she writing to?

Now Chappy entered the letter. He was standing in the street with a knife.

Only he wasn't Chappy. He was another Chappy. A

Chappy she'd engineered in her imagination. A Chappy who,
at times, ran in the wind.

It's so cold today, Chappy said after he closed the door. He
stomped his feet on the mat.

Mirror was behind the row of hanging plants that dangled
over the back of the couch. She didn't turn to look at Chappy,
but she said, Hi, Chappy. Welcome home.

The wind bit my nuts off, Chappy said. Bits of snowflake
were still in Chappy's eyelashes, like something sawed off
God's beard. Like God's breath frozen in Chappy's hair. So
cold, Chappy said.

Mirror tried to think of something warm to say to
Chappy.

She died, Chappy said.

Who died? the owl-eyed boy said.

Chappy and the owl-eyed boy were out in the big field
that rose above the ravine like a flying saucer launching pad.
The snow was up to the owl-eyed boy's knees. The owl-eyed
boy was dressed in a snowsuit with the hood up and a scarf
over his face.

She's gone, Chappy said.

Who, Daddy? Where is she now?

They were sitting side by side in the snow, having just
finished a long hike through the ravine and over the ice of
the river.

Have a piece of snow, little one, Chappy said. He handed
the owl-eyed boy a chunk of snow he'd dug out from beside
where he was sitting. It was pristine. No one had been out in
the field since it snowed last night. They were the first.

Have some cake, Daddy, the owl-eyed boy said, holding out his own piece of snow.

Chappy took the cake and bit off a small piece. Mmmm, he said. Quite good. Did you make it?

Yes.

On Wednesday, Mirror said, I got another phone call. But she could tell that, once again, Chappy was not listening.

Some years ago, Chappy said, I walked in the large coldness of winter. I don't know when this happened, Mirror, but it's still here, it's still with me. Chappy looked up. He looked up directly at Mirror. Mirror almost succumbed to her desire to interject herself into Chappy's moment and figure into his life again, if only for the moment, but she waited to hear what came next. She thought perhaps Chappy might spontaneously come out of the space he was in and rejoin her. It was not unprecedented. Yet, somehow, she held out very little hope. All that's left of the motion in that coldness, though, said Chappy, is the square smallness of warmth coming out the door behind, and that awful cold, and the snowflakes first starting. The first snowflakes.

When the wind pushed the clouds apart, the sun took a sharp piece out of the automobile. Mirror walked toward Chappy. She was shaped like a river.

After the nurses got the thing wrapped up and left them there with it, and it was just Chappy and Mirror and this thing wrapped up, Chappy said, What do you want to call him?

Mirror pulled the blanket away from his face so they could see him better. His eyes look like owl eyes, she said.

They went home without naming him. It was nine o'clock when Mirror fell asleep. Chappy sat on the edge of the bed, waiting.

God help us when the morning comes, Chappy said.

The morning is still hours away, said Mirror. Come, Chappy, and lie with me. Mirror was on the couch. They had all the lights out. The curtains were open. The houses across the street were dark. Mirror's eyes shone in the bit of light from the moon. The street lights planted variously augmented shadows about the playground out back. Mirror had a blanket up to her chin. She was lying on her side. Chappy was sitting on the other couch. The clock on the coffee table blinked red in the darkness. Morning never comes, said Mirror, her voice floating like the silence that hovers above the world when no one is dreaming anymore. But, like with Chappy and Mirror, another layer of darkness hardly mattered. Morning hasn't come yet, said Mirror.

Brown eyes, sang Chappy. Bring me down. Bring me down, baby. He emphasized the baby and stomped his foot.

What is that song? asked Mirror.

I have no idea. I've been trying to figure it out all morning.

Chappy was no longer trying to rescue himself. He was too tired to rescue himself. So he just put on more coffee and sat down to face the paralyzingly heartbreaking truth about himself.

Chappy and Mirror and the owl-eyed boy were trying to get up the hill again. This time it was Chappy who gave up first. Fuck it, he thought. He turned to go back home. He glanced over his shoulder. The hill was gone.

Chappy was doing a synopsis of the book he was reading. Mirror had her reading glasses on, but she was looking over top of them at Chappy as he spoke. The man's talent was that he could hold his breath underwater for a long time, Chappy said. I don't want to hold my breath under water any longer, the man said when he was nine years old. He gave up holding his breath. He took an office job. He lived a long life. When he died, there was no one who remembered how long he could hold his breath.

That's it? That's the whole book. Where do you get these books, Chappy?

The library.

They have books like that at the library?

Kiss me here, Chappy, said Mirror. She pointed to a place near her bottom lip. Then go to your book club. I'll be all right. I'll be sitting here, right here, when you get home. Wear your red coat. It's cold out there today. But you will be beautiful inside the wind with your red coat flapping on the way from the car to the house where the book club meets tonight.

Mirror was disappearing into her face. It was the strangest thing. If she glanced at herself in the mirror, she could barely see herself in there. Chappy said he could hear her when she talked, like someone trapped inside a closet. Like she was trapped inside her clothes, or her makeup. But the harder Mirror tried to look for herself inside her eyes, the smaller her eyes seemed to get.

There comes a time when words break free of the world and ballast themselves, seeking other words to cling to and ward off. When this happens, each word is lost as soon as it passes. But this is always the way with words. When the words break free, they leave nothing behind, seek nothing and kindle nothing. These words leave the world to be what it already was. They stand beyond, but parallel to the world, for they come themselves as absolute being. At this point, there can be no love, no hate, no attachment of any kind. All there can be is just wonder, like the open mouth of the wind, felt by all, yet subject to none.

Chappy wanted to put his thumbs on Mirror's eyelids and rub her makeup off. But he didn't. Mirror was crying so hard that her makeup was running down her face. Suddenly, Chappy could see her again. He could see her reflected in the black tears that ran down her cheeks. He could see how hot those tears must feel to Mirror. They were everyone's tears, Chappy decided. They were his tears. He put his tongue on Mirror's cheek. Took her tears inside his mouth. Climb in, Chappy, Mirror said. She laughed, but the tears kept coming.

It's a big lake. But it isn't amazing because of how big it is, or how it stretches in every direction as far as you can see. It's amazing because of that one speck of foam that pushes past the pebbles on the shore and joins with its brothers to batter the beach.

Last time I saw Heather, she was patting that stupid sheep, said Chappy.

Who is Heather, said Mirror. She was looking at a paper on the table in front of her, maybe a letter she had written the night before and was hoping to mail today. She was maybe a little distracted, and, so, not having been paying strict attention, she didn't hear exactly what Chappy said.

But the words got into her brain and she brought them back,
like candy in a window, like windy meadows come back
sometimes in your memories of windy meadows. Why was
Heather patting a sheep? That seemed odd. Mirror stopped
looking at the paper on the table. She looked up at Chappy.

I hated that sheep, said Chappy.

Onward, they say, Chappy said.
Who says that, Chappy?
But whither to?
Whither?
Blither.
De dither.

I know I'm alone, said Chappy.
Mirror looked up.
I know that I choose to be alone. Everything I do is a way
of asserting my aloneness.
You're not alone, Chappy. You have me.
It's my way of always saying, fuck you, I don't need
you.
Mirror said nothing. Chappy wasn't talking about her, she
felt. He wasn't talking about anyone. He was just talking.
Sometimes I feel afraid, Mirror. Sometimes I feel defiant.
Sometimes I can even relax and be alone in peace. But I am
always alone.
I know, Chappy.
If I meet someone who understands that, sees that
loneliness, really sees why I am so alone, what can I do with
such a person?
You can say you love me.

I love you, Mirror.

I know that, Chappy.

But so far, saying fuck you seems the only way I can really say I love you and mean it. No matter how much I love you, I can't seem to say I love you unless I say it like fucking you.

I'm sorry, Chappy, said Mirror. Is there anything I can do to help you?

You've already done enough, Mirror, said Chappy. You've made me understand that hatred is worthless. But hatred just seems to live in me somewhere. It's something I just can't ever seem to escape entirely.

The owl-eyed boy was hopping about in the hall outside Chappy's and Mirror's bedroom. He was chanting: My foot's asleep. My foot's asleep.

Chappy closed the door so they wouldn't have to listen to him.

Mirror laughed.

Chappy went over and opened the window. He opened it as wide as it would go. Bedtime was growing increasingly scary as Chappy grew older. It calmed him to hear the muted nighttime noises of the neighbourhood. People are still up, Chappy said to Mirror, but he didn't turn to look at her, he kept his face close to the screen, looking out at the street.

A garage door crunched shut. A car whooshed its tires on the street at the end of the complex. The distant sound of cars far away on the main street of town was the same as the sound of wind in the trees when Chappy was going to sleep at night as a boy at the cottage.

One side wasn't functioning properly, so Chappy forced the cloth in further, but the tinkling sound continued. Outside the window, a robin made a terrible sound, but Chappy didn't want to get out of bed to close the window. He looked at the guitar no one played anymore, sitting in the corner, on the floor.

Chappy came home after riding his bike a long way. It was dark outside and he stood in the porch light. He leaned his bike against the wall. He was wearing blue pants, baggy and spackled with mud and snow. His red and silver jacket had a hood that fell over his back. He still had his helmet on. Mirror saw him, but Chappy didn't know she was there. Mirror saw the look of riding that made Chappy's eyes look bright. Chappy undid the chin strap of his helmet and lifted it off his head. He hung the helmet from the handlebars of his bike. Mirror wanted to collect Chappy out of the story he was living and have something real outside the story. She saw his eyes in the porch light, reflecting the dark of night behind and the moon. But Mirror didn't really want to collect Chappy out of the story. She wanted him to stay the way he was, so she could watch him like that, with him totally unaware of her.

Chappy turned away from the house and looked up at the sky. It was cold and his breath made steam that drifted, lazy in the calm night air. Chappy looked up at the moon. It hung halfway up the sky. It stood like an icon, a tab of butter in the middle of a dark blue plate, a button on the night. Chappy reached up to push it, then turned. Mirror saw that he was a character in a story, and that when the story ended, Chappy would be gone, like someone dead and released, and Mirror knew that when Chappy was gone she would still be here, the book in her lap, maybe still open to the last page. Mirror knew that when that day came, she would be sad and empty, because Chappy had been alive for her, but now he was gone. Mirror could go back and read the book again, but she already knew everything there was to know about Chappy. It seemed to Mirror that she knew more about Chappy than Chappy did.

When you cry, Chappy told Mirror, it's like time travel. You always cry in the same moment you cried in the last time you cried.

Could you cry in a moment someone else cried in?

Maybe.

Maybe you could cry in a moment Bach cried in. You could cry in a moment when he finished composing his music and heard himself play it back for the first time.

You know more than the man who wrote me into this story. You knew me for a time and now I'm gone. How is that different from the conversation you have with your kids at dinner tonight and why would you rather read my story than watch your kids alive? See me from the window. Freeze. Be afraid of the deep longing you feel climbing through your body and touching you from the inside like little hands inside your veins. Your mouth slightly open, as if to whisper something, something you can't name, and you stand like that for a time at the window, watching, until finally I walk up the walk and stand on the porch with the dark, dark blue behind me. I know you want to catch beauty, like a trick you can do that gives you delight. You close the book and go toward your day. While you are gone, I bend to take off my shoes. I'm damp with sweat. You smell my sweat all day, everywhere you go: with your kids as you take them to school; as you drive to work; as you take the bus, walk, shop, eat. All day you remember me inside the book, waiting to do what I've already done. You smell my sweat and you feel me touch your arm and you pull me to you and you feel me hug you in the hall by the door and you whisper something in my ear and I don't know what it means. You imagine that you put your lips in the hollow between my shoulder and my neck. You taste salt there, but it's only ever your own salt you're tasting. You hold me tight in the spaces your mind makes for me and you want to keep me there like that, and you never want to let me go because we are remembering a story together, a story I once told you about two lovers who loved each other in a book, but never met one another – never even actually existed. Finally, you pull away and look into your day, but you have me still there in your eyes and the people you pass see you are somewhere else. They see that your eyes look hurt and alive and excited and lost. They see in your eyes the family that waits back where you've come from and the fear you feel for them and you close your eyes gently with your fingers to try to hide me from everyone you pass. Don't look away from what you see. Fill up with the hurt I give. Let strangers see in your eyes something buried so deep under the shiny surface that they have no idea what it could possibly be. They only know that if they go in your eyes, they'll never find a way out again, and you know this too, so you only let them in so far. You want to take care of me in my book back at home. But I'll always look past you, and I'll always do exactly what I did the first time, and the second time, and that can never change. Right now you hold me, and without the book there, and because you haven't finished the book, you can hope and believe that anything is possible. But, of course, it isn't. Let me a little way into your eyes, just for a while, until you pick up the book again, and we can't see each other again. Take my hand and lead me into the places you inhabit in the real world. Share me with the world. Expose me.

Bach sits in that tree over there. You see him, Mirror? His hands are those leaves fluttering in the wind.

One time, Chappy decided to try to save his marriage. He was alone in his cabin, trying to plot the trip home on a tattered map that showed where he was, but not where he needed to go. He drew a line out to the edge of the map. He grew very afraid and sad. Now it was like he could suddenly see the truth, and he could remember Mirror making all kinds of excuses not to be alone with him. He dreamed that when he got in bed with Mirror, she said, I guess I better go sit with the owl-eyed boy, and she took her book and left and Chappy found himself shivering in the dark in his cabin. He realized that every night, when he went to bed alone in the cabin, he was going to bed without Mirror, and because of this Mirror was constantly there.

*

Mirror woke Chappy up to stop him being afraid. She rubbed his arm. He crawled onto her and held her and she put her arms around him.

Chappy needed to get a better map. Until he was able to procure a better map, he must again give up trying to win Mirror back. He must stay quietly engaged in his new life in his new cabin and hope that Mirror's trust in him would grow. She had no real reason to trust him, based on all the time he spent so distant from her. But his love felt strong enough sometimes, and he kept thinking Mirror should feel it and respond. He thought she must be so deeply wounded to be so afraid.

Chappy thought of Mirror because she used to touch him a lot. Chappy cried and Mirror held him and then he stopped crying, he looked at Mirror and laughed. I think I'll go wash my face, he said. Will you excuse me?

Later, when Mirror asked him what was wrong, why he cried, he told her nothing was wrong. In fact, Chappy told Mirror, it was the nothing of everything that was making him cry.

Mirror massaged Chappy's shoulders as he sat at his desk. He closed his eyes, leaned back his head on Mirror's chest, and Mirror bent over and whispered something with her lips on his ear.

Secretly, everything continued as it had in the world beyond Chappy and Mirror, right up to the place where their cheeks stuck out a bit below their eyes, which were emeralds shining in the setting of their faces, their faces embracing the infinite, the infinite being nothing other than the climb toward heaven.

Climbing toward heaven, doing nothing on a chair.

Chappy was alone in a room and everything he was doing was the dream of a man sitting alone in a room. Mirror came home from work while the owl-eyed boy was eating and Chappy made some dinner and did the dishes and started some laundry so that the owl-eyed boy would have clean clothes to wear in the morning. Mirror sent Chappy to the mall to get the owl-eyed boy a phone card. It felt like twilight. It had felt like twilight all day. The sun seemed cloaked in various disguises, depending on where you were. At the mall, walking from the car, the sun limned some trees at the perimeter of the parking lot. Get the owl-eyed boy some cash, too, Mirror had said when Chappy was getting in the car. She'd come running out of the house, motioning for Chappy to open the car window. Go to the bank and get some cash, she'd said. He'll need some cash.

*

It was at the mall when something interesting happened.

Chappy was still a man in a chair dreaming. It was dark and it was raining and Chappy walked through the rain from the parking lot to the mall getting wet. He wanted to get wet. Getting wet, he believed, would wake him from this dream he was having.

When Chappy got inside the mall, he saw a guy he used to work with. The guy was Chappy's supervisor at the first job Chappy had. The guy was a friend, too. He lived not far from where Chappy and Mirror lived. The guy didn't see Chappy right away. Chappy thought about going on, taking care of business, not even acknowledging the guy. But, in the end Chappy decided to say hello to the guy. The guy talked for a while. He talked about work. He talked about how awful things were at work. The guy still worked at the same place he worked when he was Chappy's supervisor, but Chappy had worked at other places since. He told the guy, It's the same everywhere. This stopped the guy. Chappy told him a bit about what was going on where he was working now, but the guy had no context, and Chappy couldn't give it to him. He didn't have it in him to give this guy any context. Chappy talked very little. He listened. The guy made Chappy laugh.

Chappy had been thinking he wanted someone to come into the room with him and see the room and him in it and understand. He wanted someone to understand about him being in a room, in a chair, even as he moved through the mall and talked and purchased a phone card and procured some cash. Chappy believed that if someone saw the room he was sitting in, they would understand. But something made him know there was nothing to understand. It was just a man who decided to sit down and dream for a while. But the dream the man was having made him believe it was more and he wanted to make people see that it was more.

Chappy saw a little girl standing by some boxes, putting on her coat. The little girl looked in Chappy's eyes and he thought he might have seen something, but he kept going out into the parking lot. He turned back and looked into the store through the window and saw the little girl doing up her coat, then moving toward the door, toward where Chappy was, but she was not really moving toward Chappy. This girl was on her own journey. But Chappy thought that this little girl was getting left behind, that this little girl's journey was a lonely one. He turned back. The girl was standing in the rain, waiting to get across the road. Take care of yourself, Chappy whispered. He walked to his car. The girl seemed very beautiful standing in the rain, taking care of herself.

Chappy opened an envelope. He'd been planning all day to open the envelope. The letter inside the envelope was from the boss of the universe, although Mirror believed it was probably a letter Chappy had written and sent to himself.

Dear Chappy, the letter began. Chappy read what he'd written, what he'd tried to forget that he'd written.

The letters came back to him in the mail. Sometimes, Chappy claimed, he almost saw the other Chappy, the one who was writing these letters and might or might not be him.

*

In an entirely different way, our joints are exposed, said Chappy. Our breath is taken.

Mirror listened, tried to see where Chappy was going. So far, she didn't get it.

A while ago in history – well, pretty recently, really – said Chappy, a new chapter began in the taking of blue iron. It was a sad time.

Mirror felt worried, as this was not becoming clearer, and Chappy sounded lost inside something dense – he seemed lost inside his mind, or his words, and his mind or his words seemed too dense to traverse. He seemed to be becoming like a plan that's lost its way and is no longer a plan. He was becoming like a pan of scrambled eggs when you push them around the pan too much, or not enough, and they don't become properly scrambled.

Don't worry, Chappy said. Wait.

He seemed very earnest and it was hurting Mirror because she wanted so much to join him wherever it was he was going, but at the same time she didn't want to go to that place they'd gone in the past where nothing made sense anymore. Something was coming to an end and she wanted to crash her head on the cliff that was the ascent to the placid green meadow that she and Chappy were meant to inhabit.

In the atmosphere, at different depths, between cloud layers, the chemical differences are due to colour. All the planets combined cannot hold the mass of the sun, which is ten thousand times greater than that of Jupiter.

Mirror thought she understood some of this.

Heart of control harms your flesh, said Chappy. Humans like to explore.

You want to explore with me, Chappy.

Yes, Mirror, I do.

Me too, said Mirror. She smiled, but her face felt too flat, as though her smile were two-dimensional, and she knew Chappy needed a smile that was at least three-dimensional, if not more.

A disaster is always available, said Chappy, if what you are looking for is disaster.

I'm not looking for a disaster, said Mirror. I'm really not. It's just that... She wasn't sure just what it was.

In the kitchen or the bathroom or the garage, the limits of the possible begin to show themselves. People wake up in these rooms in houses everywhere and wonder what is happening.

Mirror laughed nervously.

Never laugh, Chappy said. Never complain. Worry a little on Wednesdays. Life is always difficult.

This last made enough sense to Mirror to give her a bit of relief. And it seemed that Chappy was through now. He seemed to have run out of words. He stood in front of Mirror, slightly stooped, his mouth open just a little. He looked like someone standing on the other side of a wall of hot wind, and Mirror felt she could not make her way through this wall without compromising herself in one way or another.

At Christie Gardens in Toronto on February 5, 2003, not two kilometres from where Mirror and Chappy lived, Wheeler thanked the staff and left.

It's time to go, Wheeler said.

Chappy stood inside the sound of trees in wind, his mind making words into life. Real life, he thought. His life, the truth of his life, was still there, listening inside his head, leaves rustling above.

Maybe that peculiar sound I hear is something trapped inside the wind, Chappy said.

If the wind stops, said Mirror, does the trapped thing escape, or does it simply disappear with the wind?

Chappy and Mirror heard music together. It might have been just wind. Something inside the wind seemed to sing.

Do you hear that, Chappy? asked Mirror.

Chappy seemed sombre to Mirror, as though the song in the wind shackled him onto some kind of thick tree of immense responsibility that made him wary and slumped him over a little. He seemed to be trying to hold himself up against some extra gravity. Then, suddenly, he looked like a small lost creature stranded at the base of a really big tree. A redwood. Or at the base of a large building, designed for large things, like an airplane hangar, and Chappy alone at the entrance where the planes went in. He looked lonely and beaten and his hair stuck up in a strange manner it had of straying along various junctions of his scalp.

How big was it? Mirror asked.

Chappy looked thoughtful, but said nothing.

For a long time neither of them said anything. Then, for a while after that, both of them said nothing. They watched each other. Waited.

Finally Mirror asked, Did you not get a sense of how big it was?

I did, said Chappy.

Often, if you asked Chappy a question and he didn't answer and you asked the question again in a different manner he would answer right away the second time.

But I'm not sure how to convey the size of it to you, Mirror.

Mirror felt good that Chappy was speaking directly to her.

It was almost as large as something I saw in 1974, encrusted in a space of light.

Mirror waited. This didn't help, but she trusted Chappy to understand this, to go on, to keep trying. She trusted Chappy to work through this without her help.

There was a halo around it, yet I don't think it was as bright as the one my dad saw in 1947. But it was about two magnitudes faster, and swelling.

Mirror continued to wait.

There were feather splotches sprinkled over with stars, leaving not-dark speckled on the sky. Chappy looked at Mirror and Mirror could see that he was proud of himself. And it was true, as obscure as his references were, he'd finally managed to touch something deep inside Mirror, his words lodged physically inside her body, and she was glad she'd been able to hold her fears in abeyance.

In the summer, the parks department hired some girls. Chappy was standing by the living room window, which was big. The light lay oblique across his face, shadowing the side of his face that Mirror was watching. She thought Chappy must have seen something outside to remind him of the girls the parks department hired, but she could see nothing out there that might have had this effect. Chappy might have just been standing by the window thinking, not seeing out the window at all. Mirror had been reading, and Chappy had been silent for so long she'd forgotten he was there, had lost herself entirely in the story she was reading. Blonde headed girls, Chappy said. They wore rubber boots, and rubber gloves that came up to their elbows, and they arrived every Friday morning and shovelled the garbage out of the garbage containers into large green plastic bags with City written on the side.

Three blonde headed girls ran through Mirror's mind.

Chappy turned to look at Mirror. Mirror had her hand on her book, holding it open to the page she was on. When Chappy looked down at the book, she looked down as well. She was tempted to go back to the story. She enjoyed being there. But she thought she should stop and hear Chappy's story. The blonde headed girls were waiting. But the book kept pulling. She slipped the bookmark in and closed it. She set it on the couch beside her. She had her legs tucked up under her. She put her hands in her lap.

There was one girl who seemed to be in charge, Chappy said. She laid the garbage containers on their sides and shovelled up the garbage in a snow shovel. The other girls held the garbage bags.

Mirror wasn't sure how Chappy made these stories seem

so compelling. The story in her book that was sitting beside her on the couch had death and love and drama, yet Chappy's story about these girls from the parks department picking up garbage seemed almost more compelling.

When they're done, Chappy said, they leave with their garbage bags. A while later, a fat guy comes along and stops at each garbage container and writes something down on a clipboard.

Chappy, who had been looking at Mirror all this time, now looked away. Mirror knew he was not done, although she couldn't have said how she knew this. Maybe it was that Chappy stood a certain way when he was in the midst of a story and another way when he was finished.

Chappy continued to look out the window. One morning, the girls came, and I was at my desk, watching them out the window. I guess they must have known I was there. They must have seen me other Fridays and they must have seen me this Friday, too. But they kept their backs to me, and it was like I'd never seen their faces. Maybe I hadn't, although I can't see how this could be. I'd watched them enter that courtyard outside my office every Friday for weeks. But I couldn't remember their faces, and I wanted to see them, but they kept their backs to me the entire time they were shovelling up the garbage. I thought I should just go back to work. There was always too much to do, and I was wasting time waiting to see if these girls would turn around. Then, just as they were about to leave, the one girl turned and looked right at my face, and her face was the face of a girl I'd once known. It wasn't the same girl, but it was this girl's face, except she maybe looked a bit older.

Chappy was struggling. Mirror could hear the struggle of

Chappy trying to tell his story. His story remained compelling, but what compelled her now was the discomfort she felt and her desire to see Chappy extricate himself successfully from the mess he was talking himself into.

If you saw this girl's face, Mirror, you'd think she'd been shovelling garbage all her life. She looked like everything she cared about was deep down inside her and she wasn't about to let any of it out.

Life culminates for Chappy at midnight on December first as he stands at the window and looks out at the rest of the sky blue objects he never often sees. The dog on fire. The crab with the chestnut clusters nearby and the play of Winchsters in the dark shadow lines of morning's approaching machinery. Methane ice crystals touch the lower reaches of sky, well beneath the white ceiling of cloud. Shades of blue as another star appears and pushes Chappy to the edge of night, to the place where we all end up at the culmination of our journeys. Chappy's fainter companion, Mirror, was long in bed, the dark curling about her wavy hair like an old-fashioned hair dryer. The bar-shaped brightness burned itself onto Chappy's retina, reminding him of yearlings embedded in their nests, the dead ones at the base of the tree in clots of earth, or riding the bumpers of four-wheel-drive vehicles.

Chappy could hear Mirror hearing the sound of shovels.

We should leave, said Chappy.

We might leave, said Mirror. Or we might not, she said.

Mirror had long ago made it clear she was in charge of leaving. Chappy could have his say, and sometimes Mirror felt the sincerity of his claim and gave in, but mostly she just ignored him.

It's an endless land out there, Mirror.

It is, Chappy. It totally is.

She could get caught up in these wild rides, too, even if, unlike Chappy, she had the presence of mind to stay her course.

They went out and ran in circles in the yard, their breath rising above them in spirals that wound into nothing just above their heads. They spelled their names backward with their boots in the snow. They taught each other tumbling motions throughout the morning and into the early afternoon, until they were too tired to continue. They rolled and stretched and shimmied.

Look how this morning can define the point of who we are, Chappy, Mirror said.

But Chappy had rolled to the bottom of a hill and could not hear Mirror. He lay still, feeling patches of snow melt on the bits of skin exposed where his pants rode above his ankles. It felt like snakes abandoning the warm bath of his bloodstream.

Mirror lay quietly in the bed listening to Chappy speak softly.

In Messier, West Virginia, six centimetres short of the dark band, but much more interesting than the dark band at low powers, the middle part of the core has two brighter portions separated by slightly darkening tips. With the silvery distance of the galaxy behind, the entire problem becomes distinctly mottled. The eastern lump is elongated near the edge, conspicuous and larger, brightening by two thirds.

Mirror felt like the angel who has fallen back on her wings and can no longer get up, now faced with the prospect that she might never fly again. She cried in silence at the void left in the wake of Chappy's voice, after his description of something she would never understand had lengthened into an interminable pain in her heart.

While Chappy was telling a story, Mirror felt a sense of new possibility present itself. It wasn't the story and it wasn't Chappy that made her feel this way. It was both. It was the fact that Chappy could tell such stories.

After the man turned into a butterfly each night, Chappy said, he clung to the wall of his cave, afraid to move.

You'll have a different teacher every year, Chappy said.

The owl-eyed boy looked at Chappy.

You're pretty quiet, said Chappy.

The owl-eyed boy never listened to Chappy anyway. Chappy blathered on.

The owl-eyed boy was playing with the elements, as he called them. These were elements that Chappy couldn't see, or even imagine.

The owl-eyed boy did talk to himself sometimes, Chappy knew. But he also sometimes did talk to Chappy as well, but he talked to Chappy about topics that had absolutely nothing to do with what Chappy was trying to talk to him about. It was like a little duet, or like warming up for a duet, with the owl-eyed boy playing one instrument and Chappy playing a different instrument, and neither of them taking any heed of the notes the other one is playing.

Hello. This is Mirror.

Hello, Mirror. Please step forward as a voice beyond denial.

Mirror stepped forward. She stepped forward into the words she was hearing in her head.

Please rescue denial as a valid activity.

Where are you going, Mirror? Chappy asked.

But this was not the right question. He understood this as soon as he asked it. Where are you? Chappy asked Mirror, and that seemed more accurate, more in tune with something that was emanating from somewhere, not from him, not from Mirror, but from somewhere nearby.

How can we threaten the poem, Chappy? Mirror asked. She looked at him. She was in the middle of the living room now, moving slowly in no particular direction, trying to get closer to whatever it was that was calling to her across the great divide of her mind, across the canyon of cranium that stood between her and understanding. How can we decollect the poem? She had her book of poetry in her hand, hanging by her side, her thumb stuck at the page she'd been reading. How can we make it our project to re-collect what we have helped to destroy? The book of poetry was a slim one, the cover a deep red, like blood before it turns black outside the body. How can we relearn love when our model for love is the project we have grown to hate?

*

Here is Heidegger's recipe for being:

1. Create a unique combination of words.
2. Take it seriously.
3. Take seriously the vague origins of being.
4. Enter into the business of getting serious about being.

Don't say shit, Daddy, the owl-eyed boy said.

Chappy stood up from the chair he was in. Sorry, he said.

Chappy loved the owl-eyed boy best when he needed Chappy most. This was selfish, Chappy knew. The owl-eyed boy was needing him less and less these days.

First, said Chappy, hear this: hear how one word meets the next in what they call authority. Do they look like people who might represent anything beyond the quotidian? What do they worship? Do they worship one another? Could a book be a city? No matter how close Chappy got to making sense of the nonsensical, Mirror still had no idea what he was trying to make her understand.

The first time I went to New York City, Chappy told Mirror, which is so far the only time I went to New York City, but there's still time, unless I die soon. I'm hoping I won't die soon. I'm hoping I'll get to New York one more time, at least, before I die.

Mirror said nothing. She was waiting to hear what happened to Chappy the first time he went to New York City. In the few days Mirror had known Chappy, she'd come to understand how difficult it was for him to get to the conclusion of a story – how difficult it seemed to be for him to get to a story at all. Mirror understood that if Chappy was going to tell a story, he was going to have to get there on his own, and nothing she could do would speed it up, or change it, so she waited.

I told my father I was going to New York City and he gave me this look. Like, he rolled his eyes. Why would anybody want to go to New York City? he was saying, but only with his eyes. But I got what he was saying. I translated what he was saying with his eyes into words I could understand. Why would anyone want to go to New York City? was the translation into words of what my father was saying to me with his eyes.

I wanted to fit in when I got to New York City, you know what I mean, Mirror?

Mirror nodded. She was growing confused. She wasn't sure if she'd got to the point of at least starting to find out what happened the first time Chappy went to New York City.

Say you lived in New York City, though. You'd be a certain kind of person, wouldn't you, Mirror? Aren't New Yorkers a certain kind of person? Chappy looked at Mirror like he was hoping for an answer, and Mirror knew he probably really was looking for some kind of answer, but she also knew she didn't have the answer Chappy was looking for.

Chappy himself seemed more confused than Mirror, so Mirror continued staying quiet and waiting to hear what Chappy would say next.

There's one thing I should tell you before I tell you what happened the first time I went to New York City. It wasn't like anything really big happened while I was in New York City. Nothing happened.

Mirror blinked.

But what is it like to be in New York City? Not for some other guy, I mean. For me, Mirror. What's it like for me?

Again, Mirror wondered if she could answer, although it was pitifully obvious that she could not know what it would be like for a guy like Chappy to be in New York City. She didn't even really know what kind of guy Chappy was where he was right now, let alone in New York City, since she'd known him only three days.

First I need to tell you what kind of guy I am, said Chappy, but without starting off at birth or anything like that. That would take way too long.

Chappy was going to hear some writers read from their books. He drove straight south till traffic backed up on the road he was on. Then he turned onto a new road and drove east. Then he turned again, onto another new road, and went south again. He was trying to get to the highway. He ended up going down residential roads all the way to the city.

The neighbourhood he was driving through was one he'd never driven through before. It was like a little business district.The business district then opened out into a valley.

He found a place to park for five dollars just east of a restaurant on a boat. The boat burned down once, but they pulled a new ship into the harbour and parked it at the dock. The new ship was as big as a cruise ship. They made this big ship into the restaurant. The food was reportedly not very good, but people loved to eat on a boat for some reason.

Chappy had to run to get to the reading on time. The first reader was R.M. Vaughan, who read a scene that took place in a girl's washroom. A guy was in the girl's washroom and he threw the girl's shoes in the toilet by mistake.

Chappy read some books by Edward Gorey to pass the time. Perfect, because they were small and had very few words and Chappy could turn the pages quietly and the pictures were sad.

The second guy read about comic books and bars with porno going on, the main character being a fornicating grasshopper who wants to be a comic book hero. The writer was an old man who said the fuck word a lot.

Soon the main writer would be on, which was good, because after that, Chappy could go home. The owl-eyed boy was trying to get his project on Lake Baikal done and Chappy wanted to help.

The guy beside Chappy was asleep. Chappy recognized some of the people in the audience by what their hair looked like.

Here's the one I want to tell, said Chappy. But that seemed to be it. He didn't actually seem to have anything to tell.

Mirror waited a little longer.

Chappy got up. That went pretty well, he said.

Mirror wasn't sure if he meant that the story he never told went pretty well, or that getting up from the bed after not telling the story went pretty well. She decided he must mean the getting up part, since he never told any story and how could he believe that a story he never told went well. Unless he meant that not telling a story was a good thing in itself. Then not telling a story might be a way of having things go well in the face of the potential to actually tell a story.

It was five o'clock. Chappy and Mirror were together in bed. Chappy stuffed the pillow in tighter to his stomach to try to get the hurting to stop. He might have gone back to sleep then, Mirror couldn't tell. She didn't think he could be asleep. He usually breathed funny when he was asleep. She couldn't hear his breathing at all.

Then it was five-thirty.

Then five-thirty-five.

Then five-forty-five.

Still Mirror didn't hear any funny breathing coming from Chappy.

I can't remember the name of the type of astrology Dad was talking about the day he died, said Chappy. He was delirious anyway. But you know how you come to believe something a person says is important if the person who says it, says it on the day he dies. Which is sort of ridiculous, since who is it really important to now that the person is dead. Right, Mirror?

It looked to Mirror like Chappy was living in something small at the moment, like a pin. He was hurting himself trying to remember, and she couldn't decide if it would be better if he kept trying to remember, or if he gave up. If he kept trying to remember, and he managed to actually remember the type of astrology his dad had been talking about all those years ago, he might feel relief. But if he kept trying to remember, and he didn't remember the type of astrology his dad had been talking about all those years ago, he would just continue to hurt till he got mad from the pain, and Mirror didn't want him to get mad from the pain.

I bought these cookies the other day, Chappy said. Everybody liked them.

Mirror thought Chappy looked quite happy for the moment, like a puppy proud of some accomplishment, like rolling over or playing dead.

It was sometimes a terrible mistake to try to make someone

stop hurting. Sometimes, a person needed to hurt for a while before they could start to be happy again for a while.

Mirror shook her head. She was feeling herself sinking into some place inside her that was scratchy, some place with cello music. She had no idea where Chappy was heading. It was like a Bach suite, hearing Chappy talk in every direction at once. Mirror sensed intelligence in what he was saying, but could not capture the specific intelligence long enough to feel at home in his talk.

It's probably too late to get any sleep now.

Probably. You want me to make some coffee?

I'll make the coffee, Chappy. You just lie here and think. I love you. Mirror kissed his cheek, then got out of bed. She pulled on her blue-lamb housecoat, and slipped on her slippers, and went down to make the coffee.

*

When I came home on my bicycle last night, Chappy told Mirror, I was breathing so hard and fast and my body felt rigid. Chappy was leaning forward with his elbows on the kitchen table, talking very quietly, with his mouth close to Mirror's ear. He dug his fingers into her arm to keep from dying while he spoke, and he kept his face close to her ear and whispered: Don't misunderstand. I don't ever get off the bike. But I have made me be like this, Mirror.

Mirror kept her head down and listened. Chappy's words entered her ear. His lips were so close to her ear. She could feel the moisture and the small wind his words made.

You might want to discuss this, said Chappy, but then he hesitated.

Mirror could see him resonating as he reconsidered his words, trying harder to get at what he wanted to say.

What already we have discussed, we might want to discuss again.

I give up. I act like I have nothing to say. You see that? Tell me to smarten up. That would be a very beautiful thing for you to do for me, Mirror.

Mirror understood just how beautiful this would actually be, but said nothing. She felt a bit of pride warming her, making her glad of who she was when she was with Chappy.

You don't have to do that for me, Mirror. You make the choice to do that. I feel the miracle of that.

Chappy went into the bathroom and cried. Then he went back to his desk and turned up the music in his headphones loud enough to hurt his ears. Then he went in the bathroom again and kicked the wall. Then he went outside and walked in the cold rain. He found Roger standing outside the coffee shop. Roger told him the cops came by all the time these days when he was standing outside the coffee shop and wrote down what Roger was wearing. This, Roger told Chappy, was so they'd know who he was if they found him dead in an alley a couple days from now.

I can't promise you anything, Chappy said. I don't know why I would ever want to shut you up again, Mirror, but apparently I'm an asshole.

Mirror shook her head and blinked her sad-looking eyes, but said nothing back to her little Chappy.

I like to not kiss at first, Mirror. I like to just know the kiss is coming and smile a bit for it, smile in my eyes and see the smile in your eyes and hold our faces close and touch your cheeks and feel my lips pull toward yours, but not touch yet, just brush enough to make me make a sound I can't describe. I like to brush our lips together like that soft and slow and touch each other and brush slow while we unbutton each other's clothes and stand just apart, only our lips touching lightly.

Okay, good plan for the meeting, Mirror said.

They were going to try another meeting in the kitchen. Mirror had been planning to sit and wait for the meeting to end, because it was Chappy's meeting and when he called a meeting, he did it so he could tell Mirror things he didn't seem to be able to tell her outside the meeting setting.

I'll go in fighting, Mirror thought. Chappy loves a good fight when he has a meeting. When Chappy has a meeting, a good fight is the only thing that cheers him up.

What happened last night, Chappy? Mirror asked. You didn't care and then you suddenly seemed to care again.

The desire came back because I let it, Mirror. I stopped stopping it.

Chappy went out to get coffee. Roger was outside the doughnut shop. He talked to Chappy for a long time. He told Chappy stuff he'd never told him about before. Chappy didn't even know Roger had a son.

I was going to call my book *Emma's Head*, Roger said. Chappy didn't know Roger had a book, either. Emma was my wife, Roger said. She could tip her head back so you could see down her neck.

That seemed weird, but Chappy kept listening.

There were lights inside Emma's neck, Roger said, and translucent bits of something floating around in Emma's body that looked like fly wings moving in a gentle wind. It was weird. Roger looked up from his coffee and Chappy nodded so that Roger would know he was still with him, even though the story was getting very bizarre.

I couldn't do a whole book on that, though, said Roger. Or maybe I could have. Every time I looked down Emma's neck it was different. But it was something different in my head, not in Emma's neck. I saw in the light and the fly wings something different every time. Not like a difference you could describe in words. Not like where you'd have a whole book with chapters and a table of contents and stuff. The book was going to be non-fiction. Roger seemed done, but something in his eyes made Chappy stay sitting, even though he was thinking he should get back to work.

Emma had brown eyes, Roger said.

Chappy wished he didn't have to go back to work. He wished he could just go home and talk to Mirror. He wanted to get Mirror to bend her head back and see if he could see down her neck.

The second day of his new job, Chappy got off his route onto a residential side street and an old man walked slowly in front of Chappy's car. The old man seemed hobbled by some invisible thing hidden inside him, like a horseshoe up a person's ass. The old man was leaning heavily on an old woman's arm. The old woman seemed hardly more capable of making it across the road than the man. Chappy stopped. The old man and old woman stopped, too. Everything in the world seemed to stop. Other people on the sidewalk stood poised. But then someone stepped off the curb and everything moved again. A man in a black hat scooped his arms around the air, like a ballet dancer, like a ballet was happening on the street, and the man lifted, pulling something invisible out of the sky, like a word.

*

The thing Mirror thought she was slithering toward faded away and Mirror stood up. She thought she had been asleep. It was three o'clock in the morning. Mirror went to the window. Across the street were other houses. There was the white house with the concrete addition. Mirror knew they needed salt at that house to keep the concrete from icing up. There were a thousand things people needed. Salt was just one of the things people needed. Sometimes it seemed like people needed so many things. Would Chappy and Mirror ever get all the things they needed in order to be able to touch that place they'd been aiming for since they got married?

When the fridge comes on, Mirror knows this is her cue to ascend the stairs. She has no idea where she'll be this time tomorrow. Right now she knows for certain that she is on the upper level of her house. But that is all she knows.

Listen to this, Chappy told Mirror. He read from the magazine he was holding. He held the magazine in one hand. He held his other hand up behind him, like he was fencing. He thrust forward at what he preceived to be key words in the passage he was reading.

Mirror felt Chappy's precipitous descent. Perceptions, however, are suspect most of the time. Sometimes, however, Mirror wholly trusts perception.

When Chappy finishes, he stops reading, but stays in fencing position. He looks from Mirror to his magazine with what Mirror thinks is glee.

The fire alarm sounded at six o'clock. There were many dishes in the sink. Chappy could hear a dog. It was somebody else's dog.

The dog was out in front of Chappy's house. Chappy went to look at it. He'd never seen a dog like that before. In one way, it looked like any other dog. But in another way, it was a completely different dog from any other dog Chappy had ever seen before.

The dog needed a bath. For a brief moment, Chappy thought about giving it a bath. But this seemed too weird, since Chappy didn't know the dog at all.

Chappy called the dog Dick. The dog's neck was thick with fur. Chappy pushed his hands into the fur and checked for a collar, but Dick didn't have a collar.

Chappy went back into the house and sat down in the breakfast nook with a pen and a piece of paper. He decided he would write a note to Mirror, asking her to please modify her behaviour in a number of ways. He would make of the note a list of things he wanted Mirror to change about herself. Chappy decided to number the list of things he wanted Mirror to change about herself. He stopped the list at ten. There were more things he wanted Mirror to change about herself, but he would make another list some other day.

Chappy went to the sink. He filled it with water. He squirted in soap. He opened the window. Cold air came in. Chappy did the dishes quickly. It was cold now in the kitchen. Chappy was wearing boxer shorts. The dog tried to come in the kitchen, but Chappy had the door closed. As he set the last dish in the drainer, he heard the dog whimpering. The phone rang. It was Mirror. Could you come and pick me up now, please, Chappy, she said.

On the way out to the car, Chappy gave the list of things he wanted Mirror to change about herself to the dog to eat. I'll give you a proper lunch later, Chappy told the dog. This is just a snack.

Everyone is sitting at computer terminals. This is a workplace, after all. Yet, someone, somewhere, is reading poetry. Someone is reading poetry quietly, almost inaudibly. But the hum of computers drowns out the sound of anything but other computers, so it is hard for Chappy to be sure. But Chappy is sure he hears poetry within the hum of the computers. Specifically, Chappy hears a poem from a magazine he has at home. He recognizes the poem immediately. He read the poem the night before while eating baked beans.

Chappy gets up from his computer. He moves along the aisles between the cubicle walls. The cubicle walls are modular, made up of temporary dividers covered in beige fabric. Nobody looks up from their computer as Chappy passes. There is no one in the aisles except Chappy. At one point as he travels Chappy believes he sees a lone fugitive darting across an aisle, looking furtive. The poem Chappy hears in the hum of the computers is about a fugitive.

Chappy stands on his toes and looks over a cubicle wall. There is a girl inside the cubicle. She has a small handheld mirror and is applying lipstick to her lips.

After wandering a long time in search of the poem within the hum, Chappy finds himself in a part of the office he's never been in. The poem is no more audible here, nor any less audible. When Chappy finally turns to return to his desk, he can no longer remember which direction he needs to go in.

The cliffs rode high above, resolving into jagged peaks among the clouds. The men were six thousand feet below the highest peak. They were aware of the peak, but they had no interest in the peak, and the peak had no interest in them. As far as the men were concerned, the peak was a dagger in God's ass.

You know those twin sisters who are on Degrassi High? Chappy said one night at dinner. I saw them at the bus stop this morning. They were jumping around, calling each other slut, and poking each other in the eye.

Mirror stirred her food around a bit with her fork and looked up at Chappy. A strand of her thick, dark hair escaped from behind her ear and fell across her face.

I'm not making this up, Chappy said. One of the twins got hold of the other one's shoe and wouldn't give it back.

Mirror pushed the strand of hair back behind her ear and forked some food into her mouth. Chappy kept his eyes on his food, but stole a glance at Mirror. She didn't look disgusted or anything. She must have got plenty of sleep last night. She seemed rested and happy.

It was a black, scuffed up shoe, Chappy said. An old shoe with a worn sole. Not what you'd expect one of the Degrassi twins to wear.

What kind of shoe would you expect a Degrassi twin to wear, Chappy? Mirror asked.

It wasn't so much that Chappy wanted Mirror to hear his story. He wanted her to hear his story, but he also wanted her to hear the secret he was holding in behind the story. The secret of what it meant to see the Degrassi twins at a bus stop.

They both had the same coats, too, Chappy said. They were jumping around, saying, You fucking slut. No, you fucking slut. No, you're a fucking slut.

Once in a while, they looked over at me, like they were

trying to show me something. Like saying each other was a fucking slut was some kind of code they wanted me to crack and they thought it was totally funny that I couldn't crack this fucking code of theirs.

Mirror laughed a little.

I was trying to read my book, said Chappy, but I couldn't keep focussed. I couldn't help but look over now and then at these two girls. I thought they were just a couple of ordinary high school twins at this point, so mostly I just went on reading my book, looking up every now and then to see how the eye poking was proceeding.

But then I noticed they were wearing the same coat, so I took a closer look. That's when I saw that they were the Degrassi twins. As soon as I figured this out, I stared at them, and I must have had a particular look on my face, because the girls looked back at me and I could see that they knew that I knew who they were. It was like I had finally cracked their code and they were saying to me, It's about time, dummy. They both got this secret smile, like they'd finally shown me something worth seeing, something good enough to get my face out of my book that I was reading.

Seeing them in person was almost the same as seeing them on TV, Mirror, only better. I could relax, just like I was at home on the couch. But then the two of them fell silent, like it was the end of an episode and I would have to wait until next week to find out what happens.

You don't even watch Degrassi, Chappy.

I didn't think so, either, Mirror, but I must watch it sometimes. How else would I know who the Degrassi twins were?

I've never seen you watch it.

Nevertheless.

They probably weren't even the Degrassi twins.

Maybe not.

Maybe you saw them on a commercial.

Chappy watched Mirror eat some of her food.

Mirror could see that Chappy was disappointed. He wanted those girls to be the Degrassi girls so bad.

We can watch Degrassi this week and see if it was the Degrassi twins you saw.

Chappy ate some food.

When the bus finally came, and we were all on the bus, the Degrassi twins sat with the toes of their shoes in the air and their green coats and that thick, kinky hair they have. I wonder if that hair is natural. Chappy looked at Mirror.

Mirror shrugged. She wasn't sure she even knew what the Degrassi twins looked like. She had this image in her head, but she wasn't sure that it maybe wasn't some other twins from TV she was picturing. It didn't really matter. Although, the twins she was picturing had very kinky hair, which made one wonder. It made Mirror wonder, anyway.

Now and then I'd look up from my book, and it was almost like having the converter in my hand, because one of the twins would tip her head and whisper something into the other one's ear and I'd feel my thumb tapping where the volume button on the converter would have been, tapping like my thumb does when I can't hear what's going on, but I don't want to turn it up too loud in case it wakes up the owl-eyed boy.

The lady went into the back of the restaurant. Chappy heard laughter.

Chappy sat up. Darkness. He put his hand out, patted the
bed beside him. No one there.

He went out of the apartment.

Out into the night.

He followed the lights.

Shops were closed. Cabs splashed through puddles.
Chappy felt like someone else. He felt like a liar.

He went back to the dark room. Got back in the bed.
He wasn't quite still. He turned his head. Looked out the
window.

There was a brown basket out in front of the house every
morning when I came out to go to school, Mirror told
Chappy. I thought it was the laundry basket. Once, when
I was in grade four, we lost all our laundry. We had to get all
new clothes. I thought it was an adventure, getting all new
clothes, but it made my mother cry. Mirror looked at the
hedge. There was no brown basket on the porch anymore.
Maybe we should go get coffee, Chappy. This seems so
unhealthy.

The man stood in the middle of the laundromat. He looked
very much like any other man in a laundromat. He was tall.
Slim. Curved slightly, with a special look to his head, the
way his head sat under his hair, and a space in the middle
to pile the laundry.

Mirror watched the man lift his hand toward his laundry
basket. The man's hand rose too far. The man let his hand
fall. The man's hand hung by the man's side.

His fingers rose slightly, loose, curled.

He lifted the other hand.

He put his fingers in his hair.

There was nothing in this man's laundry basket to make you look to see what was in this man's laundry basket.

The man looked into his laundry basket. He looked into it at length, as though he were watching a TV show. He looked into his laundry basket in a completely impersonal way, like when you see someone on TV die in an episode of your show that has really captured your heart this week.

The bras were kept in the second drawer. On top of the dresser were the paperbacks. Also on top of the dresser were the baskets of earrings, the chains, the hair clips, the picture frame with Mirror's nana in it.

The pants were across the room in the closet.

The closet was a space saver closet – built in the days when people believed fervently for a number of years that they needed to save a lot of space in their closets – with built-in drawers and hanger rods. The upper hanger rod held the pants; the lower hanger rod held the blouses. There was one blouse in the closet with a trail of frill down the front, surrounding the buttons. This was a blouse that Mirror had not worn since she was in high school. The frill ran down between Mirror's little breasts, which were new when she wore the blouse. Mirror would, as far as she could tell, never wear that blouse again.

There were three drawers in the space saver unit that held some pairs of socks and the scarf Mirror had been wearing the night her mother channelled her dead father. Mirror was fifteen when that happened.

The shoes were in a pile on the floor, below the pants, not paired up at all. When Mirror needed shoes, she pushed the pile around till she found two that matched. Then, one day, she wore two shoes that didn't match. People complimented her. Later, she saw in a catalogue that shoes were being sold unmatched at the time. Mirror tore the cups apart on two of her bras and sewed them back together. Now she wore a black cup on the right side, and a white cup on the left. Later in life, Mirror favoured cream coloured pant suits, but a very dark cream, like strong coffee with fat free cream swirled in.

At some point Mirror began to believe that Chappy had gone to the laundromat. There seemed to be some significance to certain clues Mirror was discovering around the house. Missing garments, for example. Garments that she believed she had put in the laundry hamper. As far as Mirror could tell, Chappy was not going to return from the laundromat anytime soon. He had been gone three weeks. Upon reflection, and after a brief discussion with the owl-eyed boy, Mirror had to admit that the chances were slim that Chappy would have gone to the laundromat and stayed there for three weeks.

When the laundromat reopened on the fourth day, Chappy went in again. A man in a dark blue business suit gave him a dollar. A woman with very short red hair that Chappy thought he would like to put his fingers in gave Chappy a five dollar bill then hurried out of the laundromat.

What Chappy liked about the laundromat was that it was open late at night, it was well lit and it was always very warm and humid inside, even in the middle of winter. It made Chappy feel safe to be in the laundromat late at night with a cup of coffee in a Styrofoam cup.

On the seventh day, Chappy started with dryer number six. He worked his way back till he came to dryer number one. The dryers were all empty, but he forced himself to look underneath. He found a single sock under dryer number three. Chappy put the sock in his pocket. He felt it might be a clue.

When you see the moon from the city, Chappy told Mirror, it can be a strange experience.

A man once saw the moon through the lettering stencilled onto the plate glass window at the front of the laundromat. The laundromat with the window through which the man saw the moon was the smallest laundromat the man had ever been in. Four washers, four dryers and two folding tables. There were lawn chairs folded up leaning on the back wall of the laundromat with a paper sign above them from the management saying to help yourself to a lawn chair. If you could find a spot in the laundromat that was big enough, you could unfold one of the lawn chairs and sit in it while your laundry dried. The man who saw the moon through the window of the laundromat chose a spot near the front window, by one of the folding tables. He could look out the window at the people going by. The folding table provided a perch for his coffee.

Mirror went to the window and pulled the curtain. Tonight, the moon sits incongruously above the houses across the quad, she thought. The moon was huge and pinkish. It hung like a lowercase letter, low over the townhouses across the way.

Chappy came and stood by Mirror. It makes me nervous, he said.

What happens with the man in the small laundromat, Chappy? Mirror asked.

The man in the small laundromat discovered that his laundry was gone. The longer he sat in the folding chair by the laundromat window looking up at the moon, the more he came to question things. He could no longer be certain he had ever had any laundry. This disturbed him, because it was a very small laundromat, and he should not have been able to lose his laundry there. The man had a distinct memory of putting his shirts into the washing machine, so he wasn't really convinced by his own efforts to convince himself that he'd left all the laundry by the front door of his apartment, although it was something the man could have done quite easily, being the sort of man he was.

The man walked over to machine number two. It was a front loader. He bent down to peer through the curved glass on the front door. He straightened back up and pulled the door open. He reached a hand in, felt around. He bent down again, stuck his head in. There was nothing in machine number two, but the man felt like keeping his head in the washer. It was like being in a damp cave at the back of a property big enough to lose sight of the house at the front of the lot. The house was a big, cold, brick house at the very front of the property. It was like a little saving grace, being inside that washer. It made the man feel a great sense of longing, one he longed to feel for a longer time. One he hadn't felt for a long, long time.

The man was still bent over with his head in the washing machine when someone tapped him on his shoulder. The man pulled his head out of the machine. There was a kid standing behind him. The kid was ten, maybe twelve years old. The man and the kid looked at each other. With none of the machines running, it was quiet in the laundromat.

As Chappy talked, Mirror heard piano music. Distant, probably from a window somewhere near the laundromat in the story. Some little person practicing Debussy. But apparently Chappy hadn't heard it.

What I want to know, said Mirror, is: did Guthrie ever pay for the book on astrology?

It doesn't matter.

It matters to me. It bothers me. I'd like to believe that at some point Guthrie paid for the book.

But it really makes no difference to the story. The point of the story isn't whether or not Guthrie paid for the book.

What is the point of the story, Chappy?

I'm not too sure. But it has nothing to do with paying for a book or not.

*

A lot of your stories have the main character being a writer, Mirror said to Chappy.

I know, said Chappy. There didn't seem to be much more to say on the subject. They'd discussed Chappy's penchant for making his main characters writers a number of times before. It had come up at breakfast meetings. The subject made the agenda of one meeting they'd had at the foot of the bed in the apartment they first lived in after getting married.

Chappy thought Mirror might be crying, but he couldn't be sure because she had turned her face to the window. The moon had climbed higher and grown smaller and was now white, the way you would expect the moon to be.

Do you hear piano music in your story, Chappy?

Chappy lifted his chin. Mirror saw that he hadn't shaved for days. The moonlight washed the dark from under his eyes. He didn't look so old. He usually looked so old these days. These days he looked about fifty. Maybe older.

No. I don't hear any music at all, Mirror.

I mean, in the laundromat. Does the man hear piano music?

Chappy turned his eyes down. Maybe, he said. It's very dim. I can hardly hear it. But you're right, there is piano music.

Mirror felt warm inside. She felt the wet heat of a laundromat, which she knew had its own climate. Laundromats are tropical, she said.

Chappy looked at her. Yes, he said. You're right.

Chappy was lying in bed with the owl-eyed boy. He was thinking about a story he'd read about a woman who projected images on a wall while she slept. It occurred to Chappy that perhaps he was his son. Chappy knew what it felt like to be the owl-eyed boy, talking to one of his friends. The owl-eyed boy, Chappy saw, was asleep. Eyes closed. Breathing steady. We need the goggles, Chappy whispered, still looking at the owl-eyed boy. The owl-eyed boy did not stir. Chappy and his little friend both had blond hair. They were working something out.

The best I can hope for from this busyness I'm engaged in,

said Chappy, is to look at the table across the aisle from me and see an image of myself. Chappy and Mirror were at the mall. They were in the food court. The garbage and recycle containers were orange and green. Track lights dropped bright circles onto tables, floor tiles, faces. Chappy's cheek lit up, then dimmed away as he moved his head to look around the food court while talking to Mirror. Chappy was looking at a man that he had determined was at least ten years older than him. The man had a hat on, and a winter jacket. We might smile at one another, Chappy said. We might commiserate, and that would be a kind of silence, a sad kind of silence. Mirror took a bite of her Big Mac. A glob of Big Mac sauce dripped on her chin. She stuck her tongue out and bent it down to try to get the glob of Big Mac sauce off. But her tongue couldn't reach. She scooped it off with her finger and pushed her finger through her lips and into her mouth. She rolled her tongue over her finger and sucked the sauce into her mouth. She pulled the finger clean and inspected it. She tried to remember the last time she had washed her hands.

After lunch, Chappy and Mirror left the food court and entered the tunnels under the city. They came up behind a guy who was also walking in the tunnels under the city. It was Thursday. It was snowing. Everyone was staying in the tunnels as long as they possibly could, to keep from getting wet. Chappy and Mirror were on their way to the church to hear a man play the organ. When they came up beind the guy in the tunnels, the guy seemed to sense Chappy and Mirror behind him. Mirror thought maybe she saw him glance back, just the white corner of his one eye visible around the side of his turning head, but she also believed she might only be sensing his awareness of them. Chappy pulled on Mirror to

try to go to the right of the guy, but just at that point the
guy turned his head completely around and looked directly
at Mirror and Chappy.

Chappy was trying to figure out what to do with his life. Not
in the long run. He had no interest in the long run. He had
no way of understanding the long run. He barely understood
the short run. He was trying to figure out what to do with
his life right now.

The dishes were done. He had watched an episode of
Simpsons off his four-volume DVD set of the second season.
He was watching coffee filter through the coffee maker. He
picked up a book off a pile of books and papers on the floor
by his desk. He looked for someplace to put the book. He
looked behind him. There was a bookshelf at the other end
of the room. Chappy got out of the chair he was sitting in. He
walked over to the bookshelf. He looked for a space where
he could put the book. But the bookshelf was full.

Chappy went upstairs. He went into his bedroom. There
was another bookshelf he knew of upstairs in his bedroom.

Chappy needed to tidy up. Not just the piles of papers
and books. He needed to look deeper into the depths of the
idea of tidying up and see what he could get himself to see
about tidying up. About tidying up his life.

He went to the bedroom and lay on his bed. He opened
the book he was currently reading, called *Dust*, by Elizabeth
Bear. He put the book down.

There was a pile of books and papers beside his bed.

He got off the bed now, and got on the floor.

He lifted things off the pile of books and papers.

He set what he'd lifted beside the pile, creating a new,
lower pile.

Chappy was the only man I ever knew who would put up with my desire to have more than he could give me, said Mirror. The jackets on his records were sticky from something he was constantly eating. After two weeks, I could feel this something sticky like a suit of undergarments all over my body. When we kissed, he bit my lips. Him biting my lips was my cue to bite various parts of his body. I bit off pieces of Chappy, so that when I opened my eyes I was surprised to find all of him still there.

Chappy watched the Steinbergs move out of the neighbourhood through the slats on the blinds in the kitchen window. The Steinbergs moved out on a Wednesday. They took the For Sale sign down on a Friday. There was a big hole in the grass where the pole for the For Sale sign had been. Wayne Campbell was the real estate agent on the deal. Wayne always stopped by Chappy's place to ask if he and Mirror wanted to sell. On Sundays, Mirror and Chappy had steak and eggs for breakfast – that is, if they could find steak anywhere. The owl-eyed boy had cold cereal for breakfast on Sundays, as on every other day of the week. The owl-eyed boy did not eat meat.

Seema Jordan put a motion detector over her garage, Chappy told Mirror at dinner. They were eating in the kitchen with the overhead light on and the blinds closed. It was winter, dark at five p.m. The owl-eyed boy was upstairs in his room, having eaten earlier, before Chappy cooked the hamburgers on the barbecue.

Her husband left her last April, Mirror said. She's had her unit recarpeted since.

Whenever the branches in the tree in front of her unit move in the wind, the motion detector lights go on.

Mirror looked up from her dinner, which wasn't all that interesting to her anyway. She could see Seema Jordan's motion detector lights going on and off through the slits where the blinds couldn't quite keep out the light. She felt sort of hopeless.

Sometimes, said Chappy, when I wake up in the middle of the night, I can see Seema Jordan's lights going on and off.

What about my lights, Chappy? Mirror asked.

Chappy stopped eating altogether. He had something on his fork. Something from the salad Mirror had thrown together. He saw his life like the headlight off a train coming down a tunnel. And, like any real train, the train that was Chappy's and Mirror's life together seemed impossible to get off the tracks, and the tracks seemed to lead straight down to hell.

When Chappy looked up, Mirror was eating again. The Cutahees bought a dog, she said, her mouth full of something Chappy hadn't seen go into her mouth. It's too big a dog for their unit.

For one uninterrupted three-year stretch in the early 1980s, Chappy said, no one moved in or out of our complex.

Really? Mirror poured herself a little more wine. And how did you come by that knowledge, Chappy?

I've been reading the past board of director minutes I found in the garage the other day.

Interesting, said Mirror.

I could read you some of the minutes tonight, if you'd like, Chappy said. I could bring them up to bed with us.

Okay.

Today, said Chappy, a man in blue jeans came into the complex and made notes on a clipboard. He looked at the fences, he looked at the eavestroughs. Everytime he finished looking at something, he wrote something down on his clipboard.

Did he write anything about the floodlights at the front of the complex? Mirror asked.

I didn't see him at the front of the complex, Chappy said. Why do you ask?

Someone stole those floodlights, Chappy. They're gone.

The landscaper says we have to have our Christmas lights out of the tree out front by March so he can prune all the trees in the complex.

A woman was doing something in a phone booth, but she didn't have the phone in her hand. It looked like she was just staring through the glass pane of the phone booth wall. Another woman, a woman who was in behind where the woman in the phone booth was, was harder to see. You couldn't see this other woman until you were very close. Four buses had gone by. Chappy was too far down the street,

though, so he watched them go by. In May, they initiated
the scheduling system at work. In November, Chappy got
his transfer. Six months later, he couldn't get off the Yonge
Street bus line without regretting it. The woman's chin was
breaking up. It looked like bits of her chin were breaking off
and scattering, but you couldn't see this until the last minute,
and it was her that was holding the phone and the woman
in front of her, the one who looked like the only one in the
phone booth, was just waiting. Waiting for the little girl to
hang up the phone and stop crying. It was the distance in the
woman's eyes that frightened Chappy. The sky kept getting
darker. Even when Chappy finally got on a bus, and he was
back on Yonge Street, the sky kept getting darker.

Chappy pulled the car over at an overlook. There were few
other cars. The air was cool. The sun, when it shunted out
from behind the clouds, was hot. Clouds streamed by as far
as Mirror could see. She listened to Chappy talk, but she
could not look at him. She watched clouds throw shadows
over green and brown fields. She looked to places where
the fields broke up, punctuated by little stands of wood,
or buildings – farm houses, barns, silos. Suddenly, Mirror
looked at Chappy, gauging him. How long could this go on?
she wondered. Was this some long downhill road, like the
one they were travelling when Chappy pulled the car over?
Or was this just a momentary blip?

Despite evidence to the contrary, evidence that stands
beneath the world like a flimsy structure of support, but
which is just a thing put there in the end by us – just words
concealing a vast and scattered landscape, a landscape

that precedes words, like trying to vomit out a mountain range from one of the foothills – despite all this, I believe that when you get your picture taken it steals your soul. Not irrevocably. Momentarily. Enough to sever whatever connection you have to your soul, leaving a scar, so that no one who has had their picture taken can completely re-establish the connection they once had, where body and soul were one and there were not yet two.

Mirror was between the owl-eyed boy and the wall beside the owl-eyed boy's bed. The owl-eyed boy was on his back. Mirror was on her side, her arm draped across the owl-eyed boy's chest. The owl-eyed boy lay staring at the ceiling while Chappy told a story.

Chappy stopped. For a moment there was silence and no one moved. But then Mirror shifted her arm slightly and the owl-eyed boy turned his head and looked at Chappy.

The owl-eyed boy was too young for disgust. Chappy had nothing else to give the owl-eyed boy, though. This was the end of the story, as far as Chappy was concerned, and he was not going to sell out to make Mirror and the owl-eyed boy like him better.

We were in the Dominican Republic. We decided to go on an excursion. We would go to see a waterfall. We were in a boat, like a canoe with a motor. We landed on a beach. I was thinking, How easy is this! Getting there was easy. See how easy it is, I told the guide. He asked me questions. Whatever it was he wanted to know, I didn't speak Spanish. A short hike through the jungle will get us to the waterfall, he said cheerfully.

Stephen was on a mattress on the floor. Asleep. Mary put the mattress on the floor the week before. She was sick of getting up in the middle of the night, lying with Stephen when he woke up at three-thirty.

I went out of the bedroom. Closed the door. How can you capture rain? Can you capture it in a pail? In a cup? Is it still rain if you catch it? What is it?

I kept playing little stuff. Little exercises. Little chromatic scales. A single string exercise. I was waiting for one of the kids to want something. But no one stopped me. Mary went upstairs to watch TV.

In the spring and summer, Perry Mariano drove a motorcycle. Perry and I worked together at a liquor store. I used to come home after eight hours working with Perry and sit in the living room with my wife. My wife was getting sick of sitting with me in the living room.

At home, in front of the TV, Chappy heard the woman's voice. Outside his living room, children played in the street, screaming with fear and glee. He knew they screamed for him. To bring him through her mist and land him on the new land. They screamed to pull his canoe out of the river. He could stand on the bank, see the string of water he'd once been. God sat on high. Above the clouds. Sending domes of rainfall to cover the woman and balance out the rushing force of Chappy's descent.

Chappy looked nervous. He looked red. The colour red. His face was red. Mirror's hair was black. Eighteen was Mirror's lucky number. Haircuts came in threes. Bees stung each other in the hive. How longer could you possibly talk? Chappy wondered.

The secret is everything. You write. Sometimes you write what you hear.

Call someone. Call and say, This is the secret meaning!

When we read another person's writing, we hear what the other person is telling us. We hear what they mean us to hear. We hear their story.

The project is to die. We will maintain the integrity of the project. But you'll just be dead. Try to ignore the fact that you might have collected a bit of junk along the way.

Mary once tried to do a good deed.

Books are not stories. They are not gatherings of words. They are not collages of pictures or images or symbols. They are not repositories of theme or plot. Books are just barcode numbers. Books live in computers. All interactions go on in the computer. The people inside the books, and the people outside the books, too, are silent observers.

I need braces, said Mirror. But who fucking cares. People don't care about that, do they, Chappy. People don't care about anything. I do, though. I care. Not about braces, though.

If Chappy has done a good job, unless he comes back in the evening, unless he comes back just as the sun is setting, just before it has set all the way, it won't make it too dark to see anything.

We're smiling, says Chappy. Today, we are smiling.

But what about tomorrow? Should we reach up, pluck out the eye of the eagle, swallow the delicate flesh, while the rest of the animals move out across the concrete plains?

When a story comes back to you from your past, it doesn't come back as a line, it comes back as a ball.

A little ball.

A kernel.

Everything packed in.

It's all right in front of you from the start. It crashes like a wave on your shore. And then you try to tell it.

The whole story was there all along.

Except that all you've seen are snatches.

Riding my bicycle was part of it. I went around telling everybody at school: Listen. It's *The Ballad of Dwight Fry*. You can hear it right now.

That's not *The Ballad of Dwight Fry*, some kid from the grade before me said, that's the teacher talking about Winston Churchill.

And it was. The kid was right.

I was wrong.

Again.

I see no way clear to impressing anyone anymore, Mirror. I make no attempt to do anything more than keep my teeth and armpits clean. I make the bed when you give me hell for not making the bed.

You've been very good about making the bed, said Mirror, feeling it her duty to support Chappy at this time in their life together.

They just did what you would expect them to do, said Chappy. What they always do when they see someone come over to a think tank. Which is to all swim over to one side of the tank and stick their lips in the air waiting for food. Somehow this irritated Mirror, hearing Chappy talk about

the many think tanks and all those lips sucking air from the 385
sky. Mirror was trying to figure out some way to get to the
toilet and flush it before Chappy saw what was in it.

I'm trying to prepare you for the utter inconsequentiality of
what is about to come, said Chappy. But this probably wasn't
necessary. Or even possible. The story was the one where
Chappy was standing in the elevator with his supervisor.
Some other staff were in the elevator with them. Something
came over the P.A. system, but no one could quite hear what
was being said from inside the elevator.

The men who told me about ayurvedic medicine told me that
five thousand years ago some men did something remarkable,
said Chappy. Something memorable. But I can't remember
what they did. I can't remember what the men told me about
what the men did that was memorable five thousand years
ago. Maybe they invented something.
    Maybe they invented the wheel, said Mirror.
    Maybe they just cooked something new, said Chappy.
    Isn't that what the wife does, Chappy? asked Mirror. Do
they not have a wife? Does the wife not have something to
do with any of this?

Put things on a list to accomplish. Try making a recommen-
dation. Develop a seclusion. Try to recommend a reader. Try
not to picture me in a tutu. But when you do, do you think
I look happy?

Previously filthy people were touching things only I was
meant to touch. They had the diseases you read about in

books. Leprosy. That sort of thing. But I knew they'd never been touched.

Directly over the space above Hank, it would have felt warm and pleasant to him, were he not to scratch up the injury. He sat up, cradled his wrist. He could heal it, he knew. But, if he did, he wasn't sure he would have the power to get back over to the other side. To his side. It could have been my head I hit, Hank told himself. That would have killed me. It didn't happen often. But once in a while, someone died.

About a week after Dad died, I had a dream. It's the only time I ever had a dream with Dad in it. In the dream, Dad was on the couch in the living room. This was the living room in my and Mary's house. Dad and I were trying to get ready to play some music together. I was setting up. We never played. Through the entire dream, I was setting up. When I looked up from setting up, Dad was sitting on the couch in his underwear.

*

I wish I was at the beach today, with nothing else to do but to go up to the town to visit my friend, Prissy, at the doughnut shop. But Prissy doesn't work at the doughnut shop anymore. I think I liked Prissy better when she worked at the doughnut shop. I don't know what's come over me now that Prissy doesn't work at the doughnut shop anymore. The thing is, I love Prissy because of who she is, not because she works at the doughnut shop.

One of the baby ducks swam over to the edge of the pond. It spoke to the Chappy. Save yourself, the baby duck said. Chappy asked the baby duck to repeat itself. But the mother duck came. She took the baby duck out to the middle of the pond. Chappy stood at the edge of the pond. It was late. The sun was going down. Chappy had never heard a duck talk before. He had been coming to this pond to feed the ducks for years.

Chappy didn't want to call out to the baby duck. He was afraid someone might hear him. He didn't want anyone to hear him calling out to a baby duck. He didn't know how to save himself. He supposed he could quit his job. Go back to school. But his job was a good job. It paid well. The benefits were good. It wasn't an easy job to get.

Mosquitoes were landing on Chappy's arms.

Hey, duck! Chappy called.

It was getting too dark to even see the ducks. But Chappy knew they were out there. There's nothing wrong with my life, duck, Chappy called. He listened to the echo of his voice over the water. Duck! Chappy called. Hey! Duck!

You will run out of time completely when you die.

I dreamed that I had a body, a body they could touch. They were the shadows, not I. And they saw me now. I walked among them like the Christ and they reached out to touch me, and I laughed and I scorned them, for their shadow hands could not touch me, and they suffered as I had. As I wanted them to suffer.

This is terrible, Chappy, said Mirror. I wish…

It's a dream, Mirror. It can't be undone. You have to hear it out. Either that, or you have to leave.

I won't leave.

I know you won't, Mirror. He took Mirror's hand.

For many days, I walked among the shadow people, and always they reached for me, and always they failed to touch me. In the dream, my life was over. I was very old now. I was dying.

Mirror was crying, but she was making no sound.

I went among the shadow people one last time, searching for just one hand that was real, one hand that could touch me before I died.

Chappy wanted to hurry home and show Mirror what he had

written, but the wind was strong and it took the paper out of Chappy's hand and carried it to the roadside. The rain had stopped, but there were puddles by the curb. Chappy fished the paper out of a puddle. The ink was running. The paper was soaked. The secret meaning of Chappy's four essential convictions would have to remain a secret for the time being. But Chappy was convinced he would one day convey his secret meaning, the secret meaning at the heart of his existence, in a way that would move Mirror to understand him fully, if only briefly. It would be a life's work. It would take far more than a scrap of paper with a hastily written set of life's convictions scribbled under a tree near Toys R Us. It would be his life's work. He would continue to try and try again. One day Mirror would see it like a flash of lightening. It would last only a moment. Mirror might not even recognize what had happened, but it would be enough. Enough for both of them. It would be the end in a way, but it would be a happy ending.

Epilogue

It was the first time Chappy went solo and it went quite well. For his first solo drive, Chappy drove to an ice cream place. He decided to get an ice cream. The ice cream place was a little booth in front of a barn. My dad died a year ago, the girl working in the booth told Chappy. She scooped his ice cream. She looked quite young.

Chappy handed her a five dollar bill.

You going up north to do some fishing? the girl asked.

Yes, Chappy said. Keep the change.

To Chappy, the refrigerator repairman looked tall and talked like a man who has been badly stunned by the taste of chalk on his tongue. The refrigerator repairman told Chappy about a time when there was no music playing in the background, only the click and peal of God's angels running across the clouds. Play the eyes the way you would a video game, my friend, the refrigerator repairman told Chappy. This alone will take you to the places you long to go.

Acknowledgements

"The Sun" from *Found*, by Souvankham Thammavongsa

"Crow's First Lesson" from *Crow*, by Ted Hughes

"Some Broken Thread" by Bruce Iserman, originally published in *Next Exit*

The author wishes to thank *New York Tyrant*, *Gigantic* magazine, *Buffalo Art Voice*, *Corium Magazine*, *Sententia*, *Big Other*, *jmww* and *HTML Giant* for their friendship and support.